Praise for The Gardella Vampire Hunters

The Rest Falls Away, *Gleason's publishing debut...turns vampire stories--and romances--on their ear with a decidedly dark, decidedly unsentimental Regency heroine who stakes the undead with the best of them.*

-- *Detroit Free Press*

The undead rise to great heights through Gleason's phenomenal storytelling. She creates a chilling world with the perfect atmosphere of fear and sexual tension.

-- Romantic Times

Gleason keeps upping the ante with each novel, weaving the characters around her readers with each engaging conversation and narrative, every stage set of all the appropriate gothic gloom and melting beauty.

-- Book Fetish

A promising, enthusiastic beginning to a new paranormal historical series, Gleason's major label debut follows the adventures of a conflicted young vampire hunter in Regency England.

– Publishers Weekly

Sophisticated, sexy, surprising! With its vampire lore and Regency graces, this book grabs you and holds you tight till the very last page!

– J R Ward, best-selling author, Lover Revealed

Witty, intriguing, and addictive.

– Publishers Weekly

A paranormal for smart girls who like historicals. Buffy in a bonnet takes on the forces of darkness in Regency-era London.

– Janet Mullany, award-winning author of Dedication

The paranormal world should rejoice, for a new Queen has emerged!

– MyShelf.com

...Above all, the writing is what recommends this book most. Gleason's writing is sharp and taut, which makes for excellent action sequences, and a plot that travels quickly from the start. The writing strength alone gives me ample reassurance that this potentially plot-heavy series is in the right hands. I'm definitely looking forward to the next installment.

– Smart Bitches Love Trashy Books

...Victoria is the perfect heroine. Smart, sexy, and tough while remaining vulnerable, she is the reason I love this book. Secretly I'm dying to be her, including wearing the fancy dresses and kicking undead butt. Even though Victoria is a very modern heroine for the time period, she works well with the rest of the storyline. Max is another great character, with brooding good looks and full of mystery; there is a lot in his past that I will enjoy reading about in future novels. Then there is Sebastian, but trust me you will want to read about him for yourself....

– Blogcritics Magazine

...The paranormal world should rejoice for a new Queen has emerged! Colleen Gleason has written an explosive debut novel that is assured to please paranormal fans for a long time to come. This is the first in a series that is destined to be one that will go down in history. Very highly recommended.

– MyShelf.com

With its wonderfully witty writing, action-infused plot and sharply defined characters, "Rises the Night," the second in Colleen Gleason's irresistible Regency historical paranormal series, is deliciously dark and delightfully entertaining.

– The Chicago Tribune

A tense plot line and refreshingly diverse supporting characters complete the package, giving series fans plenty to sink their teeth into--and plenty more to look forward to.

– Publishers Weekly

...Heart-stopping scenes and sexual tension. With numerous twists, [Gleason] leaves you hanging, eagerly awaiting the next installment.

– Kathe Robin, Romantic Times

Other Books by Colleen Gleason

The Gardella Vampire Chronicles
Victoria Gardella
The Rest Falls Away
Rises the Night
The Bleeding Dusk
When Twilight Burns
As Shadows Fade

Macey Gardella
Roaring Midnight
Roaring Shadows

The Envy Chronicles
Beyond the Night
Embrace the Night
Abandon the Night
Night Betrayed
Night Forbidden
Night Resurrected

The Draculia Trilogy
Lucifer's Rogue
Lucifer's Saint
Lucifer's Warrior

The Medieval Herb Garden Series
Lavender Vows
A Whisper of Rosemary
Sanctuary of Roses
A Lily on the Heath

Modern Gothic Romance
The Shop of Shades & Secrets
The Cards of Life & Death

The Stoker & Holmes Series
(for teens and adults)
The Clockwork Scarab
The Spiritglass Charade
The Chess Queen Enigma (forthcoming)

THE GARDELLA VAMPIRE
CHRONICLES

ROARING SHADOWS

MACEY BOOK 2

COLLEEN GLEASON

AVID PRESS

Cover Illustration: Ravven
Cover & interior design: Dan Keilen
ISBN: 978-1-931419- 81-9

Prologue
Terror and Hope

1821
Munţii Făgăraş
In the Mountains of Romania

AGAINST VICTORIA'S VERY VOCIFEROUS ARGUMENTS, Sebastian had insisted on being the one to wear the rings.

If he was wrong that the Rings of Jubai were all that was needed for protection, enabling the wearer to safely dip his hand into Lilith the Dark's enchanted pool, it was only right Sebastian should be the one to find out.

After all, he'd already lost half a finger—not to mention his heart, twice—in this bloody damned vampire business. There were days…oh, many of them, he wished he had turned down the opportunity to wear a *vis bulla*. It would have made his life a lot less stressful, living in blissful ignorance of the undead.

And aside from all the logical arguments he'd listed for the stubborn, loud-of-volume Victoria Gardella's benefit, Sebastian had a compelling *need* to be the one to test the pool. He didn't know why—for most often, Sebastian was more than happy to take the easier course of action whenever possible. He didn't like getting his clothing rumpled or stained.

The pool looked like glass, and the light from their dancing torches cast perfect illuminating circles over it. The water was perfectly smooth, mirrorlike in an unnatural way.

Sebastian knelt down, the uneven, rocky ground uncomfortable beneath his knees.

Victoria and their companion, another Venator named Michalas, stood guard. Neither wanted Sebastian to fall or be knocked, pulled, or otherwise introduced unexpectedly into the pool—and he sure as hell didn't trust the three vampires Lilith had sent with them. He was thankful for Victoria and Michalas standing over him as protection so he could concentrate on the matter at hand.

"Are you certain you want to do this?" Victoria knelt next to him, her hazel eyes and lush mouth much too close.

"Of course. Never let it be said I passed up a chance to be heroic." Sebastian managed a crooked smile. "I don't think the pool can be very deep—it's hardly larger than a kitchen table."

But the water—if that's what it was—was far from harmless. When Sebastian used a stick to penetrate the perfect reflection of the surface, the branch vibrated alarmingly in his hand. He pulled it out, droplets of water flinging everywhere like perfect spheres of mercury.

The section of the branch that had been submerged was charred and smoking.

"Well, that's comforting," he muttered as he moved closer to the edge. He could see every detail of his face reflected in the pool, which showed no indication its surface had just been disturbed by an inquisitive branch.

In the reflection, Victoria's and Michalas's heads were on either side of his shoulders, and the flames of their torches flickered yellow and orange above them.

Sebastian carefully lowered the little finger of his left hand— the hand without the five copper Rings of Jubai—to the water. He figured since that digit was already mutilated, cut off at the second knuckle, he had little to lose anymore.

When the blunt tip of his finger connected with the very top of the surface, he gasped. The pain was so incredible, he whipped his hand back immediately.

The end of his finger was black where the flesh had burned away. To his shock, he could even see the gleam of white bone in the center of the charred skin.

God Almighty.

"Let me do it." Victoria, of course, holding out her hand. As if he was actually going to give her the rings.

"No. It's not for you to do. The rings will protect me." Flexing the fingers on his right hand—each one decorated by a braided band of copper—Sebastian offered a quick prayer. *Hope I'm right about this.*

Then he shoved his hand into the pool.

The water remained as still as glass, but his fingers penetrated with no effort. Though he felt no pain, the edge of the water seemed to slice against his arm. But when he removed his hand, expecting to see blood, there was nothing. Not even a scratch.

Nothing splattered. Instead, the substance rolled off in strange spherical drops onto the water, then were absorbed into the mirrored surface once more.

Sebastian immersed his hand once again.

The pool surged and pressed against his arm, but there was no real pain. Just an eerie awareness of its latent power. The bottom felt sandy and smooth, without the slime of seaweed or the random bump of stone.

Victoria's hands gripped his shoulders as he inched closer to the edge. Her steadiness allowed him to reach further, but he paused for a moment, noticing the image of his face on the water—and Victoria's just behind him.

He focused on their reflections as he blindly searched the pool until he felt something sharp and pointed. He paused, observing the shape with his fingers.

It felt like a pyramid, and was about the size of his palm, and heavy. It was not the object he and Victoria were seeking—for they were looking for an orb, not a prism.

Still…Sebastian wished he had a way to remove that hard, sharp object without being seen by their undead companions.

But he had no choice but to leave it, for the vampires watched him closely, and he continued his search with no indication of what he'd found. He concentrated by keeping his eyes focused on Victoria's reflected gaze on the mirrored pool as he moved to the right side, where the shoreline bulged into a tiny cove.

The water was deeper here, and now it reached past his elbow.

Suddenly, something beneath his fingers gave way…almost like a door or release. It changed, somehow, under the pressure of his hand, and his arm slid up to his shoulder into the water. A pulse of some energy tripped through him—then he felt something close around his hand and wrist…like the sucking, sticky mud of a bog.

He couldn't move. His hand wouldn't come free; it was stuck. He forced himself to remain calm.

Something rustled in the back of his mind, near his ears… nestled in his thoughts, as if a voice was trying to speak. Sebastian blinked and shook his head, training his attention back on the reflection in front of him. He saw his face shone on the surface, and suddenly Giulia's was behind him—her long, dark hair falling over her shoulder and onto his. *Giulia.* Not Victoria.

Sebastian couldn't move his hand. He couldn't speak. Held in place, he could do nothing but stare at the reflection of the woman behind him…somehow Giulia was there.

Her lips moved. She was speaking, urgently, her familiar eyes big and dark. *Save me. Sebastian, save me.*

He cried out, reached out automatically behind him, somehow yanking his hand from the water and twisting to touch her, flinging the ball-like droplets every which way. They bounced back into the pool as he realized no one was there behind him.

No one but Victoria.

Giulia was gone…or was she?

He wanted nothing more than to save her.

Was there a way?

One

Of Prevarications and Secrets

November 1925
Chicago

YOU'VE HEARD NOTHING from Macey, then. It's been nearly a week, and you've heard nothing." Chas Woodmore paused with the whiskey glass halfway to his lips. "And so do you simply intend that we *leave* her with Al Capone?" The glass slammed back onto the bar, its contents sloshing dangerously.

Sebastian Vioget didn't have any such compunction. He swallowed his drink—a gorgeous fifteen-year-old bourbon—in one hot gulp. Its heat rushed pleasantly through him, reminding him that he could, indeed, still feel.

If Woodmore had been an undead, his eyes would have been a blazing inferno. As it was, they nevertheless leapt with roaring fury and disdain. "You're simply going to stand back and let this happen?"

Sebastian tightened his fingers around the whiskey bottle and considered how pleasurable it would be to smash it over the other man's head. In the end, he didn't. Not because he feared injuring Woodmore or starting a fight—but because it would have been a waste of good liquor.

And he would have to clean up the mess, because Temple sure as hell wouldn't.

Aside from that, with Prohibition still limping gallantly along, it would have been costly to replace the bourbon.

If only Chas Woodmore could be replaced…by someone less difficult and angry. Why Wayren had brought the man here a few years ago—literally *brought* him, through some sort of time warp Sebastian didn't quite understand—was a question to which he had yet to learn the answer. He contented himself with trust in Wayren, and the knowledge that she never did anything without a reason.

So he gritted his teeth and responded with deceptive mildness. "Let precisely what happen?"

Woodmore's jaw moved. "I know you don't believe Al Capone wants Macey for simple window-dressing. What I don't understand, frankly, Vioget, is how it happened that *you* escaped and left her behind."

"Capone's thugs caught me as I came out of the church—just as dawn broke. I had no choice but to accompany them if I didn't want to fry in the sunlight. Perhaps you feel differently, Woodmore, but the last thing I want is for Big Al to be the one who retrieves these from my damned ashes." Vioget flexed his right hand, showing off the five copper rings that had been fused to his fingers since the day he removed his hand from the enchanted pool at Munții Făgăraș.

Woodmore's gaze sharpened. Some of the belligerence faded from his face, replaced with interest. "So if Capone wanted the Rings of Jubai, he could have ordered his men to allow you to burn right then and there on the sidewalk. Curious."

"I agree."

"Then what did he want from you? And what does he want with Macey?"

Sebastian poured himself another glass and gestured to Chas's untouched one. "Not rotgut enough for your taste, Woodmore? I can't remember the last time a full glass—let alone a bottle—remained intact in your presence. Don't tell me you're cutting back. Have you joined the Temperance movement now? You wouldn't hear any complaints from me if you had. It would save me a lot of money, since you've yet to settle a bill since you arrived here."

Woodmore picked up his glass and sipped, nonchalance in his movements. "Why are you prevaricating, Vioget? What did Capone want if it wasn't the rings?"

Sebastian pursed his lips, then allowed his prickly mood to ease. "It wasn't me. It's clear he wants Macey."

Woodmore's expression darkened. "Wants her...how?"

"As his...moll. Or, more accurately, as his personal bodyguard. But one would suspect there will be other duties involved as well." Vioget kept his voice bland, carefully watching his companion.

But Woodmore's face closed up. "He knows she's a Venator."

Sebastian inclined his head. "Don't ask me how he discovered this bit of information—unless he learned it through your escapades at The Blood Club. You do tend to be a little lax while under the influence."

Both men knew precisely what Sebastian was referring to by "influence"—and it wasn't merely to alcohol—but to his surprise, Woodmore chose not to react to the dig other than to reply, "Capone has never had anything to do with The Blood Club, as you well know. And now that Count Alvisi has been dusted—thanks to Macey—Nicholas Iscariot has taken over the establishment."

"Perhaps Capone wants the club for himself. It is a very lucrative venture," suggested Sebastian innocently. "It would fit right in with his prostitution and gambling rings. Women, cards, and immortality. Pleasure for an infinity."

"Perhaps." Woodmore remained silent, possibly in reflection, and looked down into his glass. "Capone's goons did a number on you with their blackjacks. Doesn't it bother you Big Al had you worked over but didn't try for the rings? Surely he's heard about them. It must be widely known among the Tutela that Iscariot would do anything to have them in his possession."

"There's no indication Al Capone has joined the Tutela," said Sebastian. "And he's certainly not been turned. It's possible he doesn't know about the rings. Perhaps we were wrong that he's intending to ally himself with the undead."

Chas lifted his face suddenly, spearing Sebastian with cold, dark eyes. "Perhaps we were."

What does he know?

It was rare for Sebastian Vioget to be put off his game—especially since he'd been alive for more than 140 years, and immortal for more than a century—and during that time, he'd found it his particular gift to woo and manipulate and guide the people around him to get what he wanted. But at this moment, by not being completely forthright, he knew he was taking a risk that could turn Chas Woodmore from an ally to an enemy.

A more formidable enemy than he'd wish to engage—unless it came down to it.

Yet Sebastian had secrets he must keep if he ever hoped to finish the "long promise" he'd taken on 105 years ago. And so he remained silent, pouring himself another glug of bourbon with a very steady hand. Then he replaced the bottle on its shelf next to an array of decorative objects, including a marble Buddha, a jade dragon, and a square cut-glass bottle with its blue-black pyramid topper.

"And so what do we do about Macey?" asked Chas after a long, heavy silence.

Sebastian gave an insouciant shrug. "We let her do what she must do. After all, she is a Venator."

Two

A Tigress in the Den of a Lion

DECADENT, LUXURIOUS, HEDONISTIC. Smothering. Those were the words that came to mind as Macey sat next to Al Capone. Over the last three hours, a seven-course meal of pasta, soup, braised beef, and more pasta, plus vegetables, potatoes, and bread had been served to the table of five. They were in a small dining room cloaked with heavy scarlet curtains, blood-red and midnight-blue paisley wallpaper, thick Chianti-colored carpet, and heavy walnut furnishings. Massive paintings of fierce-looking Italian men in heavy gold frames studded the walls, and large vases dripping with pink and white peonies were arranged on several small tables throughout.

Firearms had been left at the door.

"This here is Macey," said Capone by way of introduction as he dug into the towering piece of tiramisu that was set before him. A tiny cup of the dark coffee drink called espresso sat next to his never-empty wine glass.

The five of them had eaten an entire meal without any acknowledgment of Macey, the only female in the room, until the dessert course.

While the men—mostly Capone—spoke of business, jazz, and politics while enjoying each course to excess, Macey had picked at her food, which had been served on hand-painted, gold-trimmed plates each as large as a hubcap. The meal was excellent, but she had little desire to eat.

She had sold her soul to the devil.

Only a week ago she'd been taken to Capone's penthouse suite, where she found Sebastian trussed and ready to die on the sunlit patio that overlooked Chicago. It was then she learned Al Capone's astonishing secret, and discovered he wanted her to work for him as his personal bodyguard.

When she flatly declined, he showed her all of the reasons she should accept his offer. Besides the bound-up Sebastian, there were photos of Macey with her friends Chelle, Dottie, and Flora, with her landlady Mrs. Gutchinson, with Dr. Morgan, her boss at the library at the University of Chicago…and with Grady.

The threat was obvious: anyone she knew or interacted with would be a target of Capone's anger—and presumably his Tommy guns—unless she accepted his offer.

So, bewildered, angry, and sick at heart, she'd agreed to the gangster's business proposition.

Sebastian escaped during their negotiation, for which she was supremely grateful, and Macey remained to live out her bargain with the crime boss.

Until tonight, Capone had ignored her, other than to keep her under a sort of house arrest at his hotel in Chicago. She'd been unable to send word to Sebastian at The Silver Chalice, and the only phone call she'd been allowed to make was to Dr. Morgan at her job letting him know she had to leave town unexpectedly. As far as she knew, no one knew where she was.

But earlier today, Capone sent one of his goons to bring her via automobile to Cicero, a small town outside the city where several of his distilleries were located. She'd been escorted into the dining room, taken her seat, and sat through the interminable meal, all without a word until now.

As if they'd been given permission to acknowledge her, the three other men at the table nodded to Macey, mumbling polite greetings as they waited for Capone to say more. Clearly having a single female at dinner was an unusual event.

Al didn't bother to introduce the other diners to her. Instead, he slurped his espresso, then stood and began to wander around the table, arms waving expressively as he spoke. "Macey is the newest addition to my staff. She has a special skill and will be providing a very specific service to me. I trust she will remain loyal regardless of any personal temptations that might come her way…just as you have, Bernardo, eh?"

Capone had stopped behind the youngest and beefiest of his companions and slapped him on the shoulder as Bernardo laughed heartily. "Right, boss. Always loyal ta da family."

Macey saw Capone shift and realized what was going to happen—just a split second before his hand moved sharply in front of Bernardo's tie. A blade flashed, whip-fast, and a stream of blood spurted free, spraying the table and its plates of half-eaten food.

Bernardo made a soft gurgling sound and that was all. When Capone stepped away, he allowed his associate to fall face-first into a puddle of blood soaking his half-eaten tiramisu.

Macey hadn't moved, hadn't made a noise—and neither had the other two men at the table. As Capone wiped the knife on a napkin smudged with pasta sauce and gravy, he looked around the table.

Gone was the affable host who'd called for refills on wine glasses and "more pasta for da boys." Now his eyes were dark, shining with violence and anger. "I take care o' my boys," he said, his words sounding more like an accusation than a promise. "As long as they stay loyal to me and my family. But when dey step over da line"—here his Brooklyn accent became thick with cold, steady fury—"I ain't got no room to forgive. It ain't da way I run my bizness, you know dere, Leon?"

The man named Leon, also thick and neckless from daily mountains of pasta, but also balding and bug-eyed, nodded quickly. He seemed unable to speak, and that pleased Capone.

"You'd never step out on me, would ya, Leon?" said Al, stopping across the table from the balding man. One hand slid into his coat pocket. "Not like Melvin, here, hm? You and Lucky Manachetti been gettin' awfully cozy lately, ain't ya, Melvin?"

"Now, wait, wait—" The man who was presumably Melvin held up his hands, his face draining from florid red to sickly white. "Now, boss, you know, it ain't what it looks—"

The gunshot was flat and sharp in the room, effectively silencing Melvin's pleadings and leaving a red hole in his forehead. The only noise left after that was the fast, rasping breathing of Leon, whose eyes became even more protuberant as he gaped at Capone. His breathing was so unsteady his shoulders actually shook.

Al slipped the revolver back into his pocket. "Have I made myself clear?" He fixed his beady black gaze on Leon, still ignoring Macey.

"P-perfectly."

"Now get the hell out of here and spread the word to da other boys. You sit at my table, you take my hospitality, and then you spit on me...I ain't giving no second chances. To no one. And you, Leon—you stay the *fuck* away from any counterfeiters. Don't think I don't know you've been sniffing around in that business. I ain't having nothing done with them."

Leon gathered his dignity and rose from the chair. When he passed by Macey, she saw the fine sprinkling of blood on his pale face and smelled the faint aroma of urine.

As the door closed behind him, she rose from her seat and looked at Capone. She made no attempt to hide her disgust, but she did manage to keep her trembling fingers hidden. The man was as violent and brutal as Nicholas Iscariot, and he'd made it clear no one was safe from his wrath—including the people she loved and cared about. And yet she had no reason to fear him. "Was that display supposed to frighten me?"

"Frighten you? Oh, no, not at all," said Al. "That was to remind Leon which side his bread is buttered on. So to speak." He looked at the bloody mess of the table and grimaced, gesturing to the spattered decanter. "A waste of good *vino*, but the message had to be delivered."

Macey stared at him, revulsion and fury churning inside her. She still could not believe this man was a Venator. He wore the blessed amulet—the *vis bulla*—that came along with the holy vocation of their family, and he was endowed with the same strength and speed and abilities as she was…

And he used those abilities to wantonly kill people—to destroy the mortals the Gardellas were meant to protect, the very lives they were meant to save.

She might have questioned whether he wore a true *vis bulla* if she hadn't remembered seeing the name Alphonsus in the Gardella Family Bible, where all the Venators—both born and made—were listed. She had also seen evidence of his superior strength and, despite his bulk, unusual speed.

"You abuse your powers as a Venator," she spat. "You've used your abilities to build an enterprise of illegal businesses—some of the worst types of businesses, ones that prey on the weakest types of people—and you've created it through violence and murder. All for greed. How do you *dare* wear the *vis bulla*?"

He swung toward her, but his expression wasn't enraged, as she might have expected. Instead, he seemed to accept her fury. "No matter what you think, there, doll, I am still a Venator," he said. "I am still bound to fight the undead."

"And to protect the mortals on this earth. And yet you gun them down, slit their throats, *shoot* them as they enjoy your hospitality—all on a whim. All because of mere insults—perceived or otherwise. You are no true Venator," she sneered.

"Do you mean to say as a Venator, you have no right to protect yourself from other mortals—only from the undead? Would you have me believe that is true of you, Macey Gardella? You're a smart broad, doll, so don't let me hear you say otherwise."

"You call this protecting yourself?" Her hand jerked violently toward the dining table bloodbath. "Not one of those men lifted a hand to you."

"You know nothing," roared Capone. "You don't know my bizness, and you don't know what those men would have done to me if I hadn't stopped them. Do you know how many sniper shots have been taken at me? How many bullets I've dodged? Do you know how many of your precious *mortals* have been caught in the crossfire because someone wanted to *kill me*? I have to protect myself."

"And why is that?" she retorted. "Because of your greed, your desire for power. Because you break the law, because you take advantage of women and sell them as prostitutes, you open gambling houses so the weak-minded will lose their money over and over while drinking your illegal beer—and you encourage half of Chicago to break the law and drink themselves into the gutter."

"Listen to me, Macey Gardella," he snarled, leaning close enough that she could smell the garlic rolling off his breath. "I provide a *service* to dose people. Prohibition ain't keeping *no one* from imbibing but those damned Temperance people—hell, you know everyone in Congress has their own suppliers on hand. Even the Prohibition agents like their beer and whiskey. But everyone knows, dey walk into one of my places, dey ain't gonna get no damn wood alcohol. They ain't gonna die because they want a drink and someone serves 'em up any damned ethanol. My beer, my liquor—it's a service and it saves lives because people trust my products. It's about regulation, Macey. Someone's gotta manage the illegal trade, or more people will die."

Macey could only shake her head. "That's a poor excuse. You're still breaking the law. You're still thumbing your nose at the authorities—"

"*Thumbing my nose?* What the hell are you talking about— the damned police chief calls *me*. I ain't callin' him. He's the one sucking my cock, coming to me, wantin' my help because he knows without me and my network, my boys—well, Chicago would be a lot more dangerous place. And I ain't just talking about the undead."

"You sure aren't. Do you even remember you're supposed to be hunting the undead? When do you have time to slay vampires when you're running your business empire?" she sneered. The fact that she shared a family legacy—a vocation to fight the malevolent, demonic undead—with the most greedy and powerful crime boss in Chicago, no matter how he protested otherwise, made her ill.

Worse, it made her question the very world into which she'd been drawn by Sebastian Vioget and Chas Woodmore less than a year ago. "When's the last time you bothered to actually kill a vampire? To actually fulfill your family legacy?"

"You're funny, Macey Gardella. You're a funny, loudmouthed, sassy broad, and I like dat in a woman—don't tell my Mae. But I don't like women who pretend to be dumb when they ain't. The first time we met, at Da Palmer—you know damned well I was wearin' undead ash on my suit. Don't pretend you didn't smell it, and see my stake. Had I known then who you were, you'd'a never left that back room without me."

"So you actually bestirred yourself to stake a vampire a few weeks ago. Why—was he planning to open a competitive dance club? Had he succeeded in booking Satchmo for an appearance before you did?"

Capone laughed heartily, his fury suddenly gone. "Dammit, doll, we're gonna have fun together, you and me." He pulled out a handkerchief to mop his damp face.

"That is about as unlikely as Nicholas Iscariot walking into a church."

He was still laughing, but then he sobered and tucked the hanky back into his coat. "You ain't got no right to hold judgment on me, baby doll. That's for the Good Lord to do—and He seen fit to give me a *vis bulla*, and there ain't no one else on dis earth who's got the right to say I ain't doing my duty. Do you know how much money I give to the poor? Do you have any idea how many meals, how many coats and shoes and homes I've given to those in need? And you ain't got no idea how many lives I've saved doin' what I do, stoppin' violence from happenin'. You ain't got no right to judge whether I'm *worthy* to wear the amulet or not. That ain't your place, and you'd best remember it."

"I won't kill for you," she said coldly. "I won't murder people. Anyone. I don't care how you threaten me."

"We'll see about that. But for now, you just wait till I need you. You live in all this luxury, and you wear fine clothes and you eat my food, and you listen to some good jazz music—that's a good idea, that, getting Satchmo back up here from N'Orleans—and you wait till I say. Because our fates are intertwined, doll, and there ain't no way around that."

It was all she could do to keep her face blank and her eyes from welling with furious, frustrated tears. She was trapped here with Capone—trapped in his world.

I was meant to fight against evil. And now I must fight to protect it.

Three

The Lonely Life of a Venator

AL CAPONE CONTROLLED his empire—and pretty much the entire city of Chicago when he was in residence—from Suite 430 at the Lexington Hotel.

The first time Macey had occasion to visit Capone's luxurious space, she'd barely noted its splendor and amenities. She'd been exhausted, wounded, and heartsick when she arrived and found Sebastian Vioget beaten, bound, and ready to sizzle in the sun on the penthouse patio. The only thing on her mind then was getting them both out of Capone's clutches safely.

But over the last five months, since Big Al brought her to the bloody dinner in Cicero, Macey had become all too familiar with the man's Chicago headquarters. Every time she passed through the hotel lobby, she encountered the gangster's lieutenants—who of course had no idea she was anything other than a simpering moll who enjoyed the clothes and food Capone provided. There were armed guards at every elevator entrance as well, and though each of them knew her by name and sight, not one of them realized she was stronger, faster, and surely more intelligent than any of them—.45-caliber revolvers notwithstanding.

The closer one got to the heartbeat of Capone's enterprise inside the Lexington, the more bodyguards there were. And once she crossed the threshold into the infamous Suite 430, she had to take care to avoid the numerous padlocked canvas bags stacked around the room—each one holding untold amounts of cash—waiting to be taken to the bank. No wonder he didn't want anything to do with counterfeiters—he had enough cash he didn't need to print his own.

It boggled her mind how much money the gangster known as Snorky made. And that he really did donate a significant amount to the poor—including serving a huge Easter feast for anyone in need.

Regardless, the last few months had done nothing to change her opinion of the gangster, Robin Hood gestures notwithstanding.

"Baby doll," Al greeted her. "Are you ready for tonight?"

He sat, heavy and solid, behind a desk strewn with papers, a half-empty plate of pasta, and a glass of wine. His dark hair was slicked back, and his clean-shaven face nestled on a short, thick neck into the collar of his tailored shirt and suit coat. The ever-present eleven-carat diamond winked from his middle finger. One of the other gals who hung around Capone had told Macey it was worth fifty thousand dollars.

"Unfortunately, yes," she replied, wandering past a table with an open copy of the *Tribune*.

She paused, carelessly scanning the newspaper headlines. *Fateful Iroquois Theatre to Reopen as The Oriental* read one of the stories. *Third Body Disappears from City Morgue* was another; *Two Dead Near Meat-Packing Plant,* and *Explosion Near Hyde Park Leaves Two Injured* proclaimed the state of crime in the city. And the *Louis Armstrong at The Music Castle Tonight—Courtesy Big Al* story had a large photo of Capone and the famous jazz player shaking hands.

And then she saw it—what she was looking for, but despised herself for doing so—beneath the two-column, two-inch story *Houdini Will Return to Chicago.*

J. Grady.

Macey exhaled and turned away. He was still in Chicago, still writing, likely still investigating. Still alive.

Irritated with herself for caring, Macey spun and moved to the French doors that led to a low-walled patio overlooking Chicago.

She'd hardly been outside the Lexington, except with Capone, for months.

"It'll be a treat to see you all gussied up tonight, doll," Capone commented, his pencil making a scratching sound as he scrawled something over a stack of papers. "Your first time out in da public eye and all."

She held back a scathing comment with effort. Like she gave a shake about going out in the public eye. She swallowed, her throat dry and her insides empty despite the excellent minestrone and lasagna she'd recently eaten. *This is not what I thought I'd be doing when I said yes to Wayren and Sebastian.*

I didn't expect to be alone.

And confused.

"And make certain you look perfect tonight," Al added firmly, setting down his pencil. "Snorky is never seen without the most beautiful and attentive women on his arm. It would ruin my reputation to be out with a sour-faced broad."

Macey turned from the French doors. "Why do you require my attendance tonight? Surely you don't fear any vampires making their way into the heavily guarded Music Castle when there are so many other venues with victims ripe for the plucking. And Iscariot would never be so bold as to show his face." Nicholas Iscariot was, understandably, the only vampire Capone truly feared.

Macey herself had had a taste of the malevolence of the son of the very first vampire—Judas Iscariot—in the back of a limousine only a few months ago. Too often she still had nightmares reliving Nicholas Iscariot's knife slicing open her dress, leaving her torso bare to the vampire's needle-sharp fangs and lascivious mouth while two other undead held her immobile. There was still the faintest scar ringing her left areola, and one right down along her sternum.

Until today, her duties to Capone over the last few months had only required her to attend private meetings that happened or would last after sunset in unsecured locations. And, occasionally, she'd attended him in this very suite of rooms. There'd been once she'd staked a vampire waiting in an alley outside one of his meetings. And there'd been a time when she'd sensed one sneaking through the back stairwell of the Lexington and introduced him to the point of her stake. But those and the few other incidents in which her skills had been needed had been mild and—well, boring.

Fortunately, thus far he'd not expected her to provide other, more intimate services. He seemed devoted to his wife Mae, and from what Macey heard from the other gals who hung around, none of them had been required to warm his bed either.

Thank God for small favors. It was bad enough that people assumed she took off her clothes for the man. Especially since it was rumored he had the clap.

Why had Capone been so intent on keeping her cloistered away until tonight? It was simply a jazz concert—and it wasn't even the first time rising star Louis Armstrong was coming to Chicago, though Capone had brought him here—so she didn't see how her presence would matter.

Unless Big Al was waiting for something big to happen.

But for now, you just wait till I need you, he'd said that night in Cicero. *You wait until I say.*

It wasn't just because he wanted her to protect him. He wanted Macey here because he believed a prophecy written by Rosamunde Gardella back in the 12th century referred to the two of them.

> *From the deepest bowels of*
> *madness and grief shall the*
> *dauntless one root, who shall*
> *go forth to lay bare from the*
> *earth this condemned evil. The*
> *dauntless one shall make the half*
> *of the whole, and the whole shall*
> *be formidable as the ocean and*
> *unyielding as the mountain.*

You, doll, are the dauntless one, he'd told her. *And I am the other half of the whole.*

Was it true? Why did he even think he was the one referred to in the prophecy? Was it merely due to his inflated self-importance? *Since I'm a Venator and a powerful man, the prophecy must refer to me.*

Macey wished she could talk to Wayren, or even Sebastian, about it. She needed to find a way to communicate with him and Chas and Temple; but so far, she hadn't been willing to test Capone's threats against her friends.

Every time she thought it was time to change that, to take control of her situation and try to walk away from the Lexington Hotel and to give Capone the boot, she remembered seeing Chelle on the table in the morgue: torn and bloody, hardly recognizable. Destroyed. It was because of her connection to Macey that had happened. And it was because of who Macey was that her very best and oldest friend Flora was now an undead.

Simply knowing Macey had destroyed two of her friends so far. How could she risk others?

As a not very subtle reminder, Capone kept the photographs he'd taken of Macey and her friends on the grand piano in his living room. Framed. Taunting.

If she misstepped, if she angered Big Al, she had no doubt he would take out his anger on someone she cared about. Sebastian and Chas she wasn't as worried about; they were well able to take care of themselves—although Chas was just as susceptible to bullets as she was—but it was Temple, Dr. Morgan, and Dottie…

And Grady.

"Seven o'clock, Macey. Be ready. Gus will come for you. And wear the silver-blue dress I had Marshall Field's send for you. With the sapphire and black evening coat. I'll send some jewelry. You bring stakes." His eyes swept her, considering. "And don't forget the special corset I had made for you. Wear it, just in case."

"Whatever you say, Scarface," she said, deliberately using the nickname he hated.

Then she left the room.

One of the benefits of being on Al Capone's personal bodyguard payroll was the furnished apartment room in the Lexington.

A year ago, Macey would have been struck dumb by the luxury and splendor in her small, private suite, but now she despised every moment she spent inside it. Part of the reason was because of what the space represented.

But the other reason was every time she looked out the window she saw the red and white *Tribune* sign. At night it was even worse, for it lit the night sky like an accusatory beacon.

Even when she drew the curtains, the insidious glow shone through.

Now, she ducked through the door just long enough to retrieve her pocketbook. It was only two o'clock—five hours before Al required her to be "gussied up." Macey was damned if she was going to sit around eating bonbons and gossiping with the other gals today.

She was going out, tailed or not.

As always, she'd trained this morning in a room Capone had set aside for her to do so (and presumably him as well, though she never saw evidence he used it), but somehow even that exhausting workout hadn't drained her of the frenetic energy, dissatisfaction, and unease that seemed to prickle through her like a warning.

Pocketbook in hand, Macey ignored the elevator and bounded down ten flights of stairs in her low-heeled Mary Janes. It was the easiest way to get out of the Lexington unnoticed by any of Al's goons—for they tended to try and tail her on foot or in their sleek black autos. The last time she'd attempted this sort of escape, they'd been behind her all the way to the library and back. Today, she didn't care whether they did or not.

The sunny April afternoon was mild, filled with Chicagoans enjoying the advent of spring. Macey didn't have a destination in mind; she just wanted fresh air, and the opportunity to clear her mind after being cooped up in Big Al's presence for months.

She managed to dodge notice of the guard at the secret back entrance because he was flirting with one of the other gals. Well, necking with her was a more accurate term. Macey slipped past them quickly, and was on the busy street in a flash.

She walked aimlessly, briskly, and without a plan, and after a while, she was surprised to discover her path had brought her to a familiar building. St. Patrick's was a small, unassuming church, one of many in the city named after the Irish saint, and although Macey wasn't Catholic, she had been inside several times.

Something had drawn her there in the past, just as something had brought her here now.

Despite her previously steady stride, now her paces were more hesitant as she climbed the steps to the entrance. The heavy wooden door opened silently, and Macey slipped into the dim worship space.

Silent. Still. Empty…except for a hunched figure a few rows from the altar, wrapped in a dark shawl, hands folded in prayer.

Candles flickered from the alcoves on either side of the double columns of pews, surrounding statues of the saints. More candles burned on the dais. Sunlight filtered through the large stained glass window above the altar, splashing colorful shards of light over the rows of benches. Because it was Easter, pots of lilies and vases of other spring flowers were arranged throughout the space, filling it with their sweet, fresh scents.

Macey could hear her own heartbeat as she made her way down the center aisle, wondering why she'd come here of all places.

Welcome.

No one was there, but she *heard* the greeting deep inside her. It had been like this before, when she came here after learning about her Venator heritage. When she didn't believe she could be a vampire hunter, when she disbelieved the tale Sebastian Vioget had told her, when she was certain there had been a mistake, that she was *not* the daughter of a famed vampire slayer.

Help me. She thought those words now, not certain why or to whom she was speaking…but if her adversaries were half-demons spawned by the Devil, then being in a holy place made sense. She drew her strength from the blessed silver amulet that pierced her skin, the *vis bulla* forged from metal in the Holy Land.

Macey sat in one of the pews halfway back, on the side opposite the other occupant of the church, and closed her eyes.

What am I doing?

Silence. But it was a strangely peaceful silence, not one filled with expectation, nor even curiosity. Just…stillness. Peace.

Yes, it was peace—for the first time since Al Capone drew her into his web. For the first time since her friend Chelle had been mutilated by Nicholas Iscariot, and since her best pal Flora had been turned undead.

For the first time since Macey realized what it truly meant to be a Venator—the loneliness, the sacrifices, the life of violence— she felt a semblance of peace.

Something stirred the air. She heard the rustle of clothing, felt the warmth of a presence.

Macey's eyes flew open. "You," she whispered, looking at the elderly woman. A quick glance toward the front told her this had been the same figure kneeling in prayer only moments earlier.

"You've returned," said the woman. She was so old, Macey couldn't even guess her age. Surely she was at least ninety. Maybe even a hundred. Her face and her body bespoke of age and fragility. Her skin, papery thin and crisscrossed with an infinite number of wrinkles, appeared soft and translucent. A hint of sparse white curls framed her face, peeking from behind the dark shawl she'd drawn over her head and shoulders.

But it was her eyes that drew Macey: her dark, fathomless eyes that glinted with intelligence and comprehension and *life.* They were familiar to her, as if she knew the person living behind them…but of course she didn't know this woman. She had only met her twice.

"I…I don't know why I'm here." Macey stumbled, somehow compelled to speak. "I just…needed to get away."

"You may always find strength and sanctuary here." The woman's eyes narrowed on her. "And do you still have the rosary? The one I gave you?"

Macey stilled. She hadn't thought about it for months. Not that it mattered to her, not that she had any use for it—except that she had. The first night a vampire had attacked her, she had used it. After fumbling through her first slaying of an undead, she'd arranged the string of beads on her windowsill in hopes it would keep any other vampires from attacking her.

"I don't know," she stammered. "I think…I left it…at home." She closed her eyes, suddenly assailed by the memory of the last time she'd been home—home being her flat in Mrs. Gutchinson's house.

Mrs. Gutchinson.

Tears threatened and nausea roiled in her belly. Macey blinked rapidly to stave off her emotions. Her elderly landlady hadn't deserved what the vampires had done to her. No one deserved to be tortured and mutilated in that way, especially a weak and helpless old woman.

"That's why you must do what you do," said her companion. As if she read her mind.

Macey blinked, staring at her. "How do you know—what do you mean?"

A sad, very sad, smile curved the woman's thin lips, temporarily smoothing some of the deep wrinkles around her mouth. "Keep the rosary near. You will be in need of it." She covered Macey's hand with her soft, slender one. Instead of being cold, as elderly hands often were, it was warm, and her touch sent a gentle, comforting jolt through the younger set of fingers.

Then the old woman pulled to her feet, slowly and with great care. Before she turned away, she looked at Macey—her eyes the same height as hers, though she stood and Macey sat. "Be safe and be strong. There are many who wait for you to act."

With those cryptic words, the woman left her, shuffling slowly and steadily down the row toward the main aisle.

Macey opened her mouth to ask more—at least the woman's name—but then something changed her mind.

It's time to go back.

Yes, it was time to return—to go back to her flat. To face her old life once more.

Perhaps then she could figure out a way to dislodge Al Capone from her world.

✝

Macey climbed out of the cab and stood in front of Mrs. Gutchinson's brick boarding house. The blue paint trim was peeling, but all of the shutters were intact. None of the windows were broken, and the flower garden along the front was just beginning to sprout springtime green. A *For Sale* sign had been halfheartedly affixed to the inside of one window.

Her knees trembled and her insides churned like an old-fashioned butter maker. The last time she'd been here, Grady was with her. And horror waited inside.

She'd just come from the morgue, where she'd identified the torn and tortured body of one of her best friends. Chelle had been brutalized beyond belief at the hands of Nicholas Iscariot—a warning to Macey from the malevolent vampire.

That day, beneath the overcoat she'd borrowed from Chas, Macey's clothing was in tatters from the onslaught of Iscariot and his knife. She'd only escaped because of his help, a fact that he drove home repeatedly—and unnecessarily. She'd learned her lesson…but it was too late to help Mrs. Gutchinson.

Now, steeling herself, Macey strode boldly up the walkway to her old apartment, wondering who—if anyone—would answer the door to her knock.

"Hey! Who're you?"

The peremptory voice startled her, and, mortified at her unsteady nerves—what the hell kind of vampire hunter was she anyway?—Macey turned to see a tall, skinny man of fifty or so standing at the fence that separated the two yards. He had an Adam's apple the size of a plum. Beneath a Cubs baseball cap, his face was in dire need of a shave. His shirt hadn't seen an iron in some time, but at least he was clean. And he had good teeth, except for them being tobacco-stained.

"I'm…I live here," she said. "But I've been away for a while. I just got back."

"Then ya don't know about it all, then? She was murdered in there, back last fall, and ain't nobody been in there since. That Gutchinson lady who owned it. Place's empty as a graveyard." He looked away, and Macey saw a brown stream of saliva shoot from his mouth before he turned back. "Who wants to live in a house where the lady got cut up into shreds? Just like that man what had all those girls in his house over on the South Side, kep'em there, cut 'em all up—"

"I've just got to get some things," Macey said, leaving him rambling on as she hurried toward the front door.

Well, that answered at least one of her questions. No one was here to stop her from going in.

The door was locked, but she had her key and it still fit. She ducked inside and closed the door behind her, then stilled. It was silent as a graveyard, just as the neighbor had promised.

The frayed carpet smothered her footsteps on the treads as she climbed the two flights to her flat. The house smelled of must and dust, and beneath it all lingered the scent of blood, the essence of death.

Or maybe it was just her imagination.

The door to her flat was locked as well, and when she turned the key and the deadbolt clunked open, Macey became aware of her suddenly clammy palms and racing pulse. Irritated with herself—she was a Venator, for pity's sake!—she shoved open the door.

Her apartment looked just as she'd left it. The curtains at half-mast, the brightly colored rag rug flipped up at the corner. Her bureau was cluttered with bottles, feathered and flowered hair bands, and a small jewelry box—now thick with dust. A few blouses and a dress were still slung over a chair. Her closet door sagged half open, revealing a tumble of shoes on the floor. The tiny kitchenette was dusty, with a spoon and a single cup still sitting in the sink, now bone dry months later.

And there was the bed in the center of the small room, the headboard tucked against the wall and a small table next to it.

Mercifully, not only had Mrs. Gutchinson's body been removed, but so had all of the bedding on which she'd bled her life away, along with the horrible ropes that had bound her frail wrists and ankles to the bed posts. Macey swallowed hard, forcing herself to look at the mattress—which had been covered by a clean blanket—and remember.

This is what my life is. This is what happens to people I care for. This is why.

A flash of anger shot through her, fury tinting her gaze red. It wasn't bad enough that she had to fear the brutality and violence of the undead against her and those she knew…but now also one of her own. Another Venator, another who carried the same legacy in his blood, was just as much a threat to her as the half-demons she hunted.

How could this be right? How could this be fair?

How could she survive this?

Thoughts in turmoil, Macey stepped further into the room, her attention settling on the dresser and the single photo that sat on top. Half the picture was torn away, but the part that remained was the image of her mother Felicia. A disembodied arm was slung around her shoulders, and she looked right at the camera, laughing at something. She had been beautiful—and Macey had some fuzzy memories of the woman filled with life and energy, blond-haired and blue-eyed…so very different from her bookish, dark-haired, dark-eyed daughter.

Macey's hands were steady as she picked up the frame and pried off the back, pulling away the cardboard mount to reveal the other half of the photo. She sank onto the dress-strewn chair, examining the photo with new eyes as her discarded clothing slipped down from the back of the seat.

The man known as Max Denton had been dark and devilishly handsome. In this photo, with the woman he loved, the mother of his only child, he grinned rakishly, showing white teeth and a deep-cut dimple in his clean-shaven face. With his tailored suit and informal pose, he looked more like a well-heeled swell than an infamous vampire hunter. But apparently, her father had been legendary in his vocation.

Especially after the vampires had brutally killed his wife Felicia.

Macey glanced toward the bed, her stomach cramping unpleasantly. It had been horrifying enough for her to find her nosy but harmless landlady torn to pieces…and even more terrifying to see what the vampires had done to her friend Chelle.

How much worse it must have been for Max Denton to discover his wife tortured in such a manner.

The loss had destroyed him. Driven him mad with grief and fury.

And he'd sent his eight-year-old daughter Macey away to live with a string of relatives in England, New York, and finally to a tiny town outside Chicago.

She'd never heard from him again. He'd never even bothered to write. To ask after her. To let her know he still loved her. To acknowledge her existence.

She stared down at the photo for a long time, sifting through her memories and emotions…basking in the memories of her anger, loneliness, and confusion.

He'd abandoned her. Discarded her. Ignored her.

And until now, Macey hadn't understood. She wiped her eyes and dug for a handkerchief in her bureau drawer.

She would *never* risk someone like that. No matter how lonely she was, no matter how much it hurt her…or them. She wouldn't be like her father.

A sound caught her attention and she turned toward the apartment door, listening. The scuttle of a mouse? Some other critter who'd taken up residence in the abandoned house?

There it was again…the faintest scuffle.

Macey rose, looking around for a weapon. Not a stake; it was broad, sunny daylight, so she didn't expect a vampire. She wasn't afraid of anything or anyone else, except a bullet, and even then—

The door to her apartment swung open silently and there he stood.

Grady.

Four

In Which Mr. Capone Receives a Set-Down

"WHAT ARE YOU DOING HERE?"

Grady didn't respond other than to stare at her—almost as if he were seeing a ghost.

Macey couldn't look away either. Seeing his name in print was a poor substitute for looking upon the man himself. At first glance, he hadn't changed—not a surprise. It had only been five months since they'd parted in front of the *Tribune* building. He still wore his thick, velvet-brown hair cut in a fashionable style—short around the ears and neck, longer on top so it dipped and waved over his temples and occasionally fell into his brows. He was dressed in a white shirt, tie, and brown coat with dark trousers and spats. His fingers, curling into themselves and the brim of his fedora, were ink-stained.

But as he stood in the doorway, it was his eyes that caught and held her attention. Those blue eyes, today stormy and dark like Lake Michigan on a winter's morning, were filled with relief and confusion. And something else—anger? Disappointment?

"Macey," he said at last. "I'm so damned glad to see you. I'm so glad you're all right."

Still clutching her handkerchief, Macey stuffed the two parts of her parents' picture into her pocketbook. "What are you doing here?" she asked again. Her heart thudded hard and she fought to keep her expression empty.

"You haven't been home for months." His voice was tinged with anger. "And you ask me what I'm doing here?"

Then she understood. "You've been watching my—this apartment?"

He nodded, stepping into the room. The door swung closed behind him. "I figured you had to come home some time. Mr. Talbot—the bloke next door—he was happy to keep an eye out for you if you came back. He called me. Fortunately, I was in the office and could come right away."

"Why?" It took all she had to keep her voice even and disinterested.

"*Why?*" He stepped closer, his eyes glittering as he tossed his hat onto the bed. "How can you be asking me that? After what you went through, after what happened *here*, and to you, after what we—Jesus, Macey, we were—we *slept* together. We made love. You—we—" He shook his head as if to clear it. "After all of it, you climb into a gangster's limousine and disappear for five months and you're asking me *why* I am here? Why I've been desperate to see you?"

She didn't move quickly enough, and he was there, his hands gripping her shoulders, his face so close to hers she could see the beginning of stubble on his chin. "Do you really not know? Do you really think I wouldn't care?" The flavor of Ireland thickened his voice as his fingers—warm, strong—burned into her skin through the thin cotton of her blouse.

Macey struggled to keep her breathing steady and her expression unmoved. Her pulse pounded in her throat, and she hoped he couldn't see it. Grady was close...so close. He smelled like pine, fresh, and like damp worsted wool, and ink, and something else...something evocative and familiar. Something that made her insides slide deliciously.

"Macey," he said, his voice gentling as he probed her with his gaze and stepped closer. Now she could feel the crease of his trousers brushing against the hem of her skirt, his shoe nudging hers. "Say something, lass."

"I…" Her voice dried up, and before she could try again, he bent his head.

Grady's lips were full and warm, fitting tenderly over hers in a soft caress.

Oh.

Her eyes sank closed and her hands landed on his broad, strong chest. Warmth and the thud of his heartbeat seeped into her palms. He angled his mouth, tasting her more deeply as she opened to him, her body leaning into his long, muscular one. Slick and smooth, their tongues and lips tangled together as all thoughts, all hesitations evaporated from her mind. Pleasure surged through her—gentle, hot licks filling her from chest to belly and lower. Oh, oh, *yes.*

She forgot where she was, *what* she was, and sank into this man…this familiar man, with his knowledgeable touch and sensual mouth and stormy, demanding eyes. She felt hot and sleek and alive, and…

Yes. She *felt.* She could still feel. She wasn't dead, wasn't as empty as she'd feared. She wasn't her father, cold and unfeeling.

The thought of Max Denton was like a bucket of ice water dumped over her head, and Macey stilled, then pulled away. Grady released her and she stepped back, refusing to allow herself to pant even though she was out of breath from the rush of pleasure.

He stared at her from the distance she put between them, his lips full and damp, his eyes dark with heat and wariness. His cheeks were ruddy with desire, his tie askew from her hands.

"That's enough," were the only words she could pull from the whirlwind of her mind, from the wants and needs and warnings fighting within her. Damned if her hands weren't trembling a little as she held them up to stave him off. She lowered them, her breathing under control, her flushed cheeks cooling.

Grady eyed her as if she were some sort of feral animal. "All right, then, lass. No more kissing…for now," he added, his voice hitching a little. "Why don't we go and grab a cup of coffee, and you can tell me about where you've been, what you've been doing all these months."

"*No.*" The word was flat and hard and angry. She had to make herself feel anger and determination. And nothing else. She could allow herself to feel nothing.

Grady's attention had fallen on the mutilated photograph on her bureau, and he picked it up. "Who's this?" He flattened the picture, then looked up at her.

"My parents."

"Your *parents.*"

"On their honeymoon," Macey felt compelled to add. "My mother was killed a few years later by the vampires. Brutally. It destroyed my father. I hadn't seen him since then. He died in the War."

"I'm sorry." Grady looked as if he were about to say something else, but Macey didn't want to talk about her parents, and she certainly didn't want to talk to him any more. The longer she was with him, the more difficult it was to remember what she had to do.

She took the photo from him. "Look, it's been nice chatting with you, but I'm leaving. I just came to—to get something," she said, suddenly remembering that that *was* why she'd come. To find that rosary the old woman had given her. "And then I'm leaving. And I won't be back. And I won't be…seeing you anymore. All right? So there's no reason for you to keep watching this place."

"Why? Dammit, tell me *why*, Macey. At least tell me what changed—why you practically leapt from my bed, and then disappeared. Is it him? Are you with him now? Is that why? Or is it something else? You forget, I know your secret. So it can't be that."

"Yes, I'm with him. I'm working for Al Capone." She knew as she said it what effect it would have on Grady, who loathed the gangsters, who hated how they skirted the law and acted like celebrities, and enjoyed the adulation poured upon them by the people of Chicago. Not to mention the violence and control they commanded. She knew it would effectively end the possibility of anything between them, ever.

And she must use it to drive a wedge between them.

"Capone?" Confusion knotted his expression. "You're with Capone?" He grimaced. "I knew Woodmore was a gangster. He brought you there, didn't he?"

"Chas?" Macey didn't know why it took her so long to catch up—maybe it was the residual effect of that hot, sexy kiss—but when she did, she shook her head violently. "No, I'm not with Chas Woodmore. He's not—he's not part of that. He's not a gangster, I told you that before. He's a—"

"Vampire hunter. So you said. And you're a vampire hunter as well. Don't forget—I read the book about your family. *The Venators.* Which brings me to—what the hell are you doing with the likes of Al Capone?" His voice was filled with loathing, and yet there was a thread of pleading woven in there. Of course he didn't want to believe Macey would ally herself with the gangsters. But it was imperative he did.

"I work for him. Personal bodyguard." She forced herself to sound blithe, to keep her voice steady and cool. "The paycheck is better than anything I could get anywhere else—you can't imagine the style he keeps me in. Being a Venator isn't a paying job, you know."

Grady blanched. His eyes never left her, and now they narrowed in anger and disgust. "I don't believe you. Correction: I don't *want* to believe you."

Excellent. Almost there. She gave the wedge one last blow. "You're such an idealist, Grady." Her laugh sounded appropriately derisive. "I've moved up in the world—simple as that. And I've left behind this rathole of a place, secondhand and over-made clothes, and scrimping for my next pair of shoes."

He stared at her for a long moment, and it was all she could do to keep her expression haughty and matter-of-fact. Her knees trembled, and her insides roiled, but he couldn't know that.

"I've never been so disappointed in anyone in my life," he said at last. His voice was so quiet, yet the words roared incredibly loud, filling her ears. And then they settled inside her like a heavy kettledrum.

His face grim, he turned to leave. "Be safe, lass. And if you ever need anything…you know where to find me." He was out the door before she could say another word.

She managed to hold back the tears, to keep herself from collapsing into the chair, shaking, until she heard him leave through the front door below. Only then did she peer out the window from behind the curtains to watch him drive away.

No, he wasn't driving away. She'd driven him away.

Now he'll be safe.

Please keep him safe.

The special corset Capone had had made for Macey was horribly uncomfortable. Heavy, hard, and restrictive of movement. Supposedly, it was bulletproof.

She put it on then almost immediately took it off. "I'm not going to wear that," she told herself in the mirror. If anything went wrong, how the hell was she going to do anything about it if she couldn't move?

I'll just have to take my chances.

She had to admit, however, the blue-silver dress was gorgeous. Capone was a natty dresser, and he clearly knew how to pick women's clothes as well as his own.

The frock was made from a gossamer steel-blue fabric that hung long, loose, and lean from shoulder to just above the knee. There were no sleeves, and the neckline was a long, narrow vee that ended at the bottom of her breastbone. At the top of each shoulder, the fabric was gathered into elegant pleats and moored by palm-sized dark blue flowers. Each was trimmed with crystals and jet beads. Silver, blue, white, and clear beads glittered in a fleur-de-lis pattern over the entire dress, and with every movement it rippled and shone like moonlight over water.

Beneath the dress, Macey wore a silvery shift of watered silk with a low scoop neck that showed the tops of her breasts, which she'd confined by a lace-trimmed side-tying corset that allowed freedom of movement, and, more importantly, the ability to draw in a full breath as well as bend and twist. The evening jacket Capone had chosen for the ensemble was made from sheer midnight-blue material also embroidered with beading: black, cobalt, and midnight. Its sleeves were long and wide, resembling those of a kimono, and the jacket, which hung open like a robe, fell in points past her knees.

Macey pinned a cerulean-blue flower in her short, ink-black curls, tucking it just above and behind her left ear. She tucked a filigree silver cross on a chain beneath her clothing, preferring the element of surprise to a badge of identification. Sparkling blue crystal earrings and a wide sapphire cuff—with real gemstones— as well as long dove-gray gloves completed the accessories sent by her employer.

Her stockings were sheer, shot with silver threads, and ended above her knees, where they were held in place by black garters. A flash of them would be revealed every time her skirt rode up upon sitting or climbing into a vehicle. Into one of the black straps she slipped a special stake. It was the shape of a flattened oval, similar to a drafting pencil, and about the width of her two fingers. Its point was long and sharp. Into the other garter, she slid a knife in its sheath. There was also a small opening in the side of her frock that looked like a pocket, but was just a circular hole made from thread through which she could hang a stake. With the dress being loose, it wouldn't ruin the way it hung.

And then there was her pocketbook—long and shallow. Perfect for a stake, her lip color, a few bucks, and a tiny derringer.

She had just slipped on dark blue shoes—lower heels than fashion generally dictated for obvious reasons, and decorated with sparkling pink flowers over each foot's arch—when a knock came at the door.

Seven o'clock. Right on time.

Macey had met Gus before—he was the one who'd driven her to Cicero, and the other few times she'd been transported somewhere at Capone's whim. Neither of them felt the need to speak as he gestured for her to precede him into the elevator, but she was fully aware of his appreciative look sweeping her from head to toe. She filed that away for potential future interest and swept into the elevator.

"You look stunning," said Capone when Macey walked across the Lexington's lobby to meet him. He took her arm, leaning close enough to mutter for her ears only, "And little do all da boys know, you're deadly in more than looks, ain't ya, doll?"

"Da boys" were stationed around the lobby and in the alley Capone used for entrance and exit, because it could be closed off on either end for protection. Each of the dark-suited men were armed, a fact which was obvious by the bulges beneath their suits, the way they stood, and, in some cases, the firearms poking boldly from between shirt and waistband.

One of them opened the door to a sleek black limousine, flanked in front and behind by two other vehicles.

"I didn't wear the corset," she said as she settled into the seat across from Big Al. "I couldn't move in it."

Capone looked as if he wanted to retort—he did not like to be naysaid—but then pursed his lips. "Suppose I best look at changing that then. Ya ain't no good to me if ya can't strike out when necessary."

Macey hadn't been inside Capone's personal limousine before, and she looked around at its luxury. The engine purred as the vehicle slid away from the curb, and her employer noticed.

"Ya don't need to worry when you're in my car," he said—as if the thought had crossed her mind. But maybe it should have, for as he had pointed out previously, Capone had been the target of assassination attempts by competitors multiple times over the last year. "It's got reinforced doors, and the glass is so thick no damn bullet's gonna pass through it. Cost me twenty grand, and General Motors made it specially for me—one of a kind. I even had 'em put special combination locks on the doors so no one's gonna be able to slip a bomb inside for me. And Johnny and the others are in front and behind us—we'll get to the Castle safely, don't you worry, doll."

"What do you want me to do tonight?"

He seemed neither surprised nor irked by her demand. "Watch. And do whatever has to be done," he said with an impatient flap of his hand. "But make it quiet. Don't be disrupting the damned show, you got it?"

"Are you expecting undead to be there? How on earth would they get past your boys?"

"I prepare for the unexpected, so what I *expect* is irrelevant. I'm hosting Satchmo tonight, sweets—the last thing I wanna be doin' is worrying about whether there's an undead lurking about. That's your job. You got that?"

"I got that." Macey settled back in her seat and realized for the first time how incredibly quiet the vehicle ran, and how she didn't feel even the slightest bump on the road. As the sights of Chicago rolled by, she smoothed the skirt over her thighs and adjusted the flower in her hair, watching the street and business names to orient herself to their location.

"Damn, you got some nice legs there, doll," said Al. His voice was as objective as if he was talking about the taste of coffee. "You got a whole 'nother set of assets than my boys an' their guns. Use them wisely."

Macey saw no reason to respond, and soon the limousine purred to a halt in front of The Music Castle. Lights shone everywhere: from streetlights studding the sidewalk, to the colored marquee of the club's name, to a trio of spotlights that circled and dodged like manic fireflies around the entrance to the venue. *Al Capone Welcomes Louis Armstrong*, announced the sign, punctuated by a frame of gold light bulbs that looked like a moving rectangle. People gathered in front of the theater, but eight burly, ferocious-looking men were arranged to keep the bystanders at a safe distance from the new arrivals.

Macey followed her boss out of the limo, and she felt as if she were being physically pelted by flashes of camera bulbs. One of his goons helped her slide from the low vehicle, then Capone offered her his arm. Instead of escorting her inside, however, he paused to greet the crowd thronging the sidewalk.

She stood there, the sultry April breeze ruffling the hem of her frock and tousling her curls as Big Al held court with his admirers. Jovial and expansive as usual when greeting the public, he answered some questions from bystanders, made a few jokes, and accepted the offer of a light for his cigar from one of his bodyguards.

"Hey, Snorky! Who's the dame?" asked someone whose face was obscured by the bright spotlights and the continuing flashes from photographers.

"This here's my escort for the night," Al replied, tightening his grip on Macey's arm, as if expecting her to flee. "Don't she got a nice look to her?"

Someone hooted and whistled, others cheered, and another person shouted, "The broad's sure got some sweet gams on her!"

"What's Mae gonna say, Snorky? She gonna make you go to confession again?"

Some of the crowd laughed, for Capone was known for going to confession weekly. He chuckled too, gesturing with his cigar. "Well, Mae ain't gonna know if none of you tells her! Anyway, she knows my heart belongs to her, even though it's nice for a little variety now and then, eh, boys?" He leered at Macey, and some of the men in the audience cheered, while a few whistled catcalls.

Her cheeks were hot with fury, and it was all she could do to keep from shaking off the odious man's arm and showing him— and the rest of the men—a little *variety* of her own.

As if sensing her rising ire, Capone chomped on his cigar, and, with a mere look, indicated to his goons that the interviews were over. He whipped off his fedora and adjusted his white carnation boutonniere as they strode through the double doors thrown wide.

As soon as they were inside the theater, Macey shook off his arm and rounded on Al Capone. "I am not your dame, your broad, your doll, or your anything." She was shaking, and though she was less than a third his size, the height of her shoes put her almost nose to nose with the fiercest gangster in Chicago. She could smell the wine and garlic, as well as the expensive vetiver and sandalwood cologne, that emanated from his person. "I am here to fight the vamp—"

"Shut up," he snapped, his voice low and furious. A sharp gesture kept all of his handlers—and therefore the bystanders—at a distance. His fingers closed tightly around one of her wrists and he brought it down between them so she was forced closer to his body. "I know that. But you gotta role to play, and I expect you to play it. Otherwise, people will ask what you're doing with me."

"I won't pretend to be your whore," she responded from between clenched teeth. She could see the pores in his skin, the stubble on his clean-shaven chin, a tiny clump of pomade near his temple. "I'll walk on your arm, as your escort, but if you ever refer to me as anything more, I'll expose you and everything else right then and there. I don't have anything to lose, Scarface, but you sure as hell do."

His eyes flashed with cold, violent fury. He moved closer so she could feel the metal of his hidden revolver pressing into her hip. "Don't you fucking threaten me, Macey Gardella. I have you in the palm of my hand—"

"You need me. For the prophecy," she spat. "Don't think I don't know that."

"I do—God help me—but that don't mean I don't have my ways of makin' you behave. You think you can threaten me, doll, you think you can disrespect me, you got a lot to learn. I got ways of making people cooperate. And I ain't above using 'em."

She glared at him, cold and furious, and yet deep inside, aware how thin the ice was on which she tread. He would do it. She knew he would. Damn him.

Think of Dottie, and Dr. Morgan, and Grady.

Sebastian. Chas. Temple.

She lifted her chin and pivoted away from Capone, presenting him with her back. Still furious, she looked around the lobby of The Music Castle, which was thronged with people dressed in furs, diamonds, and other finery.

And that was when she saw him.

He was watching them—as was everyone else in the lobby, though most were pretending not to—from his position leaning against one of the huge potted ferns that created private alcoves in the corners of the room.

Macey met his eyes coolly and gave a brief nod of acknowledgment. Then she accepted Capone's arm once more.

"Our seats are waiting," muttered her escort. "Now behave yourself, Macey."

"Of course," she murmured between stiff lips. She'd sit down, all right. She'd play the game for a few.

And then she'd excuse herself to slip away and find out what Chas Woodmore was doing here.

As Grady drove past The Music Castle, he recognized Al Capone's limousine parked at the curb. The crowds gathering on the sidewalk in front of the nightclub indicated the gangster had either just arrived or was preparing to exit his vehicle.

Grady's hands tightened on the steering wheel. He accelerated a little more than was strictly prudent considering the number of pedestrians about, and rumbled past the public display without slowing down. He simply couldn't imagine Macey Denton working with that mobster, being around the bootlegger, taking part in his sordid life. It made him physically ill to imagine her as one of those gawking, shiny-eyed molls who worshipped gangsters and found their money, brutality, and power exciting.

Surely she'd been lying.

She'd definitely been hiding something—but what? He knew all about her secrets, he knew about the danger of vampires—though he'd never encountered one himself—and he knew about her family legacy. He knew what beauty was beneath her dress, and how she looked when she came, and the way her already wild and curly hair was even more tousled and sexy when she woke. He knew she was very smart and bold and even a little sassy.

Well, a lot sassy.

And brave. She must be brave, to have faced vampires more than once—Venator or no.

But something was there in her face: something closed off. Something had changed her. And other than those few moments of hot, passionate bliss when he'd had her in his arms today—smelling her, tasting and touching her, relieved she was alive and safe… Other than when he'd first caught her off guard, Macey had been hiding something behind those incredible dark eyes of hers.

Bugger it. He had to put her out of his mind, at least for tonight. He couldn't afford to be distracted; he'd been waiting for this opportunity for two weeks.

Several miles from the rowdy Music Castle, in a scrubby, run-down area near a row of warehouses, Grady parked in dark shadows to hide his automobile from streetlights and moonbeams alike. He had a small notepad tucked in his pocket, along with several pencils. He also carried a torch—they were called flashlights here in the States, something he occasionally remembered—and was well equipped with a variety of other tools and accoutrements.

He didn't walk on the edge of the street, instead keeping close to the shadows cast by the large, rectangular buildings and avoiding the single streetlight on this block. The sound of water rhythmically lapping nearby docks mingled with the distant roar of automobiles, honking horns, and even a possible gunshot. Or two. The area smelled rank from degrading waste and the burp of coal smoke spewing from a factory two blocks away.

"Are you sure you want to go down there by yourself?" Linwood had asked when Grady told him of his intention earlier today. "If you're about waitin' till tomorrow, I'll go with you. Two's better in number."

It might have been a good idea for his uncle the cop to accompany him, but Grady was determined to go tonight. Partly because his editor wanted the story, and Grady was hoping to break it open. Besides that, he had to do something other than sit around and stew about Macey.

And besides *that*, the foul streets of the poorest part of Dublin had been far worse than anything Chicago had to offer. Though he was loath to admit it, the bootlegging gangsters like Capone and his ilk did have a code, and they usually kept their violence to themselves. And, to some extent, their business enterprises helped alleviate some of the economical strain the Volstead Act had unwittingly put on the country.

Grady had been taking care of himself since he was ten—at least when it came to mortal threats. And he had a pretty good idea how to keep the undead at bay as well, thanks to reading a good portion of *The Venators*. Case in point was the silver cross he had tucked into the pocket of his open coat and the stake slipped securely into his belt loop. Though vampires had no need of printed bills—real or fake—it paid to be prepared.

The warehouse that was his target sported broken windows, their jagged glass pieces glittering with snatches of moonlight. The painted sign on one of the brick walls that had once clearly advertised *Speedman's Boots: the best hob-nailed toes in the business, don't you know!* was dingy and peeling, not very readable in the dark. Everything around the building was desolate and still.

But Grady knew better.

This building was the hub of a smart, efficient operation whereby dollar bills were being washed clean of their printing, and then reprinted as tens. It was a particularly clever setup, for one of the most difficult parts of a failsafe counterfeit operation was producing the special fiber-threaded paper on which U.S. currency was printed. These crooks had figured out a way to reuse the paper to print a higher denomination on it.

Grady had been following the trail of these faked ten-dollar bills for almost a month, trying to find its origin. Linwood had put him on to it, knowing his journalist nephew not only liked an investigative challenge, but also that Grady—like his uncle— was one of the minority when it came to disdaining bribes and avoiding corruption.

Grady's patience and doggedness had paid off, for he'd managed to befriend one of the men he was certain was a key player in the counterfeit ring. Since he wasn't the fuzz, it was much easier for him to make inroads with the group. He'd overheard a conversation between the suspected ringleader and a likely colleague—which was how Grady had come to believe something was happening at this very location tonight.

Now, he skirted the warehouse, edging along the rough brick wall until he found a promising point of entry: a window obscured by shadow, tucked into the corner of the building, and with a huge chunk missing from the glass. The broken window was three stories off the ground, but that posed no problem.

He removed his shoes and tied them together, then slung them around his neck, socks stuffed inside. Then he pulled on a special pair of gloves with sharp metal points at the tip of each finger. Now, barefooted, he reached as high up into the grooves between the bricks as he could. Curling his fingers tightly into the gritty cement, he began to carefully scale the wall.

If anyone had seen him, he would look like a human fly, clinging to the side of a building and liable to tumble to the ground at any moment. But with his agile toes and strong fingers, along with the assistance of the glove's metal tips and the deep wale between each row of brick, Grady felt quite at ease as he climbed.

After all, he'd been doing this sort of thing since he was ten. Of course, back then it was climbing down inside a chimney to sweep it clean. Or…when the opportunity arose…to slip into a house unseen and nick some of its valuables. And he hadn't had the fancy gloves back then either.

When he reached the window ledge, he paused for a moment to rest, listen, and take stock. This was the most difficult part— getting through the opening in the shattered glass without cutting himself or, worse, announcing his presence by knocking shards to the ground or interior floor. He knew the warehouse wasn't empty—during his circuit of the building, he had seen the faint glow of light deep inside.

Despite the precariousness of his position, Grady had chosen well—for as it turned out, he didn't have to try and climb through the jagged glass hole. He reached in, found the latch, and flipped it open—all while his toes clung to the rough edge of a brick and one hand gripped the ledge.

Then, holding his breath, balancing carefully, he inched up the window sash, prepared for any squeal or creak that would give him away. It stuck a little, but was silent except for a very low, moan-like noise. When it was open far enough, Grady slipped through the opening.

He landed on a dusty, dark floor and once again paused to get his bearings. He needed to find the culprits and witness them doing their business. Once he clearly saw what was going on, then he could call in some of the detectives or at least a beat cop. If he were lucky, Linwood would be available by then.

Moving silently as a cat, he navigated through the old building, down two flights of stairs to the level where he'd seen the glow of light through a dingy window. As he drew closer, he heard the familiar rhythmic thud of a printing press, and the clatter of other mechanical tools through the walls and floor. He smiled in the darkness. *Bingo.*

The lowest floor of the warehouse was open two stories high in the center, and split into sections by temporary walls. It was a vast space with a few old pallets of old crates gathering dust, a large mechanical engine, and other miscellaneous debris strewn about. The soft glow of light and the thuds of the machinery came from a far corner, obstructed by a row of bays for inventory that no longer existed. A large canvas tarpaulin gathered dust in the corner, next to a pile of splintered crates.

Then…voices. Too close for comfort.

Grady paused, slinking more deeply into the shadows as he strained to listen, edging along the wall to draw nearer to the conversation.

"…tonight. Ain't gonna risk…"

"…all the evidence. Don't need no fuzz sniffing…"

"…never put a finger on us." A laugh, then more… "Get the stuff out… Burn the place down."

"Right, boss."

Heart thudding with excitement and determination, Grady followed the conversation of the two men. Definitely the right call to come here tonight; from the sounds of it, the gang was moving on to who knew where.

That meant Grady had to get the cops here immediately, before the thugs set fire to the place. That alone was a terrifying thought: this old warehouse, though brick inside and steel-beamed in framework, was wood everywhere else. Dry and dusty, the interior of the place and its clutter of contents would go up in smoke in a heartbeat.

Yet he hadn't seen anyone to identify them or even what they were actually doing. He had time…the machine was still running. Obviously they weren't planning to move the equipment out before that print run was finished. Then they'd have to pack things up…

He needed to see more. At least then he could act as a witness *and* get the story for the paper. He wished he could take a photograph, but that would illuminate his presence as well as that of the perpetrators.

Soundless, he crept around a stack of crates, quickly and deftly making his way toward the corner of the room where the counterfeiters gathered. He heard them talking and joshing, and the definite noises of paper crinkling and heavy items being moved or stacked.

Grady was close enough to be able to see now, and he peered around the corner of one of the flimsy temporary walls. His pulse leapt. *Yes.* Exactly what he had expected: a small press spitting out one bill at a time, then the bill was fed back into a different press for the other side to be printed. There were two presses going on, and two men at each press taking the bills and swapping them for the other side to be printed.

A fifth man—the one Grady knew and believed was the ringleader—was helping a sixth member hang the bills on clotheslines to dry.

He was just about to ease back and make his escape when he felt something behind him.

He turned just in time to see a man, arm raised…then something struck the side of his head.

Pain exploded and everything went dark.

Five

Wherein Chas is Greatly Amused

THAT WASN'T THE BEST PLACE for a lover's spat, was it, Macey darling?"

She didn't turn from where she pretended to contemplate a painted mural of jazz musician silhouettes, though the hair prickled gently—yet didn't feel chilly—at the back of her bare neck. "Not here, Chas. Meet me at the coatroom in five minutes."

She continued on her way to the ladies' lounge, aware of the number of Capone's men who stood watchful in the lobby and along each of the entrances to the club. After attending to the sagging cerulean flower behind her ear and dabbing on a little more lip color, she pinched her cheeks and left the lounge.

Because of the balmy April weather, and the fact that people preferred to keep their furs in their own proximity, the coatroom was deserted.

Macey glanced around to make certain none of Capone's men were watching her. Then, with a neat one-handed movement, she vaulted herself over the half-wall where the attendants normally collected and returned coats. She landed solidly on the ground, and just as she adjusted her errant hair-flower again, she saw a shadow move in the back of the rows of empty coat racks.

"So what brings you to The Music Castle?" she asked Chas as she edged toward one of the inner walls, out of sight of the coatroom window.

"I heard Louis Armstrong was going to be here tonight. Thought I'd come and listen to some good jazz music." Sarcasm rolled off his very posture.

Though the only light was that which came from the lobby outside, she could still see Chas's features and expression relatively well. He looked the same as always: hard, closed-off, dark and swarthy from his Gypsy heritage, and unhappy to be there. He wore a suit and coat, like most of the men present, his of charcoal gray, with an unfashionable dark shirt—likely to allow him to meld into the shadows without the white beacon of a cotton button-down to give him away. His hair—thick, wavy, and too long—was completely out of date. He looked as if he belonged to an utterly different era. He sometimes spoke that way too.

"I'm promised it'll be a good show," she replied. Then, dropping all pretense, Macey continued, "How is Sebastian?"

"Sebastian? Ah, then you *do* care—at least about *his* welfare. He's slick and sly and impatient as ever, lulu. Oh, and he can't go about in the sunlight, you know. Poor fop."

"Now, Chas," she said, her voice dropping a little. "Jealousy doesn't become you. Of course I care about your welfare as well as Sebastian's, and Temple's too, of course—but the last time I saw him he barely escaped poofing in the sun."

"And that was, what…five months ago? Last fall, was it? Apparently your concern didn't extend to proactive communication—now that you're Big Al's sidepiece," Chas replied coolly. "What's it like, living in the lap of luxury, on the dime of the most evil man in Chicago—that is, besides Nicholas Iscariot—while the undead roam like feral rats in the underground and the rest of us try to keep them at bay?"

She caught herself just in time; her hand had jerked, ready to fly up and connect with his sharp-boned cheek, and she only barely kept it at her side. Chas met her eyes, challenge and knowledge in his gaze. "Good decision, Macey. Save your tantrums for Snorky. You were having a ripe one, too, from the looks of your little display in the lobby back there."

She drew in a deep breath, and with effort forced the fury to ebb from her body. Chas had a right to be angry, to question her. He didn't have to be such an ass about it, but she couldn't deny he had cause. And just because she was feeling a little thin-skinned tonight…

"I'm sorry," she said.

"Sorry for precisely what?"

She pursed her lips. "All right. I deserve that, I suppose, to some extent—"

"You sure as the devil do deserve that—and more. Look, Macey, the last time I saw you, we'd just battled our way out of a den of vampires and you got forced into a long black car—and I was detained from joining you. I hear from Sebastian that he nearly died and lost the Rings of Jubai to Al Capone…and then he tells me you're *staying* with him? With that bastard? What in the hell is going on—"

"Keep your voice down. He's got people everywhere—which is *why* I haven't been able to be in contact with you or Sebastian or anyone. Capone's kept me under house arrest for months now, and in case you couldn't tell, I was damned happy to see you here."

At last Chas relaxed a little. "As a matter of fact, I could. I could've sworn you looked like you were going to faint with relief when you looked over and noticed me."

She breathed a little sigh of relief. That was Chas. Furious and black-hearted one minute, ready to crack a wry joke the next. "Don't flatter yourself. I don't need to be saved. But I do need to talk to you—"

"So talk. Let's get down to business. What are you doing for Capone, lulu?"

"He wants me to be his bodyguard, his—well, his personal Venator. Mainly, he wants me around. Because he believes one of Rosamunde Gardella's prophecies refers to me…and him."

Chas's eyes narrowed. "One of Rosamunde's prophecies… about you and *him*? Why the bloody hell would he think that? And how would he even *know* about the prophecies?"

Macey stilled. "I guess you don't know. He's a Venator."

Her companion froze then his eyes widened and he began to laugh. Loudly, derisively, uproariously. His body shook and he leaned his shoulder against the wall as if needing to be held upright.

Good grief. When the dark pain and anguish that always lingered in his countenance evaporated and turned into reckless humor instead, Chas became unbelievably handsome. Impossibly good-looking—so much so that Macey's knees felt a little weak with the rest of her being in close quarters with such a gorgeous specimen of manhood.

A powerful, mysterious, gorgeous specimen of manhood.

"Keep it down," she said again, putting a little space between herself and this suddenly godlike being. He was being an ass again—which helped.

Why would a man who looked like Chas Woodmore be so lonely? So empty? Surely it wouldn't be difficult for him to find companionship, and perhaps even love. Of course, there was that underlying derision and anger he always seemed to possess.

Chas brought himself under control, but the hard light of humor still glinted in his eyes. "So Al Capone told you he's a Venator, and you believed him?" He started chuckling again, derision lighting his expression. "What a fool—"

That did it. This time, she didn't hold back. It wasn't her hand that came up to slap him in the face, it was her elbow and forearm that swung up and around sharply, catching him in the diaphragm hard enough to cut off his air—and to fully get the bastard's attention.

He grunted and jolted backward, his hand going to his bent torso as he tried to catch his breath.

"I saw his *vis bulla*," she snapped.

"I'll...bet...you...did," he wheezed. This earned him another blow, but Chas managed to catch her fist with his open palm. His fingers curled around hers and tightened in warning as he straightened. "I'm happy to scrap with you, Macey darling, but we might do a little too much damage in this small space. Then how would we explain it to your new boss?" His voice quivered with humor, then steadied. "Besides that—it's the undead we need to be showing our strength to."

She yanked her hand away. "His name is in the Gardella Bible. Go look it up. Alphonsus."

"Fuck." Chas stepped back, shock and disbelief replacing levity in his expression. "Is it true?"

"Unfortunately, I have no reason not to believe him—except for the fact that he's a greedy, brutal bastard who is using his abilities for the wrong reasons. In other words, I wish I *could* disbelieve him."

"Fuck," he said again. Then his lips twisted, turning them from sensual to flat and ugly. "Vioget must know. The *bastard*," he muttered. "I knew he was keeping something from me. Hell, that's probably not the only damn thing." His gaze flashed, and Macey realized if Sebastian was there, she would be treated to one hell of a brawl—destruction of the coatroom notwithstanding.

"You can fantasize about stabbing him with a stake later, Chas. We need to figure out a way to communicate once I leave here. I'm not certain how much freedom I'm going to have, and I…"

She stilled, and both of them turned at the same time. An ugly, insidious, eerie chill settled over the back of her neck—the prickling that announced the presence of the undead.

"Time to get to work." Chas shifted and a stake slipped into his hand from up a sleeve.

"Capone will feel it too. I'd better get back to him first."

"You do what you have to do," he said, much too politely. "By all means. Take care of your boss. I'm going to dust some undead before they do any damage of their own."

"If I don't see you again tonight—"

But he was already gone before she could tell him where and how to communicate with her in the future. *Jerk.* Macey shook her head and hurried out of the coatroom.

Though she and Chas were both aware of the mortal danger the presence of vampires portended, the other attendees at The Music Castle had no idea their lives were in jeopardy. When Macey came out of the coatroom and returned to the lobby, everything was as it had been before: gangsters standing about watching for trouble they had no concept how to combat and probably wouldn't recognize anyway, a few knots of people chatting. As if to punctuate the easy mood, beyond the two sets of double doors that led to the club itself crooned the jumpy, happy beat of a jazzy clarinet.

"Miz Macey," said one of the bodyguards as he opened the door to the club for her.

As she stepped over the threshold and into the hall swelling with music as well as spectators, Macey felt as if she'd moved into another world. It was a full-sense experience, being surrounded by this bold, new style of music, particularly as it was being performed by one of the most talented musicians in the country. With its low, blue and purple lighting fringing the edges of the room and dangling from random lamps, and the round tables packed close to each other and the stage, Capone's club immediately felt close and intimate. Add to that the low, gravelly voice of Mr. Armstrong as he sang something about a kiss to build a dream on, and the smooth accompaniment of piano, trombone, and clarinet, and the experience was stunningly sensual.

The pungency of cigarette and cigar smoke wafted through the air, weaving through the scents of lemon or peppermint pomade and floral colognes. Silhouettes of short-haired women, their nape-baring tresses topped by feathered bands or studded with glittering combs, displayed elegant necks and delicate shoulders bared by sleeveless shifts or slipping necklines. Gems glittered like random stars, picking up the cool lights as hands, wrists, and throats moved. The men sitting next to them sported their own diamond-studded rings, as well as shiny, slicked-back hair that seemed be frosted by moonlight when the lights from onstage filtered over the crowd.

Macey felt the beat of the music filling her, mingling with the heartbeat deep inside her chest, and she was reminded of a similar sensation when she'd first encountered the undead. When a vampire would focus his or her glowing red eyes on her, luring her into a thrall, their breaths mingled, and her heartbeat seemed to pound along with that of her adversary. The music took hold of her like that, for Macey had never before had occasion to hear such talent, such perfectly sensual music performed by such a master musician.

But hers was only a short lapse into the sensations of the moment, for that eerie, forbidding chill still burned into the back of her own bare neck.

Macey had hesitated just inside the door, but as Mr. Armstrong finished his song and the audience erupted into enthusiastic applause, cheers, and whistles, she made her way quickly to the table where she'd left Capone.

Not front and center of the stage, but at the right corner, directly adjacent to the musicians. As she approached, Satchmo was still bowing and accepting his adulations, but then he picked up his coronet and began to tap out the countdown for his Hot Five to swing into the next song. She recognized "Gut Bucket Blues."

"Where da hella you been?" Capone's fingers were tight around Macey's wrist as she came up next to him, before she even slid onto the edge of her chair. "You got things under control?"

She didn't bother to respond to his first question, but she did pull her arm away with a sharp twist. "I will," she said, using the opportunity to turn back and scan the audience from her front-row vantage point. Now where was that chill coming from…? "I just came back to make certain—"

Her eyes lit on a table in the back. The cold, prickly chill suddenly became overwhelming, rushing through her body as if she'd been plunged into the lake on a gray day.

Oh no.

She ignored Capone's hissed demand as she rose from his side and woodenly, blank-mindedly began to make her way back up and around the audience.

No.

It can't be.

But why wouldn't it be?

She made her way toward the group of men and women. Their round table was tucked back into a dark corner, as if to leave them to their privacy, where any sort of shenanigans could happen unseen by anyone else in the club. As if to allow its occupants to watch over the crowd as well as the musicians. As if to allow each of them ample opportunity to carefully choose and hunt his or her own prey.

And in the center of the table sat a tall, gangly redheaded woman, no older than Macey.

Flora. Once her best friend and closest confidante.

Now, an immortal undead.

Six

The Dark Pangs of Regret

MACEY GRIPPED her stake, aware that her stomach was fluttering uncomfortably. Her palms were damp, and she drew in a deep breath.

It was Flora. Her friend…and now an immortal half-demon. Someone she was bound to kill.

Every time she thought about it, Macey felt like throwing up.

Nevertheless, she approached the table of undead exuding confidence. At least, she was fairly certain everyone around the table was a vampire—but it was hard to tell for certain with so many of them sitting there. There might have been a mortal or two in the group of six.

One thing was certain: the back of her neck felt as if a brick of ice had lodged there, and the eeriness of the sensation crept into her belly.

Or maybe that was simply because she was going to have to destroy her best friend.

She adjusted her hold on the stake, hiding it among the loose folds of her flimsy evening jacket as she walked up behind one of the men at the table. He sat two people over from her friend.

"Hello, Flora."

When she turned toward the greeting, Flora didn't appear surprised. "Hello, Macey. What a pleasant surprise." Her words were neither blatantly false, nor falsely polite. Her eyes looked normal, and there wasn't a fang in sight.

Macey had a moment—just a moment—to wonder if she was wrong. If somehow she'd been fooled or tricked, and that Flora was still Flora: funny, cheerful, gawky, and loud. But the moment of crazy hope was fleeting. She knew better.

"I'm going to have to ask you and your friends to leave. Immediately," Macey said, her hand resting on the back of the chair in front of her.

"We're not going to be leaving," replied one of the others at the table—a short, dark-skinned woman with a jeweled red comb holding the hair out of her face. "We like the *jazzzzz*." She smiled, drawing out the last word, but there was no warmth in her grin. A flicker of red showed in her eyes for a moment, tugging at Macey's belly, but Macey was easily able to pull her gaze away.

The occupant of the chair she was holding twisted lazily in his seat, looking up and around at her. "Don't be a bore," he drawled. "Have a seat here, doll." He patted his lap as he made his gaze hot and red and inviting, pulling at her as if he'd slung a rope around her waist. "Don't be shy. I don't bite." He laughed, but the sound was absorbed by the music filling the air. His hand closed over hers, which still rested on the back of his chair. "Come on now, doll. Give me a warmup." His grip was uncomfortably tight.

"No thanks." Macey moved with a quick, spare gesture, plunging her stake down over the shoulder angled toward her, right into his heart. *Poof.* The vampire exploded into soft, vile-smelling ash as the rest of the table looked at her in shock and surprise, their eyes wide and red. "I told you to leave. I'd prefer not to make a scene, but I will if you don't heed my warning."

"All right." Flora stood suddenly and began to make her way around the table toward her. Her hands were raised as if to ward off her former friend from launching another attack. "All right. We're going." She glanced out into the club, then turned back to the table of the people Macey assumed were Flora's new friends.

None of them were familiar to Macey, and at first blush, they all seemed to be relatively young and inexperienced vampires—at least compared to the likes of the dusted Count Alvisi, and the terrifying Nicholas Iscariot.

"Let's go. She'll just ruin the evening if we stay," Flora was saying.

"Who the hell is she?" one of them muttered as the five remaining vampires pulled to their feet.

"Hurry," Flora muttered, pushing at one of her companions.

Macey looked over and saw Chas working his way through the tables. Flora had been looking in that direction—was that the reason she'd capitulated so easily? He had been with Macey when they first encountered Flora as an undead—when Macey had attempted to slay the ginger-haired girl and hadn't succeeded.

Had Flora seen that Macey wasn't alone, and realized she and her friends would be no match for two or more Venators?

No one else in the audience had seemed to notice the slaying of a vampire in their midst, but if a full-out brawl occurred, they certainly would. If a fight erupted, everyone who carried a revolver—which meant ninety percent of the men in here, and probably a surprisingly high number of the women—would pull out the weapon and start shooting. They'd have no idea at what or whom they were shooting—or that vampires were impervious to bullets—and who knew how many people would be caught in the crossfire.

The trigger fingers of gangsters, she'd come to realize, were very touchy.

Whatever the reason, Macey was content with letting the undead simply file their way out of the club without doing any damage to anyone—except the man she'd already staked. She brushed off the ash that clung to her beaded clothing, and realized it would probably adhere to the nooks and crannies forever. Unless she wanted to smell like dusted undead, she wouldn't be able to wear this jacket again.

She paused to determine whether the chill at the back of her neck had abated, and noticed Chas—who'd been making his way toward her—had veered to the right and was circling the audience again.

And since the back of her neck remained uncomfortably cold, Macey knew there was still work to be done. Brushing a clump of ash from the edge of the table, she turned and made her way toward the doors that led to the lobby. Chas could handle everything in here for now and she would make certain no one was lurking elsewhere.

She blinked rapidly at the bright lights that accosted her as she left the close, smoky, coolly lit hall. The eerie prickling led her to the right, toward the side doors that opened into the backstage area of the center, and she picked up her pace. The chill became stronger and more insistent.

Just as she came around the corner that led to the backstage doors, someone grabbed her arm. Macey spun, stake raised, and found herself face to face with Flora.

Her friend's eyes widened and she stepped back, hands up and palms out once more. "Don't!"

Macey halted, breathing heavily, the stake quivering in her hand.

"Please," Flora said. "Please, don't. Just…let me talk to you first. And then…" She bit her lip and stopped, waiting.

Macey lowered the stake, eyeing her friend cautiously.

Flora was still tall and loose-limbed, with carroty-red hair and freckles everywhere from her pug nose to her shoulders to her legs. She'd always been fair-skinned, but now she appeared even more washed out except for the freckles—which stood out even more on her dead-white skin—and her lips had faded to a pale melon color.

"What do you want to say?" Macey kept her voice cold. She had to keep reminding herself this wasn't Flora anymore. This wasn't her friend.

She prepared herself for anything—for the woman to lunge at her, fangs flashing, for her to sneer and challenge and threaten as she'd done before, or even for Flora to accuse her—to accuse Macey of leading her to this position, of causing her to be turned undead. But she was shocked when her friend's light blue eyes filled with tears and she folded her arms into her chest, hands gripping her own shoulders as if to hug herself.

"Help me," she whispered. "Please. Macey, can you help me?" She looked at her, eyes watery and blue—not a hint of a red glow or malice anywhere.

Still, Macey kept herself rigid, both mentally and physically. "What do you mean?"

Flora sniffled and huddled even more into herself, still fixing those blue eyes on Macey. "I…I'm frightened. I…" She was breathing heavily, nearly panting with obvious distress. "I don't…I…" She trailed off, closed her eyes, then seemed to gather herself back together. She shook her head, sending her loose curls swinging. "Never mind about me," she said, her voice steadier. "I've done what I've done, and…anyway, *Macey*. You're in danger." Her voice was earnest, and she reached out, as if to touch Macey in comfort.

Macey stepped back, still wary. Flora's expression closed off a little at the rejection, but she gave a short nod of acknowledgment. "Right. I understand."

"What do you mean I'm in danger?" It was all she could do not to shrug—after all, when *wasn't* she in danger?

"Nicholas Iscariot—you know him, right?"

"We've met."

Flora seemed hurt by her friend's continued reticence, but she plowed on. "He's obsessed with you. He's coming after you. You're all he talks about. And there's something about some rings?"

"I thought you were hanging out with Alvisi's crowd," Macey said coolly. "The way I understand it, Count Alvisi's people don't get along well with Iscariot's."

"Vampire society politics," Flora said with a wry smile. "But now that Alvisi is gone—and everyone knows you did it, Macey— that group is beginning to fall apart. Some are joining Iscariot, and others are trying to keep away from him."

"If Iscariot hated Alvisi so much, he should be thanking me for dusting him."

"Well, you know how men are. They can be real fickle." Flora's eyes lit with a moment of humor, sending a stab of familiarity and grief directly to Macey's heart. It took every bit of control she had to keep from responding to her friend's joke.

She decided to put everything on the proverbial table. "I nearly killed you, and now you're coming to me for help. Don't you find that a little fickle?"

There was a flash of something in those blue eyes—not a glow, not red, but something deep and dark and perhaps even sad. "You had your eyes closed when you struck at me. Did you know that, Macey? That's why you missed. You didn't really want to kill me."

"I could kill you now."

Flora nodded calmly. "You could. And you know what would happen to me, don't you? Where I'd go? What I'd be? And that's why you didn't do it before. Why you couldn't."

The stake was heavy in her hand. Very heavy; too heavy. Accusing by its very weight. Macey adjusted it, raising the pike so Flora could see she had no qualms about using it. "I'm bound to do it. It's my vocation. My legacy."

The blue eyes—still with no trace of red or malevolence—remained steady. "*I know.*" Her voice dropped to barely a whisper. "Macey, I'm frightened. I know I shouldn't ask. I have no right… but please…can you help me?"

"Help you how?"

Tears filled her eyes again. "I don't want to die, I don't want to be damned…I don't want to be this way. I—I made a mistake. Please…you must know how to fix this. How to fix me. Please, Macey, *help me.*" This time when Flora reached for her, Macey didn't move away. Her friend's hands closed warm and familiar around her arms as she pleaded, her teary blue eyes filled with sorrow and fear.

Suddenly realizing how vulnerable she was, Macey yanked her wrists away and stepped back. A quick look around confirmed they were alone. The moment of pause told her the temperature at the back of her neck hadn't changed.

This wasn't a setup. This wasn't a trick.

Flora had waited for her. Alone.

But that didn't mean Macey could help her. She looked back at her friend—her oldest, dearest, closest friend—and told her the truth. "I know of no way to change…*this.*"

Flora gasped and stepped back. "Truly?" Those huge blue eyes became even larger, even more frightened and shocked. "There is no way?"

"I know of no way," Macey said, her voice thick and steady. "But that doesn't mean there isn't one."

Her friend looked at her, a flicker of hope in her face. "You'll try to find out?"

"I will. If that's what you truly want."

"Of *course* that's what I want. If I had known…" Flora trailed off. "But why *would* you believe me, after the things I said and did to you? I understand that, Macey. I do. But if you could help me…" She smiled, her normal, beautiful smile that never failed to bring light to her eyes and roses to her cheeks and warmth to Macey's heart.

It did this time as well, despite everything that had passed between them.

"If you come back to The Silver Chalice with me, I'm certain Sebastian will take you in. And keep you safe."

Flora appeared startled. "You'd do that? For me? You'd let me stay with you?"

"Not with me. I'm not…I'm living elsewhere. But you'll be safe with Sebastian Vioget."

And if anyone would understand about being an undead and wishing he were not, it was Sebastian.

But that very thought sobered Macey. If Sebastian knew how to undo his undeadness, wouldn't he have done so a century ago? Then she remembered something Chas had told her about Sebastian. *He has a chance for redemption. And he needs you to help him.*

Maybe there *was* a way.

"Let's go." She gave a jerk of her head for Flora to follow her. Somehow she had to get out of The Music Castle and Flora to The Silver Chalice without Al Capone or his goons interfering.

She paused when they got near the lobby, an interesting and yet discomfiting thought occurring to her. Nevertheless, she plowed on. "If anyone tries to stop us leaving, can you…er… change his mind?"

Flora looked surprised, but then the flicker of a smile twitched her bow-shaped lips. "I can do that." She laughed, bumping companionably against Macey as they peered around the corner of the hallway, looking into the lobby.

It was like old times, sneaking around spying on Lillie Bentley and her beau Royal Yates.

Once assured there were only two potential hazards to their exit, in the form of a pair of burly guards at the closest set of doors, Macey boldly led the way across the lobby with Flora in her wake. When they got to the doors, as expected, the men brought them to a halt.

"Now where might you be going, there, Miss Macey?" asked the shorter of the two—which still put him more than a head taller than her.

"I was just taking my friend here out to get some air," she replied, and nudged Flora.

"It's awfully hot in here," said the redhead in a sort of singsong-y voice. And then she looked at the men, one at a time. "We've got to get some air."

"You should get some air," said the shorter one after a moment. His eyes had gone glassy. "Open the door for these dames, Bart."

The rush of balmy spring air was welcome, but just as Macey was about to step outside, she heard a noise behind her. A shout, and then a scream.

Then a gunshot. More gunshots.

She pushed Flora all the way outside. "I've got to go back." Her neck was still chilly, though whether that was from the proximity of her friend she didn't know. "Stay here. Don't come back in."

Macey hardly waited for Flora to respond in the affirmative before she was bolting off across the lobby, heading toward the music hall. But she was only a few steps away from the outside doors when one set of double doors burst open. Two men staggered out—and they were dragging a third one, whose white shirt had blossomed red on one side in the front. The wounded man appeared to be dead or dying, and the men dragging him were Capone's goons.

"Who's that man?" she demanded of Bart, the guard at the door. "The one who's shot?"

"Looks like Fanalucci," said Bart, squinting at the scenario. He seemed as unmoved, as if he were surveying his shirts to decide which one to wear. "He hates Big Al. Can't believe he had da balls to come in here tonight. Poor bastard. Ain't gonna have da balls to bug Snorky ever again."

Macey shook her head, stunned by the casualness of the violence, and the fact that someone had been shot during a jazz performance…and the spectators weren't running and screaming to get out of the place. What was wrong with people? Were they so inured to violence they didn't care?

The back of her neck was still frigid, and it was too cold to be merely the warning of Flora's presence. She hurried toward the music hall, where the sounds of excited, angry people poured through the open doors, although none of the audience members seemed ready to take themselves away.

"Now, now, everything's all right now," Capone was saying when Macey came through the doors. "I'm sorry about dat little disruption there, everyone. Let's just get back to the music now. We wanna get our money's worth from Satchmo, don't we? Cost me a pretty penny to bring his black ass back here to Chicago when he thought he was going to The Cotton Club in New York."

A nervous laugh rippled through the crowd, but people sat back down in their seats. Louis Armstrong, who seemed to have ducked off the stage during the altercation, walked back on to a roar of applause. He picked up his coronet and nodded to his piano player, who launched into a song Macey didn't recognize.

She was still scanning the hall, but the chill at the back of her neck had abated. If there were any undead around, they weren't nearby.

"Where da hell have you been?"

This time it wasn't Chas who spoke in her ear.

Macey turned to find Big Al nearly breathing down her neck. He looked furious as he clamped a hand around her arm and tugged her away from the door and into a dark, private corner.

"I was doing my job," she retorted, keeping her face close to where he'd thrust his.

"Your job," he said from between clenched teeth, his chin protruding belligerently, "is to *protect me*, first and foremost. I don't know where you were, but—"

"I was dispatching a tableful of vampires," was her even reply.

"You missed a few. And one of 'em nearly put a damned bullet in my face." His eyes bulged and his temples dripped with perspiration. He whipped out a handkerchief and mopped his face roughly.

Macey drew back a little. All right, so maybe he had the right to be a little annoyed. Still. "You're a Venator. Did you stake him?"

Capone looked as if he were about to explode. "In front of everyone here? I can't do that. Why the mother-fucking hell do you think I've hired you, ya damned broad? I can't shove a goddamned stake in an undead's chest in the middle of one of my clubs. How the hell would I explain *that*?"

"So where is he?" Macey's knees *might* have been trembling a little in the face of the violent fury directed toward her by the most dangerous man in Chicago, but she wasn't about to show it.

"I put a damned bullet in him. You just saw him being escorted out by Rudy and Sam. Now you're going to have to finish him."

Macey blinked, trying to understand. "But bullets don't affect the undead…"

Capone gritted his teeth and spoke sharply and succinctly. "They do if they are studded with silver. It'll keep him immobile and he'll appear dead until you can dust him. No pulse, no nothin'. But the minute the bullet's taken out, he's back to normal."

It took her a moment to process this, and that bit of information answered a whole lot of questions she'd had and never asked. So that was how Capone was killing his vampire enemies.

How many of his dead rivals had already been *un*dead, shot with the special bullets?

"Where are they taking him?" Macey tilted her head as the sound of sirens streaked through the distance. The warning was high and loud enough to be heard above the crooning of Louis Armstrong's horn.

"To da morgue, of course, ya dumb broad. Where the hell else do they take a goddamned corpse? And now I've got da fuzz coming in here and messing with my club—" He cut himself off and got in her face again. "You fuck up like this again, and I'm gonna—"

"What?" she fired back. "You're gonna *what*? Don't forget, Scarface—I know your secret. Maybe you shouldn't be threatening me quite so much anymore." Her fingers itched to slam her stake into the man's barrel chest, vampire or not.

The police sirens were so shrill, she knew they had to be just outside the front doors.

Al stepped back. His eyes glinted coldly. "You don't wanna play dat game with me, Macey Gardella. I don't lose. And I don't back down. And I'm a hell of a lot smarter than you."

"We'll see about that," she muttered as he turned away.

Seven

An Unbearable Reality

MACEY WAS ABLE to slip unnoticed out the side doors of The Music Castle as the fuzz arrived. Bystanders, both in and outside of the club, gathered to see who got shot or arrested, and they crowded the sidewalk outside.

Traffic rumbled past, and the marquee lights flashed red, yellow, and blue over the tops of the cars, pedestrians, and the few bushes that managed to exist on the street. Above, a half-moon glowed in a dark blue sky, surrounded by a freckling of stars and some dark wisps of cloud. People walked by, chatting and laughing across the street and around the corner, and the smell of coffee rolled from the open doors of a nearby cafe.

Macey looked around for Flora, pausing to let the night breeze filter over the back of her neck and then to determine if there was another, ugly sort of chill that portended the presence of her vampire friend. At first, when she didn't see Flora, Macey thought she might have run away.

But what would have been the purpose of doing so? She'd already had the opportunity to escape from the threat of Macey and Chas—why would Flora have stayed if she didn't truly want to talk to Macey, if she didn't truly want to warn her…and ask for her help?

Uncertainty niggled at her. Could she trust her old friend? She fully understood that when a mortal was turned, he or she ceased being the person they'd been. The soul was lost, and the need and obsession for blood and violence took over their lives.

Yet Sebastian Vioget had existed for more than a hundred years as an undead without taking one drop of human blood. He fought alongside the Venators. He *was* a Venator—he'd been one before he became undead.

Could a vampire change? Could a vampire control those urges? Could a vampire be saved?

"Macey!"

Her heart leapt and she turned. Flora emerged from the shadows, tall and slender, eyeing her nervously. "Is everything all right?" her friend asked.

"It's fine. I have things to do, so let's go to The Silver Chalice so I can get back to work."

"I was afraid you'd changed your mind," Flora said as they fell into step together. "And decided not to help me. I don't want to go back."

"Where have you been staying?" Macey asked. "Now that Alvisi is gone."

The count had been the one to turn Flora undead when he hired her to work at his Blood Club—a nightclub that offered mortals and immortals alike the opportunity to mingle, feed, have sex, and enjoy other hedonistic pleasures. Unfortunately, The Blood Club and the few other establishments that catered to this sort of entertainment were also more like feeding farms and slaughterhouses for the undead. A good number of mortals who entered those places never left again. Some died, some were recruited to join the vampire-protection society known as the Tutela, and a select few were turned undead.

At the original The Silver Chalice in London, on the other hand, Sebastian Vioget hadn't allowed that sort of mingling and feeding. Back then, he served both undead and mortal, but he hadn't ever, as he put it, procured or pimped for either side. There'd been no violence, no shedding, spilling, or sucking of blood in his place unless it came from the jugs of animal blood he kept for his own sustenance. None of that was true at his new establishment here in Chicago. He was the only undead who crossed the threshold there.

"I sort've ended up in Iscariot's camp," Flora told her as they stopped at a busy intersection. "He knows about you and me—our connection. He's anxious to get to you in any way he can."

"Including using you."

"Yes." Flora looked at her sidewise as they started across the street. Someone honked at them, and there was a shrill catcall-type of whistle, which they both ignored. "That's why I wanted to warn you. Iscariot is planning something big. He's determined to kill you and Sebastian Vioget. He says there are some rings, and the only way to get them is to slay Vioget."

Macey gave her a wry smile as they turned onto a side street. "Vampires have been trying to dust Sebastian for over a century. He's not very easy to kill." She saw something moving in the shadows ahead and narrowed her eyes. The back of her neck was still chilly, of course, because of her friend's proximity. But was the prickling getting stronger?

"Well, I've heard he's very handsome. And very sexy. If I were around him all the time, I know where I'd be looking to have some…fun." Flora gave her another side look, and even in the glow from a weary streetlight, Macey could see the glint of humor and bald curiosity in her eyes. Once more, she felt a stab of grief for the loss of their friendship.

"Someone's up there," she murmured to her companion. "Ahead. Just beyond that parked car. Two or three of them, I think."

Flora's grin grew wider. "They think we're going to be easy pickings, don't they? Two gals out alone? Let's give them a surprise." She picked up her pace with a conspiratorial giggle.

Macey smiled too. It'd be easy as pie for her and the fast and strong undead Flora to combat anyone who attacked them.

As long as it isn't Iscariot.

Macey shoved away the thought, but it returned with surprising force, and she stopped suddenly. An ugly feeling swept her and she eyed Flora with suspicion. Had she lured her out here, away from Chas and everyone else, so Iscariot could grab her?

Flora stopped too and turned to look back at Macey. "Don't tell me you're afraid!"

"No." Macey forced herself to concentrate, to feel and open her senses to determine whether there were any other undead in the area…or any other sort of threat. But even if she didn't sense any other vampires, it could be members of the Tutela waiting up ahead to force her into a dark automobile…to wrestle her back into the vehicle of terror where she'd been helpless at the brutal hands and fangs of Iscariot.

Nothing. She felt nothing. No sense of foreboding or apprehension. She began to walk again, her attention now on high alert and her eyes constantly scanning the shadows, parked vehicles, and doorways. Nevertheless, she dragged out the silver cross from beneath her dress and slid one of the stakes from her garter. A mortal could be stabbed with it just as easily as an undead. She was prepared for either consequence.

Once Flora realized her friend had started walking again, she began to put on what Macey could only describe as a show—the show of an innocent, oblivious woman strolling along a dimly lit, deserted street, completely unaware of the dangers ahead of her.

The gangly redhead fairly danced along the sidewalk, turning backward as she skipped in happy circles to talk to Macey about nonsensical things—about the cute delivery boy who brought the milk every day, or their old piano teacher back in Skittlesville, or anything she could think of to make her appear distracted.

It worked, and when Flora, with Macey several wary paces behind, reached the parked car they'd been watching, three men stepped out from behind the shadows.

Macey's fingers tightened around her weapon, but there was no sign of glowing red eyes, no increased chill at the back of her neck. And when she peered closely into the windows of the parked car around which the men had been hiding, she saw no sign of anyone lurking inside. Iscariot wasn't waiting, and surely more than three measly men would have been sent to capture a Venator.

She relaxed slightly, just as one of the men lunged for Flora's arm.

Her friend gave a convincing scream of surprise, but it was cut off when her assailant clamped a hand over her mouth. "How's about we go for a ride, doll?"

Before Macey could react, one of his companions accosted her, hands on his hips, standing directly in her path. He loomed over her, blocking the dark sidewalk.

"Hey, little lady," he drawled. "You and your friend are gonna join us for a bit of entertainment. We could use some dames to *heat* things up." He reached for Macey's arm, his smile wide and lascivious.

Before she could retort, the third man slipped up behind her and Macey found herself sandwiched between the two. A quick glance indicated that Flora's adversary was manhandling her—or so he must think—toward their parked vehicle.

Macey allowed the greedy hand to close over her arm, cutting off a startled shriek of her own as she slid the stake into her pocketbook and exchanged it for the derringer.

"No thanks," she said once her fingers curled around the heavy metal weapon, which was hardly larger than her palm. "We've got other plans."

She moved quickly, exuberant with the freedom of her abilities, sliding her gun-filled hand out of the purse and whipping it around into the cheekbone of the goon behind her—who'd had the audacity to slide his hands around to fondle her breasts!

He grunted and stumbled back as his companion used the grip on Macey's arm to fling her sharply toward the parked car. But she was anticipating this, and Temple had taught her to use the momentum against an adversary. She turned sharply, ducking low and fast under his arm. He tripped as she spun him around, then gave a choked cry of shock as she moved on, leveraging *him* up and over onto the ground with a sharp thud.

"Keep your hands to yourself," she told him, placing her foot on his heaving chest. Her chunky heel, a short one tonight due to the possibility of this sort of activity, pressed firmly into his diaphragm. "And learn some manners."

Out of the corner of her eye, she saw the third man—the one whom she'd clocked with her tiny firearm—rushing toward her. Still pinning the panting man with a superhumanly strong force, she turned calmly and displayed the derringer. "Did you want a second round?" she asked brightly. "Or would you prefer I simply empty *this* round into your belly? Small bullets notwithstanding, I hear a shot to the stomach is a very slow and painful way to die."

The attacker caught himself just in time, and he seemed to get the picture. "All right, lady, geez," he said, holding his hands up in surrender.

"Get out of here, and take your friends with you." Macey gestured with the gun, removing her foot from where she'd been pressing it slowly and steadily into the other man's abdomen.

They wasted no time disappearing into the darkness, leaving Macey to realize Flora and her assailant had disappeared. Probably into that dark alley.

She had a moment of uncertainty, wondering whether her stronger, faster companion—who was able to enthrall at will—had really been overpowered by her attacker. The chill at the back of her neck was still present, so Flora couldn't be far away…

Just then, the slender, long-limbed figure of her friend emerged from the shadows between the two brick buildings that formed the alley. She fairly swaggered out into the glow of the streetlight, and Macey turned cold when she realized Flora was dragging the back of her hand over her mouth.

She'd just fed.

All at once, the scent of blood was in the air—as if it had been waiting for Macey to recognize it. Pungent, coppery, the smell rose above the smells of vehicle exhaust and rotting garbage, and even the essence of urine that tended to pervade the alleys and entryways of side streets like this.

Gorge rose in Macey's throat, putrid and burning, and she swallowed it back with difficulty. All at once, the knowledge that her best friend was required to subsist on the lifeblood of living beings rushed to the forefront of her mind. Their moments of being carefree, companionable, and silly drained away.

Macey couldn't pull her attention from Flora's mouth. Though she saw no trace of blood or fangs, she knew what the woman had done. That she'd *bit* into human flesh, that she'd sucked and licked and *taken* from a person.

And what had happened to her victim?

Was he dead? Left for dead? Had he somehow miraculously escaped?

Her stomach lurched again.

"You took care of those two without batting an eyelash, did ya?" Flora said, lively and loud as ever. "That was fun. We make a good team, don't we, Macey? Even now!"

Macey felt lightheaded. "Where is he?" she managed to ask from between dry, stiff lips.

"Where is who—oh." Flora paused, then gestured to the alley with a casual thumb. "There."

Without another word, Macey strode past her, the handkerchief hem of her dress fluttering wildly about her calves. She made her way between the two dark buildings in the narrow passageway filled with garbage and other waste. The stench of blood was strong, and she could hear the gasping breaths of the man slumped against the wall.

As she went to examine him, she felt a presence behind her. The back of her neck grew eerily chilly, and Flora's long, angular shadow fell over them.

Macey couldn't bear to acknowledge her friend's presence. Instead, she hoisted the man up, then flipped him over her shoulder. She staggered a bit at the sudden addition of weight, but once steady, it was no great task for her to stumble out of the alley toward the street.

"I had to eat," Flora said. Her voice was petulant and defensive.

Macey closed her eyes for a moment, then walked past Flora, making her way back toward the busiest street. Blood from the victim seeped into her shoulder and along the loose material of her evening jacket, all the way through to her skin. She felt it oozing warm and wet, and the rusty stench filled her nostrils. The victim shuddered and gasped against her, his arms dangling, and occasionally one of his legs tightened as if he were trying to gather up the effort to free himself.

Once at the sidewalk, Macey let him slide down onto his feet. She held him upright with a strong arm as she waited to flag down a taxi. While she waited, she dug a vial of salted holy water from her pocketbook and dumped it onto the victim's wounds. He bucked and shuddered as the water hissed into the night air, but Macey held him firmly.

Fortunately, it wasn't long before a cab came along, and she whistled shrilly.

The vehicle pulled up and she wasted no time easing the man into the backseat. She tore off one of her stockings and wrapped it around the man's neck to stanch the blood as much as possible. Then, instead of getting inside, she hobbled to the front on her shoeless foot and spoke to the driver. "He's been injured. Get him to St. Joe's Hospital right away."

The cab driver opened his mouth to argue, but she tossed two dollar bills into the seat next to him—a very generous fare. "Do it, or Al Capone will find you. I have your car number."

With this threat, she pulled back out of the cab and it squealed away. Tomorrow, she would go and check on the man.

But for now, she had to decide what to do about Flora.

Heavy of heart, ill in her stomach, Macey went back to where she'd left Flora.

But when she returned, her redheaded friend was gone.

Grady abruptly became aware of his surroundings. He was sitting on the floor, slumped against the wall, arms immobile behind him. There was a thudding—seemingly everywhere— reverberating both along the floor on which he sat, and the wall against which he leaned, as well as at his temple.

He forced his eyes open and realized the thudding was only on his temple, though it felt as if it were coming from everywhere.

The place was dim, with a soft yellow glow to his right. Shadows moved quickly, bending and lifting, carrying bulky objects. Grady immediately knew where he was—in the warehouse, where the counterfeiters had been. Where they planned to remove their equipment and burn the place down.

Damn.

If the thudding of the printing presses was gone, that meant the gang was finished, and it looked as if they were packing things up…

Grady pulled experimentally on his wrists and was rewarded with a soft rattle, and the feel of metal biting into his skin. Handcuffs. Better, in this case, than being confined with rope—though either option was workable.

He smiled grimly and, using the wall, began to struggle to his feet. As he did so, he realized the handcuffs were locked around the pipe he felt directly behind him, which ran up and down along the wall.

A trickle of cold swept down his spine. Had they meant to leave him here to burn when they set the place on fire? That would make them murderers as well as counterfeiters.

His jaw set against the dull thud of pain, he managed to pull himself upright. Being attached to the pipe made it slightly easier, because he used it for leverage. Once standing, Grady set about extricating himself from the handcuffs.

He bent at the waist and, before he began to work his cuffed hands down over his rear, he toed off both shoes. His stockinged feet made it easier for him to step out from between his bound wrists with first one foot, then the other. He was huddled on the floor by this time, due to the connection to the pipe, but once he'd stepped out from between his arms and turned, he was facing the pipe, hands in front of him.

After this, it was child's play to release himself. Acutely aware that the sounds of movement had ceased, Grady slid the cuffs back down the pipe to the ground and retrieved one of his shoes. They were special shoes, designed by Mokana, and had hollow heels. Inside the heels were several useful objects, including lock picks.

When the great Houdini made his escapes from handcuffs and other bindings both in public and in private shows for law enforcement officers, he was normally stripped down to his skivvies. He was therefore unable to make use of special shoes like these, and found different ways to secrete the necessary lock picks on his person. But in this case, Grady's captors had no reason to suspect he was outfitted with devices created for the business of magic and illusion.

In very short order—he timed himself once the pick was held tightly in his teeth, and was pleased it took fewer than eighteen seconds to pick the lock; a personal record for this type of padlock—the cuffs popped open. He was free. He put his shoes back on and tucked the cuffs into his pocket.

Now to catch some counterfeiters…and would-be murderers.

It was just about that time he smelled smoke…and when he looked over, he saw the dancing glow of flickering flames where the gang had been, only minutes earlier.

Damn.

He had a choice: go after his captors or attempt to retrieve some of the evidence they were trying to burn. Neither way was an obvious home run when it came to getting what he needed for the cops.

Grady ran toward the flickering shadows of flames, and when he got closer, he saw that the fire was relatively small—hardly larger than a generous campfire. They'd just started burning a pile of debris, but it was near a wooden bay and a pile of crates. He didn't smell anything like accelerant.

Presumably, the "evidence" was somewhere in the fire, or nearby…and then he remembered the large tarp. Spinning, uncaring whether anyone was around to hear him—though he sincerely doubted it—he dashed back the way he'd come and found the canvas cloth. It was large and heavy and dusty—but exactly what he wanted.

Despite the canvas's bulk and weight, Grady caught it up and ran back to the fire, which had grown significantly in size as it caught on to the old, dry wood. He unraveled the canvas and tossed it on top of the blaze…

And with a whoosh, it settled into place, smothering the flames. Panting, Grady waited, but all was still. The fire was out, smoke filtering out through wrinkles in the heavy, thick canvas, and he had reason—not for the first time in his life—to be thankful he'd been introduced to Harry Houdini at the beginning of the Great War.

Otherwise, Grady would certainly be on his way to a too-early grave.

Eight

Brawl in the Powder Room

A S IT WAS A FRIDAY night, The Silver Chalice was packed with patrons. Macey could hear the sounds of revelry even from the street level, where a chalice-shaped newel topped the wrought iron gate that enclosed the stairwell leading from the sidewalk down to the entrance. That decoration was the only indication of the pub's location, and one had to know it existed in order to look for it.

A bar owned and operated by an undead had no need of windows. It was also tucked down beneath the street for privacy and security, its entryway a dark, seedy-looking area surrounded by a no-nonsense wrought iron enclosure.

Macey pounded down the dark, narrow stairway in her clunky-heeled shoes. Noise and light spilled from the ajar door, and a bulky shadow stood, arms folded, in the underground alcove next to it. He was smoking a cigarette and spewed out a long stream of smoke as he eyed her.

She ignored the man and pushed open the door. Immediately, her attention went to the bar counter, where the tawny-haired Sebastian Vioget stood. He was a study in gold, honey, and bronze, from the tips of his thick, tousled hair to the warm glow of his still sun-kissed skin, to the topaz of his eyes. One of the most angelic-looking and handsome men Macey had ever seen—and he was an undead vampire.

Sebastian was pouring a row of drinks, his white shirt open at the throat and sleeves rolled up to the elbows. Amber-colored liquid—highly illegal, of course, and knowing Sebastian, most likely straight from France—splashed into the shot glasses. He never had to worry about The Silver Chalice being raided by the fuzz, for all he'd have to do was give the cops a good, long look in the eyes and they'd be putty in his hands.

Macey took a step over the threshold. The door swung shut behind, and the noise and smells of the pub surrounded her: loud conversation, laughter and whistles, music from a piano, and the scents of smoke, alcohol, popcorn, and peanuts.

Sebastian stopped suddenly, frozen in his movements, then fairly spun around toward her. Their eyes met across the room, over the heads of his patrons sitting at scarred, round tables and along the broad, glossy-topped bar.

Macey felt the weight and power of his tiger-eye gaze from where she'd paused at the entrance. His eyes flashed gold, then became orange and red and hot. The tug was so strong, the sensation so sudden and intense, she felt as if she'd been dropped into a murky pond of warm water: everything around her slowed and became muted…lights, color, sound… She was trapped; she was falling. She was flushed and loose and—

"Well, look who the cat dragged in." The tense words were accompanied by a tall, slender figure who stepped in front of Macey, interrupting the powerful thrall that had settled quite over her so unexpectedly.

She shook her head, heart thudding. How had that happened? *What* had happened? She blinked hard, and the world settled a little more.

"Temple," Macey said, looking up at the elegant woman who'd positioned herself between her and Sebastian.

"I'd ask where the hell you've been for five months," said the woman, whose dark, almond-shaped eyes scored over Macey with concern and some ire, "but we can catch up later." And then she relaxed a little. "That's not your blood."

For the first time, Macey realized how she must appear—and that, in turn, made her understand why Sebastian had reacted the way he had. Maybe. There was blood all over the side of her neck and throat from Flora's victim, which she'd slung over her shoulder. She shivered a little, for the dark intensity in his gaze had made even her—an experienced Venator, a friend and colleague of his—feel lost and out of control.

Sebastian was just as powerful, it seemed, as Nicholas Iscariot. Perhaps more so, for he wore the *vis bulla*—and had power from both evil and the divine.

"Even so," Temple said, her slender, dark fingers tight around Macey's arm, "let's get you cleaned up."

Macey still felt a little out of sorts as she went with the other woman to wash up in a private powder room.

"What happened back there?" she was compelled to ask as her companion handed over a wet cloth.

Temple met her eyes in the mirror. "You walked in smelling of fresh blood."

Macey shook her head as she scrubbed at the blood, which had begun to dry in places and was sticky in others. It stained her clothing, and between that and the undead ash caught up inside the beading and lace, this outfit was definitely going in the trash. "That seemed an awfully strong reaction for someone who's managed not to feed for more than a hundred years. Surely Sebastian doesn't react that way every time he encounters fresh blood on a human." She knew he kept a stash of fresh cow's blood procured from the stockyards for his sustenance.

"Geez, sister, you don't get it, do you? I said *you* walked in covered with fresh blood. It ain't anyone else would have that affect on Sebastian Vioget but you, Macey Gardella Denton."

She felt the blood drain from her face, then whoosh back up again, hot and fiery. "Oh."

Temple didn't seem angry as much as intent on making Macey understand. "You are the spitting image of Victoria Gardella, but with the eyes of Giulia Pesaro—a perfect combination of the two women he loved. The two women he's sacrificed everything for—

including his soul. It was because of them he allowed himself to be turned undead."

Now she felt cold and unsteady. Nauseated. Chas had said something similar to her once… *I warn you—don't allow Vioget to see you bloody like that. He'd be on you in a heartbeat. The blood, and the fact that you're the spitting image of your great-great-grandmother.*

"Right," Macey managed to say around the lump in her throat. The problem was, the heat in Sebastian's eyes hadn't been as frightening as it had been alluring. She still tingled a little, still felt the titillation of need…

Or maybe it was simply because she'd been lonely, separated, and angry for months. Because she'd finally learned what it truly meant to be a Venator: no attachments.

An image of Grady, his expression shocked and repulsed as it had been earlier today, floated in her mind. Macey ruthlessly pushed it away.

Temple thrust a wad of clothing at her. "Here. It's probably a little long for you and'll be tight over the tits, but it's better than what you're wearing. Smells like vampire and blood. Which means you must have a story, now that you've decided to grace us with your presence again."

Before Macey could reply, Temple continued, "About Sebastian…look, sister, I'm worried about him. And you know me—I don't worry too much about anyone. But lately, Sebastian's been—"

The door opened. "He's a bloody damned mess—no pun intended."

"Lordy, Chas," Temple snapped, partly in surprise, partly in irritation. "Macey's in her altogethers and here you are, busting in for a peek."

"Though it wasn't my intent to peek," he said, crowding into the small chamber with them both and bringing the scents of smoke, undead ash, and damp wool, "one can't be looking a gift horse in the mouth—or so they say."

Macey, whose cheeks had flushed hot yet again, had been in the act of finding the head and armholes of the new frock Temple had given her, and stood there in no more than her side-lacing brassiere, which covered her from breast to thigh, and briefs.

She spun around with a huff, partly to hide her cheeks as much as the rest of her, and scrabbled through the flimsy material of the dress to find the opening. "Go away, Chas."

"Not a chance. You and I have some talking to do, lulu."

She yanked the frock over her head and, locating the holes for her arms, turned back as the fabric fluttered down over her torso. It was tight around the bust, and would have been tighter if she hadn't been wearing the side-lacer, which flattened her a little.

"Thanks, Temple," she said, turning back and ignoring the new arrival. "I didn't think about there being blood on me. I'll be more careful next time." Surprisingly, the pretty blue flower was still attached to her hair, out of place but still clinging to a few strands. She leaned toward the mirror to adjust it.

"That assumes there will be a next time," Chas said. "Temple, you'd best go see to Vioget." He gestured to the door.

The woman glowered at him. She was as tall as Chas, and her café-au-lait arms and legs were slender but shaped with smooth, lean muscles—unlike Flora's, whose freckled white limbs were merely thin and gangly…yet that much more powerful. Temple appeared ready to argue, but there must have been something in Chas's expression that caused her to fold, for though she gave him a sharp, displeased look, she reached for the doorknob.

"Better me than you, I suppose," Temple muttered, and left in a swish of understated fury.

Macey took a step to follow her, but Chas moved neatly to block the way. "Why in such a hurry to escape? Are you afraid I'm going to want to finish our little scrap in the coatroom? You seemed raring to pummel me before." His eyes lit with danger and challenge.

She gritted her teeth. "What do you want, Chas?"

"We didn't finish our conversation."

"I don't know what more there is to tell you. I am committed to working with Al Capone, and—"

"Yet here you are, somehow having slipped the noose—so to speak—so very easily after claiming your inability to do so for five bloody months. One can only assume you misjudged the ease with which you could escape Capone's influence."

Grady's face wavered in her mind, followed by the threatening, determined countenance of Al Capone. She might be smarter than he was, but he had Tommy guns and goons and contacts everywhere.

"I have to go back. I can't stay."

"Jesus, Macey, are you a Venator or are you a bloody damned *girl?* Don't tell me you're afraid of Al Capone, Venator or not!"

"It's not me I'm afraid for, you jackass!" Macey was so furious, tears stung her eyes—which made her even more angry.

"Well it's sure as hell not me or Vioget you're protecting, so who the—*oh.* Jesus *Christ.* The Irish bastard, is it? You went and fell for the damned mick, didn't you? Jesus, Macey! And as a result, Capone's got his own little Venator bitch all decked out and collared up, ready to do whatever he says."

Red tinged her vision and Macey grabbed him by the front of his coat. She whipped him to the side, slamming his broad-shouldered body into the corner as hard as she could. He crashed against the wooden wall, and it splintered a little beneath the force, but she was already shoving open the door.

She didn't get a toe over the threshold when Chas yanked her back, dragging the door closed behind her in one breathless movement.

"We aren't finished," he panted as he pinned her against the wall, his fingers angling just beneath her throat and holding her there with a wide, flat hand. Her heart pounded against his palm.

"Take your hands off me," she snapped. She had no fear of him—it was pure anger that fueled her. Anger, and something beneath her skin that was just fighting to be set free. Something that sizzled and tingled and burned.

"Only one hand is on you," he taunted, showing her the other that was free. He swung neatly aside when her knee jacked up, grinning when she missed—but the smile faltered when she hooked her foot around his knee and yanked, thanks to a neat move Temple had shown her months ago. He didn't fall, but she jolted him off balance and they tumbled into each other, crashing into the wall.

She spun away, pulling loose from his grip, and bolted to her feet. She stood there, panting, hands on her hips. "Don't touch me again."

His smile taunted her. "I told you before—the life of a Venator is lonely." He was out of breath enough to make Macey feel as if she'd won that round at least. "You can't be with the Irish bloke, Macey. You know you can't expose him to that sort of threat—whether it comes from Iscariot and his ilk, or that bloody Capone. You're on your own, lulu."

Nine

IT TOOK SEBASTIAN LONGER than it should have for his fangs to retract and his pulse to settle back into place. The sight of Macey—bloody and disheveled, eyes bright and determined, lips full and lush and beckoning, her scent carrying to him all the way across the room—standing there had tipped him into a vortex of need and desire.

He had to curl his fingers into the edge of the bar counter to keep from launching himself over it…to her. It wasn't because he hadn't seen her for months. It was simply because she was there.

Ready for him.

Damn it. *No.* Never that. *God help me.* Sebastian broke out in a cold sweat at the thought.

But the dreams about her had been taunting him for weeks now…and here she was, in the flesh. Returned at last.

No.

Thankfully, Temple realized what was happening and she broke the connection in her understated but effective manner. He owed her one.

Chas Woodmore…not so much. He'd been sitting at the end of the bar counter, having just arrived from somewhere and in a particularly foul mood—even for Woodmore—when Macey walked in.

Even now, Sebastian remained unsteady and off balance. He poured a too-large glass of the bourbon he'd brought in—

smuggled was too complicated a word; he'd merely shipped it from France and convinced the customs officers it was nothing but a case of communion wine (the ability to enthrall did have its benefits)—then set the glass aside.

The last damn thing he needed was to impair himself even further.

He looked up as Temple came into view without Macey and Woodmore. She met his eyes and seemed relieved that he at least *appeared* steady, but ire flashed there. Sebastian didn't have to think hard to wonder who had caused it. Woodmore was even more of an arse than Max Pesaro had ever been, and that was saying a lot.

"We're closing up," Sebastian announced loudly, aware of the alarming thuds now coming from the private rooms he kept adjacent to the pub. "Everyone out."

The bitter grumbling that started was put to rest as Sebastian scanned the place with an unyielding expression. He didn't even need to spark a glow in his eyes. "Your accounts will be settled later," he added, knowing half of them never would. That, too, helped clear the place more quickly than anything other than a warning of "Fire!"—or "Raid!"—would do.

Just as the last few patrons made their exit, Macey stalked out of the back rooms with Woodmore in her wake. She was, thankfully, cleaned up and no longer looked as if she'd been devoured by a lustful vampire.

Sebastian relaxed even more and trusted himself to pour a finger—just a finger—of the bourbon in a fist-sized glass. Then, thinking even more clearly, he added a large slop of fresh cow's blood to the whiskey and sipped.

Immediately, the lingering tension and the need for sustenance eased even more…though as Macey walked across the pub toward him, the low, golden light made her look even more like Victoria. Victoria'd even had short hair like that for a time, when they were in Prague to retrieve the second Ring of Jubai, and it sprang up the same way in thick, inky curls around her jaw and bared her long, slender neck.

Sebastian's fangs pulsed, threatening to erupt again, and he surreptitiously reached for the *vis bulla* dangling beneath his shirt. The extra jolt from holy silver against the pads of his fingers served to remind him of his promise and gave him a surge of strength, so by the time Macey climbed onto a stool in front of him, Sebastian was able to smile at her with ease.

"Well, now—to what do we owe this pleasure, *ma cher*?"

"I'm sorry I haven't been in contact," she said immediately.

He noted an unusual bashfulness clinging to her, and recognized it was a little difficult for her to meet his eyes. Devil take it. Had he frightened her, or was it Woodmore who'd done the honors? He'd told no one about the dreams, that was damn well sure. Despite her reticence, there was a sort of underlying rage clinging to her as well as Woodmore.

A little uncertain himself, Sebastian chose not to reply; instead, he brought up three more glasses and poured a round for the trio now settling on stools at the corner of the bar. Temple, Macey, and Chas, clustered one by two.

Woodmore and Temple sipped without hesitation, but Macey looked at the bourbon as if it were poison.

"Come now," Sebastian told her smoothly. "Let's not be shy and demure, *petit*. We all know you left that carriage behind some while ago, and you clearly need a bracing drink. No one will know. And then you can tell us what happened."

"I'm sure Chas would love to fill you in. I...I can't stay." She looked as if she were about to slide off the stool.

A snort from Woodmore drew Sebastian's attention, and he moved automatically to refill the man's glass. "Macey claims Capone is a Venator." His lethal gaze settled accusingly on Sebastian. "A fact I suspect is not news to you, Vioget."

Sebastian shrugged. "I suspected, but didn't know for certain. There is an Alphonsus listed in the Bible."

"A prevarication if I ever heard one. Not that I expected anything more from you," Woodmore replied.

"I don't understand. How can he be a Venator—be like us— and not do his *job*?" Macey seemed to have decided to stay. She sipped her drink, and Sebastian was pleased to see a little more color returning to her face. He avoided looking into her eyes for too long, however, knowing that was a trip he dared not take.

Not when he was feeling this vulnerable.

"Why don't you ask Vioget here about Venators who shirk their duty?" Chas was clearly still in a foul mood, and he was doing his damnedest to bring Sebastian down into it as well. *Bastard.* "I'm sure he can enlighten you."

Sebastian swallowed his fury. "Woodmore is referring to a period of time in which I declined to employ the stake," he replied. "For a number of reasons that are no longer relevant, more than a century after the fact. But to answer your question, Macey, it's actually not all that surprising for someone who's been granted the power and abilities we have to use them to benefit themselves, rather than for the purpose for which they were given. It's much easier—and less dangerous—not to hunt the undead, but instead use the *vis bulla* for other reasons. We all have free will, you know."

Macey nodded. "Have there been other Venators who…well, became villains? Used their abilities for selfish reasons?"

"Unfortunately, yes. I haven't ever encountered them myself, but there was Frederick, for one. Surely there were others, but history isn't one of my strong suits. Now, back to the most pertinent question: why do you think Al Capone is showing so much interest in you?"

"He believes one of Rosamunde Gardella's prophecies applies to us—to Big Al and me."

The absurdity of the idea was beyond comprehension. "Indeed? And did he happen to tell you which one it was?" Sebastian didn't attempt to hide his derision. If it was true Capone was one of them, Sebastian found it difficult to believe he could be much of a scholar about the family legacy. The bastard struck him as someone who had even less time for such mundane topics as history as Sebastian did.

"I have it written down," Macey replied. "But it's something about a dauntless one. He claims I'm the dauntless one, and he is the other half that makes the whole. But I don't know what would make him believe it was about him."

Sebastian looked at Temple, who nodded and rose gracefully from her seat. "I'll see what I can find. Don't wait up for me, boys."

Out of habit, Sebastian watched her tall, elegant figure as she walked across the pub. How did women manage it on those high, chunky heels—especially to appear both graceful and sensual at the same time? Her hips moved sleekly; the silk of her dress slid over a sassy arse with every step. She was a hot piece, and he knew she found him attractive. But it wasn't Temple he wanted.

Hell, it wasn't even Macey. Not really. Not when it came down to it.

Not even Victoria, if she walked in the pub right this moment—well, perhaps that wasn't strictly true. After all, he *had* loved her. Although, after more than ten decades of self-examination, Sebastian supposed part of the motivation for that love might have been to taunt Max Pesaro.

But it was Giulia who filled his dreams. Giulia who held his heart. It was for her he'd done this.

But by *God*, if it didn't end soon, Sebastian didn't know if he could manage it.

What if it were another hundred years before his "long promise" was fulfilled? What if Macey walked in here again, all blood-covered—and with her own blood this time? Sebastian lifted his glass and took a long draw.

God help me. I'm done with this. I don't know how much longer I can go on.

Ten

Of Questions, Answers, and Assumptions

MACEY TOOK ANOTHER DRINK of whatever it was Sebastian had poured her. She was warmer now, looser…yet beneath it all she felt a sense of foreboding. The clock was ticking. What would Capone do when he realized she was gone?

How long did she have before he made good on his promises? Maybe he'd think she'd gone to the morgue to take care of Fanalucci's body? If he did, that would give her more time… wouldn't it?

Chas, who seemed to have shed most of his angry, challenging mood, fixed Macey with his attention. "What happened with your friend Flora at The Music Castle? Yes, of course I bloody well recognized her."

Macey nodded and collected her thoughts—or tried to. This was the reason she'd come here tonight anyway. Even without Flora, she had questions. And she needed to talk to Sebastian and Chas—the only two people who really understood her situation. Temple, too, of course, but she wasn't a Venator, and so she couldn't wholly understand.

This time, Macey took a big gulp of the whiskey—or whatever it was—and drained the glass. It burned her throat and she had to stifle a cough, but even as her eyes watered, she set the glass down with a thunk. "More."

While Sebastian, who didn't bat an eyelash, filled hers and Chas's glasses, she began to talk—grateful to be able to do so with two people she trusted.

If only Wayren were here.

"Flora wants me to help her. She wants me to save her from her—uh—undeadness, I guess you'd call it. She realized she made a mistake in getting turned"—Chas made a rude sound, but Macey ignored him—"and she wants to get away from Iscariot and the life of a vampire. She says she's afraid of him."

"She damn well should be," Chas muttered.

"And she said—which is no surprise to me—that Iscariot is after me, and after the Rings of Jubai." Her attention slid to the five copper rings that glinted on Sebastian's hand. "I was going to bring her here tonight—I thought she could stay here with you," she said, looking at Sebastian. "Since you…well, you might understand her predicament."

Chas slammed his glass on the table. His eyes burned, dark and intense. "No. He doesn't understand her predicament because Vioget here made a *conscious decision* to relinquish his soul in an attempt to save the soul of Giulia Pesaro—who was a vampire, as you may or may not know, and thus her soul was damned.

"He didn't choose to become undead on a whim, because he wanted to be immortal, wanted the power, thought it would be *fun*—or to get *back* at a friend." He nodded at Macey, who was surprised he even knew Flora's anger with her had been part of the reason she was susceptible to the lure of the undead. "So, no, Sebastian doesn't really 'understand her predicament,'" he said, mimicking Macey's words in his low, gritty voice.

"Well now, Woodmore," Sebastian said after a startled moment, "I didn't realize you had an empathetic bone in your body. To surprises." He slopped more whiskey in everyone's glasses and lifted his own. "*Salut.*" Then he looked at Macey, capturing her with his warm gaze—though this time, without the edge of the thrall. "And why did you not bring this Flora here after all, then, *cher?*"

"On the way here, we were set upon—or at least, they attempted to set upon us—by three thugs. Of course I—we—fought them off, and when I went to look for Flora, she was gone." Macey hesitated and lifted her drink.

If she told them what happened, she sensed Chas would be even more accusatory. And what would Sebastian think?

"Ah, I see. She took the opportunity to partake from the man who made the poor decision to attack her, didn't she?" Chas spoke before she could make the choice. When she looked at him in surprise, he made an impatient gesture. "It's obvious—you showed up here covered in someone else's blood. Is he alive?"

"He was…when I sent him to the hospital in a taxi. I didn't really know what else to do." Macey's hand was a little unsteady when she lifted her glass again. When was the last time she'd had something to eat? The whiskey still burned when it went down, but she was beginning to appreciate its warmth.

It dulled everything.

And yet it heightened her senses.

She drank, dimly aware of her two companions trading glances.

Irritated, she set the empty glass down with a dull thunk and gestured to it. In for a penny, in for a pound, she figured. Tomorrow would be soon enough to face the impossible choice that had become her life.

"*Is* there any way to help her?" She pointed to Chas. "*You* told me *he*"—she gestured to their host—"needed my help to save his soul. If it's possible, then why can't I help Flora?"

"That's assuming your friend really wants help to save her soul, and isn't working for Iscariot." Chas, of course.

Macey bristled. "As if I haven't thought of that—"

"I'm not certain it is possible." Sebastian's voice was low, tinged with an emotion Macey couldn't quite identify. Fear? Despair? "To save a soul that's been—what do the Dracule call it, Woodmore? Damaged? Yes, that's the term. Damaged. I am acting on faith and hope, and the interpretation of a prophecy.

Even Wayren can't—or won't—tell me what the result will be. I won't know until it's all over."

"Until what is all over?" Macey demanded. She was *sick* of prophecies and unanswered questions, and answers she didn't want to hear or think about. And she sure as hell didn't want to leave here and go back to Al Capone.

"This. My life. Such as it is." Sebastian smiled his gorgeous, charming smile. "And believe me when I say I am more than ready for it to be done."

Macey didn't quite know what to say to that. She'd known Sebastian—and Chas, for that matter—for less than a year, and already she couldn't imagine life, or being a Venator, without either of them. She simply didn't know enough, have enough experience—and she would never rely on Alphonsus to help her.

And the thought of facing Nicholas Iscariot on her own was hair-raising.

"That makes two of us." Chas's voice was gritty. "To clarify, Vioget—I speak of wishing for my own time on earth to come to an end, not the demise of your charming self."

"Well, isn't that nice, to know both the men I rely on the most have death wishes."

"You rely on us?" Chas, of course, seized Macey's comment like a dog with a bone. "I would never have guessed. I thought for certain we'd been replaced in your affections by that fat Italian bastard."

He might have been baiting her—he probably was—but this time, Macey didn't let his comment get to her. She merely turned toward Chas, leaned in closely enough to smell *him*—whiskey, wool, smoke, and something spicy—and batted her eyelashes. Yes, literally batted them. There was that saying about honey instead of vinegar, right?

"Of course not, Chas, sweetie. You could *never* be replaced in my affections. After all, I have you to thank for dragging me out of Iscariot's auto, don't I?"

His throat moved, his lips quirked, and his eyes flashed dark just for a moment. "Be careful, lulu," he murmured. "I can play that game." He lifted his glass, his knuckles brushing her cheek she was so close, and looked at her over the rim as he sipped.

Warmer and more lightheaded than she had a right to be, Macey eased back and turned her attention to Sebastian. He was watching the two of them, his mouth set in a half-smile, his eyes glinting with pleasure. The man definitely appreciated the fine art of flirtation.

"Perhaps you should ask Woodmore here about his own charmed life, *ma petite*. I'm not the only one who doesn't belong in this age. He has his own role to play—and one about which he's been particularly closemouthed. If you can imagine that." Sebastian's gaze narrowed with pleasure.

Macey was getting a little dizzy, transferring her attention from one to the other…or maybe it was the whiskey. "All right then, Chas, 'fess up, why don't you?"

He'd settled onto his elbows, leaning on the bar counter, looking down at his perpetually full glass. "It's Wayren's fault. She gave me the opportunity to leave—"

"It was more like an escape, *non*?" Sebastian said helpfully.

Chas shot him a look of loathing. His jaws were obviously tight when he spoke, for his words came out clipped and sharp. "It was a long time ago, and I had finished with…what I had been doing—"

"Which was what?" Macey was genuinely curious, even though she could tell Chas didn't wish to talk about it at all.

Sebastian came to Chas's rescue. "He was hunting vampires, but a different breed of them. They're called the Dracule, and unlike those of mine and Iscariot's ilk, the Dracule *can* be redeemed. Some of them, anyway." His smile was pained. "What Woodmore isn't saying is that he had his heart broken, and he was running—"

"I'd finished a difficult task in Paris," Chas interrupted flatly, taking over the narrative. "And the way it all worked out was not what I had hoped. The woman I—well, things were rather… unpleasant—"

"Unpleasant? The way Corvindale made it sound, you were even more of a cold bastard than you are now. And coming from him, that's saying a lot." Again, Sebastian with the helpful comment, but this time he softened it with a splash of whiskey into all three glasses. "Alas, that's what a broken heart will do to a man, *non*?"

"As you well know," Chas replied evenly.

"I don't deny it."

Macey shook her head. It was as if they were speaking in a foreign language, and that, combined with the drink, made it difficult for her to follow their conversation. So she jumped in. "Are you saying…Wayren brought you here? From *where*?"

"From 1803. London, to be exact. Though I spent quite a lot of time in Paris," he added, bitterness in his tone. "Beneath the streets, hunting the infamous Cezar Moldavi. And his sister."

"Are you saying Wayren brought you through *time*? She can *do* that?" Maybe it was the drink, but Macey actually found his tale believable. Maybe she'd read too much Jules Verne.

"Apparently so," Chas said, looking back down at his glass. "I didn't really care to know the mechanics. I was simply ready to… move on. So, under the tutelage of Max Pesaro—"

"*That* I would have liked to see," Sebastian commented slyly. "You and Pesaro in the same room. It would have been quite entertaining to watch the two of you manage your—"

"—and his trainer Kritanu," Chas continued from between gritted teeth, "I went through the Trial to become a Venator, and I was granted the *vis bulla*. Then Wayren brought me here. She hasn't been specific about my purpose, but I think she simply wants me to play nursemaid to Vioget here. To protect his pretty face and form from the ugly undead." He grinned darkly.

"Nursemaid my arse," Sebastian growled, the bottle clinking as he refilled everyone's glasses.

"Why else would she have offered me this?" Chas replied companionably, lifting his glass. When he set it down, it was empty, and he spoke to Macey. "It's five years I've been here in Chicago, watching over the fanged one here. But I've traveled more than a hundred-twenty years, if you go by time measured in stars and planets."

"You were in love with a woman in Paris, and what happened? You were hunting vampires, so, what? She got destroyed by the undead?" Macey couldn't help but think of her own father's story—and that of her mother.

That's what happens when a Venator loves someone. Her stomach churned in an ugly swirl, and suddenly the whiskey didn't look quite as appetizing.

As if reading her mind, Sebastian clunked a small bowl of peanuts in front of her. "Eat, *cherie.*"

Chas had given a short, hard laugh. "Oh, no, it wasn't as *simple* as all that," he said, real venom in his voice…but even in her state, Macey could hear the deep, raw pain he tried to hide with the bitterness. "Narcise was a vampire herself. A Dracule. And that, Macey darling, is the irony of the two men upon whom you rely the most—as you put it. The pair of us—we are the epitome of irony: the vampire hunter who *becomes* a vampire, and the vampire hunter who *loves* a vampire." His eyes were bleary as he looked up at her. "Is it any wonder we're finished with this world?"

Just then, the outside door rattled violently.

"We're closed," Sebastian called.

The door rattled even louder, and someone shouted back from beyond.

Sebastian rolled his eyes and slipped from behind the counter. "I know I serve the best, but when I'm closed, I'm closed. Bloody fools."

Macey looked at Chas. "I'm sorry."

He smiled tightly and lifted his glass. "It was for the better. I'm here now, and not just as window dressing, as they say at Marshall Field's. Wayren, sly as she is, hasn't told me anything other than I'm needed."

"Will you go back when—well, after you're done here?"

"I sure as hell hope not."

"Macey." Sebastian's voice was tight and sharp, and she looked over. He'd stepped back to allow a small group of people to enter.

Five men, three women—all seemed raucous and happy… until she recognized two of the men. Capone's goons.

And then she looked at the women, who were clearly drunk, hanging on their companions as if they were drowning.

The bottom dropped out of her belly, and all the whiskey inside surged and churned alarmingly.

"*Dottie,*" she whispered, bolting to her feet so quickly the stool crashed to the floor. And the other two women were friends of hers as well—Mandy and Clara.

They all appeared to be having a fun time…except for the thugs, who made a point of revealing the guns they had tucked in their pants.

Capone's message was abundantly clear: her time was up.

Eleven

A Revelation Above the Fold

B EFORE I GOT coshed on the head, I saw their faces," Grady told a trio of cops, which included Linwood. "I can identify five of the gang members."

After successfully smothering the fire, Grady had called the fuzz and directed them to the warehouse while he headed into the office to write his story, in hopes of making the early edition… and possibly the front page.

Once a news hawk, always a news hawk.

Now, he and the authorities were standing in the *Tribune's* office, shortly after dawn. The towering building, finished only last year, still smelled of fresh paint and new plaster.

"You really do have nine lives," his uncle said, shaking his head. A smile flickered at the corners of his mouth.

Lieutenant Jameson Linwood was the only family Grady had, and vice versa. Grady hadn't even known he had an uncle when he left Dublin to make his way to London, just before England got involved in the Great War. For his part, Linwood, who was barely a decade older than Grady, had no idea what misfortune had befallen his much older sister after she ran away from home, for he'd been a mere toddler at the time.

While working for a textile merchant, Linwood met and married an American girl. He moved to her hometown of Chicago, joined the police force, and had been here ever since.

He had pale, gingery hair and a spectacular number of matching freckles, which for the most part were limited to his muscular forearms and shoulders—with only a smattering of them decorating his forehead and hands. Though of average height, Linwood had the broad shoulders and build of a heavyweight boxer. Though uncle and nephew shared a name, the only physical feature they had in common was the color of their eyes—blue, though the elder relative's irises tended more toward cornflower than his nephew's.

"Explain to me again how you didn't get burned alive," said Officer Trudell, one of the few on the force Linwood and Grady would trust with their lives. "They had you handcuffed to a pipe? Who do you think you are—Houdini?" He laughed, slapping his uniformed leg.

Grady merely smiled and exchanged glances with his uncle. Linwood was one of the few people who knew the brilliant escape artist and magician was his mentor. "It doesn't matter now. You have evidence, and I can identify them—one of the men has a deformed earlobe, which will make it easy to spread the word on the force."

"And the misprinted bills—tens being printed on bleached-out singles. What a damned good idea if I do say so—for a counterfeiter." At the new voice, Grady turned to Robert McCormick, former war hero and owner and managing editor of the *Tribune*. The newsman, who was taller than even Grady and sported a neat black mustache, was appropriately called the Colonel. With black-tipped fingers, he held a folded paper that smelled of fresh ink. "Glad you were able to save some of them from the fire, ace. The picture of the bills—and your story—made the front page."

"Above or below the fold?" Grady asked with a grin, taking the hot-off-the-presses early edition. He didn't mind when the ink transferred liberally to his own fingers—hazard of the trade—and answered his own question. "Hmm. Below it is. Well, maybe someday you'll be finding my stories a place on the top," he said with a grin at his boss, flipping the paper so he could see just what *had* made it above the fold.

"You'll get the top when there's an arrest," replied McCormick.

But Grady wasn't listening. His surroundings had fallen away somewhere far from him, and the conversation around him became murky as he looked at the front-page article that had not only usurped the position he'd hoped for, but fairly stabbed him in the gut.

There, splashed on the front page in a huge photo, was Al Capone…with a smiling, stylish Macey on his arm. *Satchmo Stuns While Big Al Brags: Armstrong returns to Snorky's Music Castle.* Grady read on:

> *While Louis Armstrong and his*
> *Hot Five played to a packed club*
> *last night, Big Al squired about a*
> *mysterious new dame on his arm.*
> *When asked about his lady, Capone*
> *merely grinned and said, 'Don't tell*
> *Mae!' Later that evening, gunfire*
> *broke out in the club, temporarily*
> *halting Satchmo's performance…*
> *but the sweet sounds of his coronet*
> *were only delayed a short time, for he*
> *swung back into the show with gusto*
> *after the wounded Danny Fanalucci*
> *was removed from the club. When*
> *asked about the altercation, Capone*
> *said, 'Someone draws a gun in my*
> *place, he's not gonna be welcomed*
> *back.' The animosity between the*
> *two men is well known. The status*
> *of Danny Fanalucci's health is not*
> *currently known, but bystanders*
> *indicated he was shot in the chest.*

Grady felt a roar of emotion build inside, and he returned the edition to McCormick ever so calmly. "Better luck next time," he said slowly, as if the words were being pushed out through a thick stew.

His companions didn't seem to notice his reaction, though Linwood did give him a close look. But then Trudell reminded Grady he needed to give his formal statement, as well as work with an artist at the station to describe the gang members so drawings could be made.

Grady had no arguments about keeping his mind otherwise occupied. That was what he'd been doing for the last five months: trying to forget about Macey Denton.

Now he had even more reason to do so.

If he could.

Macey had been to the Cook County Morgue only once before. The memory was not one she cared to revisit, for on that occasion she'd had to identify the body of one of her closest friends.

Chelle had been captured and fed upon—brutally and liberally—by Nicholas Iscariot, and Macey had visited the morgue to confirm it was her friend whose body had been discovered dumped in an alley. It had been the morning after Macey herself had been attacked by Iscariot, and she was exhausted, hurting, and heartsick.

Thus it was no surprise she wasn't anticipating the act of stepping into the cold concrete room nestled in the basement of a building adjacent to the police station. For obvious reasons, she'd waited until well past midnight to leave Capone's Lexington Hotel suite to venture into this morbid chamber.

Big Al had been less than pleased with her disappearance from The Music Castle during the Louis Armstrong performance, a fact which he subtly reminded her by adding several new photographs—framed, of course—to the gallery of what she'd begun to think of as hostages to her good behavior. So when he'd blandly suggested tonight was the night to finish off the undead Danny Fanalucci, who'd been trapped in a state between undeath and death thanks to the silver bullet lodged in his chest, Macey had thought of Clara and Mandy and Grady and had no choice but to agree.

The subterranean corridor was lit by exactly two lights: one at the bottom of the stairwell, and another halfway to the entrance of her destination. The hallway could use a sweep, but there weren't any cobwebs, nor did she encounter any sign of mice or rats or other creatures. As she drew closer to the morgue, Macey felt the eerie chill settle over the back of her neck. Fanalucci was definitely still present.

County Morgue was painted on the frosted glass window of the door. She used the key Capone had given her, and the unlocked knob felt cold and uninviting when she closed her fingers around it.

The space was dark and still, and the back of her neck prickled with the awareness of an undead. The room smelled of death—though, being from mortals, it was a different scent than the repulsive one that clung to the undead or their ash—accompanied by the pungent aromas of chemicals and industrial alcohol (which was still legal, of course). There was a sharp, biting scent she couldn't identify, and also a damp, earthy essence.

Ashes to ashes…dust to dust.

Perhaps some of the corpses here were already beginning to decompose, ready to rejoin the earth.

Dead bodies were brought to the morgue to be officially identified, then kept until they were retrieved by family or taken to the funeral home. In some cases, a corpse might be examined in order to determine cause of death.

The place was dead silent. Macey smiled grimly at her private joke—surely it wasn't the first time someone had said or thought it—and pushed the light switch. There were no windows in the eerie room, so no one would come to investigate the midnight illumination.

The walls and floor were unpainted concrete. Columns of forbidding metal doors lined one wall, stacked three on top of each other and four across. Those would be the body drawers, on which each corpse could be rolled out on a morbid tray. There were also four so-called slabs, or tables, lined up in the room—each one a steel tabletop mounted on a massive lever in the floor that raised, lowered, or tilted the body as necessary. Only one was currently empty.

Aware of the insistent chill on her neck, Macey glanced at the three sheet-covered bodies that adorned slabs. Might as well start there. She slid the stake from its mooring beneath her dress and approached the first corpse, whose toes were uncovered on the foot sporting a tag. *Guernsey, T.*

The second toe tag read *Fenilworth, B.*, and the third bare foot was clearly that of a woman.

She turned to the wall of drawers and noted they were labeled on the exterior, which should make it easy to find…ah, yes. *Fanalucci, D.* Middle drawer, third column.

When she pulled it out, the drawer gave a low, protesting groan, adding to the atmosphere. Macey eased the sheet down to his shoulders and looked at Danny Fanalucci's body with curiosity. He certainly appeared dead. His skin was a pale grayish-blue and his eyes were closed. He wasn't breathing, and there was no sign of a pulse in his throat. She lowered the sheet to his belly, unmoved by the thick, dark hair that grew over shoulders, arms, chest, and abdomen.

The gunshot wound was in the right side of his chest, probably puncturing a lung but not lodging in his heart—as her stake would soon do. The hole was dark and deep, and she wondered how far into his organs and tissue the bullet had penetrated (she wasn't about to turn him over to see if there was an exit) and whether, if it were somehow dislodged, Danny Fanalucci would spring to life—fangs and glowing red eyes and all.

She had to give Big Al credit. This was a brilliant way to get rid of vampires without drawing attention to the fact that they were being slain—and without drawing the attention of the general populace to the fact that the undead walked among them.

Something stirred the air, and Macey looked up from her examination of the wound. The hair on the backs of her arms prickled with warning.

Nothing seemed amiss, and yet…

She straightened, tightening her grip on the stake. Rotating in a slow circle, she looked around the room, listening, feeling… waiting.

Something was wrong. Something…

The lights shuddered, then dimmed, but remained lit in a dull golden glow. An awful chill rushed over her neck and shoulders, surging through her body as if she'd been thrown into the deepest, coldest part of Lake Michigan. Macey could hear her own breath—strong, measured—and felt her heartbeat pounding steadily…

She became aware of another presence. Someone—or something—approaching.

Another strong heart pounding, somehow melding with the rhythm of her own…and another breath, fighting to merge with hers…

She remained very still, standing in the burnished glow of a room as the ugly chill settled over her, permeating her skin through to her bones and muscles…

The lights went out, plunging the room into full darkness. Macey made no sound, though terror shuttled through her. For at last, she'd recognized the sensation.

She'd felt it once before, on the most terrifying night of her life.

When the door opened, a sliver of light spilled into the morgue, surrounding the tall, angular figure standing on the threshold and obstructing the details of his face. All she could see was his black hair, ruthlessly parted and combed close to his scalp. It gleamed richly, as if it were wet paint.

"Macey Gardella. What a pleasant and unexpected surprise," said Nicholas Iscariot in his too-smooth voice. He stepped into the room, and his long, slender hand moved in the vicinity of the light switch. The bulbs popped on with audible reluctance, barely illumining from dull orange to a mellow golden glow. She had the impression he hadn't actually *touched* the switch.

"Isn't the very nature of a surprise, that it's unexpected?" Macey managed to find her voice. And by God, her words were rock steady. "And in my case, it's most certainly not a pleasant one." Her fingers around the stake had become numb with tension, yet through her shock and terror, Macey focused on a beacon of clarity and determination.

Her heart still beat in its own rhythm despite his powerful pulse fighting to control it. No. She wouldn't allow it. *Never again.*

Iscariot closed the door with a dull thud. "A pedantic Venator. How amusing. Although one shouldn't be surprised, for of course, the first time we met was when you worked at the library. You were utterly naive and innocent then, weren't you?"

Macey took care not to look him in the eye, or even near his face. She kept her attention focused over the corner of Iscariot's left shoulder. Two of the sheet-covered slabs were all that separated her from the most powerful vampire in the world—the son of the man who'd been the first of Lucifer's immortal, half-demon creations: Judas Iscariot.

She knew with a sudden, stark clarity that only one of them would leave this room alive. A rush of fear shuttled through her, and she went cold with terror. Ruthlessly, she beat back the weakness and replaced it with determination. She would win.

He should be just as terrified of her, just as wary and on edge as she. For Macey was the daughter of Max Denton. She carried the blood of the great Victoria Gardella and the incomparable Max Pesaro.

It was her destiny to put an end to Nicholas Iscariot. *That* was the meaning of Rosamunde's prophecy. She was certain of it.

And the prophecies…it was imperative they were fulfilled.

Though Iscariot had taken her off guard, this time she wasn't outnumbered. And she wasn't confined in the small space of an automobile, held down by countless hands…

"In light of the stake in your hand, I can only suppose you've come to finish off Fanalucci," Iscariot said, moving toward the open drawer. "It's a clever stunt—using silver bullets." He looked at her sharply, and Macey almost got caught in his lethal gaze. A shimmer of softness teased at the edge of her consciousness, and she pushed it away. "Surely that wasn't your idea."

Interesting. Did he not know about Capone?

"In light of your unwanted presence, I can only suppose you've come to identify the body...before I dust it to ash," she replied evenly. "Make it quick, Nicholas. I haven't got all night."

He looked at her. His thin lips flattened into a small smile. "You weren't so bold the last time we had occasion to meet, Macey Gardella. I find I like this aspect of you much better than the sniveling, shivering, fainting girl you were then."

She measured the distance and height of the sheet-covered slab between her and Iscariot. If she launched herself over the body then levered herself to the right—

"I don't think so," murmured Iscariot. Suddenly he whirled... and was gone.

It was impossible—but he was there, and then in an instant, he wasn't—he was over *there*, and Macey spun to find him standing behind her, on the other side of the room. Had he flown? Cold shuddered through her. How could she fight a vampire who flew? Who could turn lights on and off at will?

The empty slab cut through the space between them, but Iscariot was closer than he'd been a moment before. She could *smell* him...a sort of earthy, oily, dark smell that made her insides churn.

"Do you feel it?" he said in a low, lisping voice. "I know you can feel it...you can feel *me*." His eyes glowed bright—a strange combination of red ringed with cobalt blue. They caught her unawares and tugged...as if a hook pierced her belly and reeled her closer.

Her breathing clogged, and her vision softened at the edges... She felt it happening, and fought, *fought*...

Iscariot chuckled, low and gritty, and Macey curled her fingers around the stake, around the edge of the empty slab next to her. She held tightly, focusing on the cold metal, the smooth wood, her feet planted on the floor… *No.*

"Macey," he whispered. "I remember…do you?"

She struggled to blink her eyes, to close them against those twin beacons of red flame eclipsed by bright, burning blue… mesmerizing, lulling, and luring…

Suddenly, she felt a stinging pain down the front of her torso, from breastbone to belly. She clapped a hand to her abdomen as the scar he'd left with the tip of a knife throbbed and burned in reminder of that terrifying night. Fear shuttled through her again, fighting to overcome her determination.

"I see you *do* remember, my lovely Venator. The blood of Max Pesaro runs in your veins…and I've tasted it. Do you remember? Oh, yes, I see how well you remember…" He smiled, and Macey felt another sharp pain streaking around the front of her left breast.

She shuddered, her knees buckling, her breath thick and slow, but she caught herself at the edge of the metal table, gripping it as if the slab was an anchor. Her veins pulsed and surged as if responding to his thrall. The pain slicing down her torso stung and burned, and she was aware of blood dampening her frock in a long, thin line right down the center and around her left areola. It was as if Iscariot was pulling the life force from her with every beat of her pulse…*tug, surge, tug, surge*… Softly, gently, incessantly.

"It's unbelievably perfect, isn't it, my lovely Venator, that I should be so fascinated by the progeny of the man with whom my sister Lilith was obsessed. And that I should be the one to destroy both father and daughter of that selfsame legacy."

Father. Legacy.

The words penetrated Macey's fog, and in that instant, something changed. Determination edged back blind fear. The metal slab felt more firm, her grip less desperate.

"You killed my father." The words came from far off, dreamlike, but they came nevertheless. And with them, the stake became more solid in her grip. Her feet rooted more sturdily on the concrete floor. "And my *mother*." The foggy edge of her vision turned clearer. Her mind latched on to fury in the place of susceptibility.

The tips of his fangs showed now. "Oh, yes, Felicia. She was *luscious*. Quite honestly, nearly as delightful as you—all springlike and fresh, and a little bold on the tongue. But, unfortunately, your mother was merely a mortal. There wasn't enough of her to…well, for someone such as I to appreciate. And it was all over much too quickly. But it was worth it, lowering myself to partake of her…to see Max Denton destroyed."

Macey swallowed the bile surging into her throat. Now more than ever she was certain she would slay the repulsive, evil creature smiling at her from across the room. His lips glistened, red and reptilian, and his stark, angular countenance appeared as cold as marble…except for the eyes. They glowed strong and bright, teasing and beckoning Macey…the strength of their thrall wavering at the edge of her vision.

"And yes, I killed your father—but not in the way you imagine, my bold stake-wielder. No…he lives on in his own private Hell: alone, guilt-ridden, empty. But still upon this earth. I suppose he must wish for his death every day, as one does when one loves too deeply and then loses all—simply because of one's own folly…but I cannot wish him anything other than such a fate."

Macey went cold and still. "My father is alive?"

This made Iscariot laugh, his eyes squinting closed for a moment. It was a reprieve from that dangerous, insistent gaze. "And so no one has bothered to tell you that, have they? They've sent you off to fight their battles, armed with the righteousness of avenging the death of your parents—despite the fact that it's a lie." He shook his head. "You poor darling. I almost feel sorry for you."

"Enjoy your pity while it lasts," she managed to say. "Because it won't be long before you've joined Lilith the Dark in Hell. And I'm going to be the one to send you there."

Iscariot smiled, fully displaying his fangs as well as a horribly attractive dimple in his cheek. "One must have dreams, then, mustn't one? Do you think your father, and Sebastian Vioget, and even Chas Woodmore have not also promised the same? And here I am." The smile widened. "I have more powers than my sister ever dreamed of…and when I have acquired the Rings of Jubai and the secret they protect in the Pool of Samung, well then…" His laugh was delicate, genteel. "I will, quite literally, rule the world. There will be no more darkness—for me, anyway."

Iscariot lifted his hand, his fingers curling up like elegant talons. He beckoned for her, the motion smooth and alluring. His nails were long and sharp, and they glinted like mother-of-pearl beads in the dim light. "Come here, Macey Gardella Denton… come to me." His eyes glowed brighter than ever, like a blazing fire and a flash of blue. "Come."

She released the metal table that separated them, her hand going to her throat, the stake clattering to the floor at her feet.

She took a step. Then another.

Then another.

His cold, powerful presence wrapped around her, and still she went to him.

Twelve

A Dark Battle

"NOW, MACEY," Iscariot coaxed. "Come to me. I can smell you, and now I will taste you once more."

Macey's fingers curled around the neckline of her dress, tangling in the heavy chain beneath it. She felt the unyielding edge of the empty metal table as she made her way along its length toward him…step by step.

Father. My father is alive.

The words burned in her mind. *Our legacy.*

Her hand gripped the edge of the table as she came to the end. She was almost to Iscariot, close enough she could feel his heartbeat more strongly…she could see a small mole on his face, see the way his nostrils flared as he scented her… His eyes were narrowed with anticipation, and his tongue slipped out to moisten those skinny lips, running over the tips of his fangs.

And then she *moved*: yanked the chain from beneath her frock and simultaneously rammed the table toward him with every bit of strength she owned.

The metal corner caught him in the abdomen just as her large silver cross came into view, tumbling forth to dangle between her breasts. Iscariot's shocked cry was cut off as the heavy table knocked the breath out of his lungs. He slammed into the wall behind him, doubled over, and shoved the table back.

Macey whirled away, swiping her stake from the floor in a smooth move as her cross bounced and swung as if it yearned to lunge for him itself. By the time she swooped upright, Iscariot had recovered. His eyes were furious: red and blue. His lips were peeled back, revealing long, terrifying fangs. The sight of the cross had paralyzed him, but not for long.

He lunged toward her, and Macey somersaulted over one of the bodies, dislodging it as she landed on the other side of its slab. The corpse tumbled to the ground in a morbid show of stiff limbs, and she barely missed her feet tangling in its sheet.

Iscariot hissed and swiped his long-nailed fingers at her, catching her bare arm across the slab and leaving three long streaks.

Macey gasped at the sudden streak of pain even as she grabbed his arm on the downswing, yanking him toward her. He didn't expect this, and lost his balance for a moment—but that was all she needed. Macey yanked the cross from her neck and slammed it against his cheek. He screamed, and his flesh sizzled as he twisted away, sending her spinning into the wall. She crashed into the cement block and whirled just in time to see Iscariot leap into the air.

Macey froze as he seemed to hover near the ceiling for an interminable length of time, then suddenly...he was gone. The only thing left was an ugly swirl of black smoke.

She spun wildly, looking in all corners of the room, stake in a death grip, cross in hand, eyes wide. Nothing.

Everything was still but for her panting breaths and the sounds of her feet scuffing the floor.

Silence. Nothing.

She held her breath, listening to her body: the sensation at the back of her neck, the prickle of hair along her arms, the putrid scent of burned vampire flesh and embalming fluid...and there was nothing.

He was gone. Could he really be gone?

Her fingers shook and her knees trembled and she waited... and waited.

Iscariot had gone.

All that remained was the eerie chill of an average undead—Danny Fanalucci.

Macey wasted no more time. She turned to the vampire and plunged her stake into his heart, shoving it through tissue and breastbone until she felt the little *pop* that told her she'd hit her mark.

Fanalucci seemed to shudder, and his eyelids fluttered—and then, just as she withdrew her stake, he exploded in a cloud of foul-smelling dust. Something metallic clinked onto the floor.

Coughing, panting, her knees still terribly weak, Macey brushed the ash from her dress and shoulders. She considered—briefly—sweeping it up, but there wasn't all that much of it, and vampire dust would disintegrate for the most part anyway. Besides, she wanted to get *away* from here.

She shoved the now-empty drawer back into place with a dull metal clang and looked around the room one more time.

Empty. Silent.

And yet the essence of malevolence and dark power remained.

Anger and residual terror fueled Macey as she left the morgue and stalked along the dark, deserted streets. Her knees still shook and she felt vaguely nauseated—and more than a little stunned that she was still alive, all things considered. But more than that, she was blind with fury.

She could have hailed a taxi, but part of her almost *wished* she'd encounter someone who meant her—a female alone—harm. She had a lot of pent-up energy ready to explode. Nevertheless, she made it to the wrought iron railing topped by an ornamental goblet with no incident.

She clomped down the stairs with unsteady knees and had her fingers on the door to The Silver Chalice before she realized what she was doing.

"Damn." She snatched her hand away and looked down at herself: disheveled and streaked with blood. Her own blood this time. She was still rattled from the encounter with Iscariot, still disbelieving he'd actually left—disappeared in that curl of smoke.

She couldn't go into the pub looking and smelling like this. But by God, she was going to speak to Sebastian—or Chas.

The door opened, narrowly missing slamming into her at the base of the small, subterranean stairwell. A man staggered out and she grabbed him by the scruff of the shirt.

"Go back in there and fetch Chas Woodmore."

The man blinked, and tried valiantly to focus on her. "Chats *who*? You need more wood?" His eyes fell to her neck and then her bloodstained dress. "What in hell happened to—"

"Chas. Wood. More. Fetch him now." She spun him back toward the door and shoved him back through, hoping Chas was, in fact, inside.

But it wasn't yet near dawn, and surely he was out hunting vampires, saving innocent mortals from their rapacious fangs.

Which was what Macey was supposed to be doing instead of kissing Al Capone's ass.

That was her legacy. The one she shared with her *father*… Was it possible he was still alive?

But instead of doing her duty—ridding the world of as many vampires as possible—she was fumbling around at the whim and will of a brutal gangster…and losing her cool when confronted by a powerful undead.

She couldn't deny she wanted to be sick at the thought of Iscariot's hands on her…his fangs, driving deeply into her throat and drawing her lifeblood out in long, whistling drags. Her insides were like a mass of writhing snakes, and cold terror still lingered like an icy finger tracing her spine.

But she'd *burned* the creature. She'd *burned* him.

"Macey?" Suddenly Chas was there—clearly surprised, but not displeased, to see her. "It *is* you."

She gathered her thoughts and looked up at him as the man whom she'd sent to collect Chas brushed by in a cloud of drunkenness to make his way up the steps. "Why didn't you tell me my father is alive?"

Chas frowned. "What the hell are you talking about?"

"My father. *Is he alive?*"

"Hell no, as far as I know, he isn't. What makes you think otherwise?"

A wave of emotion shuttled through her. Something between relief and anger and what doctors called "shock." Chas, at least, hadn't been lying to her.

Either that, or he was a hell of an actor.

"You look like you've just come from doing your job," he added. "It's about time you told Al Capone to fu—"

"I was at the morgue. Iscariot was there. He…" Her voice wavered, but damned if she was going to let herself show any more weakness than she already had tonight. "He told me my father is still alive."

Chas's eyes narrowed as a range of emotions rushed across his face. "You escaped from Iscariot? Don't tell me you killed him—Christ, did you?" His eyes widened.

Macey shook her head. "We fought, and then he just… disappeared. In a puff of black smoke." She kept her voice steady with effort. "After I smashed this in his face." She produced the cross.

The door opened before Chase could reply. Noise and the sour stench of stale beer poured from the pub as three patrons angled their way none too gently through the bottom of the narrow passage.

"We better get out of here before Vioget gets a whiff of you," Chas said. "You can tell me everything."

"No," she replied. "And since I can't go in there now, you'd best find out from Sebastian whether he knows."

She'd barely put a foot on the lower step when Chas took her arm. "Where the hell are you going?" When Macey turned, he must have read the answer in her face, for his own expression darkened. "Back to Capone?"

She shook free of his grip and stared him back down. "We all have our faults and weaknesses, don't we, Chas? I'll be in contact as soon as I can."

Without another glance, she clomped up the steps. Yet, though she could leave behind her fellow vampire hunter, as well as the man she thought of as her mentor, Macey knew she was neglecting even more than that.

She was abandoning her family legacy.

THIRTEEN

A Coming to Terms

MACEY HADN'T MADE it to the end of the block when she felt him behind her.

She spun just as Chas lunged. "You're not going back there." His grip was painfully tight around her arm as he put fingers to his mouth and gave a sharp whistle.

"Let me go." She gave a rough jerk to pull free, but he was strong and very determined…and maybe she didn't really have the desire to fight that hard.

At least, that was what she told herself as he muscled her toward the black car that rolled up silently. She made another token protest, which Chas ignored as he unceremoniously bundled her into the backseat.

"Who the hell do you think you are? Al Capone?" she muttered as he shoved her legs out of the way and climbed in after her.

"Bite your bloody tongue," he said, then spoke to the driver, whom Macey recognized with a start as a regular at The Silver Chalice. "My house."

"Since when do you have your own private automobile?" she said, hoisting herself upright onto the seat next to him. The vehicle was not a luxurious stretch like Capone's, so there was only the one bench seat in the back.

"Not mine. Vioget's. A recent acquisition—after his unexpected ride in Capone's limousine. But he lets me use it as necessary." Chas settled into the corner. "I'm sure he'd approve of this trip."

He slung his arm over the back of the seat, and when one finger brushed against her shoulder, he didn't seem to notice. Nor did he move it. He did, however, seem to be noticing everything else. Macey watched silently as his eyes tracked from the windows on each side of the auto, then out the windshield, then back again. He was on guard for Capone's goons.

And perhaps for Iscariot.

Macey couldn't control a little shudder, and she reached automatically for her cross. The one that surely had saved her life. She still felt a twinge pulsing from the scar Iscariot had raised down along her torso.

"Cold?"

"No."

"You can relax now, you know." He gave her a little poke at the back of the shoulder.

Five months ago, Macey probably would have argued with him. She might have retorted she didn't need anyone to protect her or take care of her, and she didn't need to relax.

But she'd changed.

Chas felt the tension ooze from Macey's body as she finally let go of everything and slumped further into the corner. Her fingers uncurled and her eyes drifted closed. He set his teeth grimly and continued to watch the shadows and streets, to read the back of his neck and listen to his instincts…watching and waiting for danger in both mortal and immortal form.

So Max Denton was still alive…if Iscariot could be believed. He wondered what the hell Denton was thinking, abandoning and ignoring his daughter for more than a decade.

Sometimes life is too painful to remain part of it, isn't it, Chas?

Wayren's words to him—oh, more than a century ago, after everything had happened with Narcise—suddenly rang in his mind.

Well, he couldn't argue with that. He was fortunate Wayren had given him an out, a detour…an escape. He wondered what Max Denton's escape would be. A dark, violent, solitary life… then death?

Well, hell. Just like the one Chas was living.

The car eased to a halt in front of St. Anselm's Church. The cross atop its squat spire made a nice shadow in the middle of the street, and, occasionally, that shadow fell across the window of Chas's upper-floor apartment in the building next door. A nice little deterrent for the undead.

Chas slipped Ned a few bills as well as a message for Vioget. Of course, Sebastian paid the man a salary, but Chas saw the value in having his own relationship with the driver. At the sound of Ned's murmured thanks, Macey blinked and shook her head as if to clear away the cobwebs, but Chas didn't risk the delay of waiting for her to haul herself to her feet. Instead, he tugged her out of the backseat and ushered her through the hidden doorway that led to his place.

It wasn't until he got her inside his small apartment and turned on the lights that he saw the blood. It wasn't as if there was that much of it…it was just *where* it was. In a long, neat line down the front of her dress, bisecting her torso. And there was a rusty ring around one breast.

"Christ," he said to cover his shock, "this is getting to be a damned habit of yours, arriving at my place looking half dead."

She looked up at him from under a tangle of dark curls, her eyes gleaming with something almost unholy. Her fingers trembled a little as they gripped the back of the sofa, but her voice was strong. "Let's be honest, Chas. I'm here because you want me here—not because I need to be here, or because I need you."

"Is that so?" He pulled out the glass Mason jar labeled "vinegar" from under the tiny sink in his kitchenette and unscrewed the top. The whiskey—good stuff, but not as good as what Vioget served—sloshed into two fairly clean glasses as silence reigned. "Drink up." He shoved one toward her.

To his surprise, she stepped away from the sofa and leaned against the counter, taking the glass. She swallowed a healthy sip, watching him over the rim with those big, dark eyes. When she lowered the glass, her lips glistened invitingly and she was still looking at him. Very pointedly.

"Is that an invitation?" he said.

"The life of a Venator is a lonely one. Or so you've pointed out to me numerous times."

She threw his words back at him without coyness or invitation, and Chas mentally shook his head as he lifted his glass and drank. Damn, she was getting to be a handful. Give the woman a *vis bulla* and a pair of hot, velvety brown eyes—not to mention a reason to go a few verbal rounds with him—and he was very nearly in over his head.

He itched to touch her…no, to be more specific, he itched to shove her against the wall, tear off that stained dress, and drown their respective sorrows in a blur of heat and passion. And from the look of her expression, she wouldn't mind some mindless sex one bit.

"We both know it's been brewing for a while," she said, holding his eyes with hers. They were firm, cool, steady—almost emotionless. "You and me. And now, here we are, with no Sebastian and no Temple and no Capone. No one to interfere, and the sun'll be rising any minute now—so no more hunting the undead tonight. So why don't you follow through on your offer and show me your *vis bulla*, Chas? And maybe I'll show you mine."

"I've already seen yours, lulu. *However…*" He set his glass down with a soft, deliberate thunk. Still watching her, holding her gaze meaningfully, he removed the drink from her grip, saying, "Let me take that for you. It'd be a waste to spill such good contraband."

He'd barely released the glass onto the counter—sloppily enough to slosh a bit—than he was dragging her to him by a fistful of her dress.

Macey met his mouth eagerly, her lips firm and mobile. She tasted of whiskey and salty perspiration, and her powerful, lithe body felt terrifyingly slight in his arms. She was damp and a little sticky, scented with blood and sweat—probably even tears as well—but she was warm and ready, soft and curvy, and the essence of female musk clinging to her skin was enough to make Chas exhale with relief. He was very ready for this…and was growing more so as she pressed against him, her hands gripping his shoulders, her hips flush against his.

Though small and slender, Macey was as strong as he, so Chas had no compunction about being a little forceful, a little rough, and a lot demanding. He kissed her hungrily, delving with a strong, thrusting tongue and nibbling at her lips. She seemed to enjoy it, gasping a surprised laugh against his mouth when he yanked her dress open. Buttons flew, and the lace and cotton tore a little when he pulled the neckline down over her shoulders. They were delicate white shoulders…marred by two small wounds on one side of her neck.

Chas paused when he saw them, and then noticed the slender red scar trailing from the top of her sternum down behind her undergarment…and another around the front of one breast, encircling the areola. Even in the hazy moment of lust and desire, he recognized the marks weren't exactly fresh…yet they still oozed blood.

Macey didn't seem to appreciate the halt to things, for she took matters into her own hands and began to work at the buttons down the front of his shirt. "Where is it, Chas?" she muttered, pulling the cotton down over his shoulders and then plucking his undershirt from the waistband of his trousers. "Where is your hard-won *vis bulla*?"

But she'd already found it—her fingers quick and nimble, sliding under the cotton of his shirt to capture the small silver cross he wore pierced through the upper lip of his navel—just as she did. When she touched it, Chas felt a sizzle shoot through him that had less to do with lust than blatant power. He gave a little laugh as she gasped in surprise—for a Venator touching a *vis bulla* would always cause a spark of energy—and pressed her hand against it and the vibrating muscle of his belly. The power leapt between them again, sending a strong rush of pleasure funneling sharply to his straining cock.

He released her hand and brought Macey up close along his body, angling one of her thighs along his hip so she could feel his arousal as he deftly unlaced her brassiere. She was panting a bit, soft, sexy little sounds that made him want to yank off the rest of her clothes and toss her on the sofa and make her moan a little louder.

When he peeled her undergarment down far enough to uncover her breasts, he gave a low hum of delight at the curvy, perky sight. Macey shifted impatiently against his johnson, using the waist of his trousers to pull him closer, even grinding against him a little. Well, a lot, actually.

"Whoa there, lulu," he murmured, shifting away a little as he slid a hand up under her dress to bare a slender, muscular leg. She was warm and soft, and he itched to touch her right where she was lush and hot and wet. "Let's not rush things."

"I don't mind rushing things," she told him, reaching for the fastening of his trousers and ripping it open.

For the first time in a while, Chas looked down at her face. Even through the fog of lust and need, he registered the expression there: dark, set, determined, and needy.

Just the same, he supposed, as the look on his own countenance. "All right then," he muttered, propping himself against the back of the sofa and pulling her along with him. His trousers sagged and he let them fall around his ankles as she dragged his boxers out of the way. Skirt high on her thighs now, his hands holding the flowing fabric out of the way, he hoisted her up onto him as she gripped his shoulders.

"*Oh*," she said as he slid home, deep and slow, into her warmth. The sound penetrated his fog of lust and he wanted to drag more from her: more pleasure, more soft gasps and sighs, more nails digging into his skin, more hot, sleek kisses.

He moved, carefully at first, but that foolish restraint lasted only a moment. She was clearly impatient, and so was he, and Chas saw no reason to hold back. Macey used her feet for leverage against the sofa, and they slipped into a fast, hard rhythm laced with sighs and moans of building pleasure.

Chas saw her eyes flutter just before she came, her head tipping back as she gripped his shoulders, her mass of dark curls bouncing and tumbling around her cheeks and chin. As she shuddered against him, hard and sharp, he let go with a long, low moan of relief and pleasure, and it mingled with her own gust of release.

He managed to keep hold of her with one arm braced around her waist, though his knees buckled a little and his stockinged toes curled with pleasure. Breathing hard, damp with pleasure and exertion, he sagged against the sofa, eyes closed, and fought off a riot of conflicting emotions that threatened to shatter his bliss.

Macey shifted against him, sending a little twitch of lust into the depths of his belly, for they were still joined. He came out of his moment of half-consciousness to help her to her feet, not quite ready to look at her yet. Not willing to see what was in her eyes and expression…and certainly not wanting her to see what was in his.

He spewed out a mental breath, shoving away guilt and remorse and a whole lot of other things, and focused on the fact that his body was still humming pleasantly and Macey didn't seem to have any problem with what had just happened. Except that… *Damn it to hell.*

No condom. No bloody damned condom. Chas went cold, and the last remnants of pleasure were gone. Just like that.

"Well," Macey said, jolting him from his dark thoughts. Her voice was breathy and low, and she was looking down at the tatters of her frock instead of up at him. "I think I might need something to wear."

He found his voice. "I didn't use a condom."

Now she looked up at him, tucking her short curls behind an ear.

"I—uh—it all was—rather unexpected," he added, desperately wishing the whiskey was within reach. "I don't usually…need…" *Fuck. Shut the fuck up, Woodmore.*

She shook her head. "It's all right. Temple gave me—well, there's a concoction to prevent pregnancy. Victoria Gardella used to use it too, and I suppose her daughter did as well."

Chas couldn't quite control a blast of relief, but he hoped he managed not to appear too giddy. "Good." He felt as if he should be saying or doing something to alleviate the tension between them—why the hell was there tension after *that*, anyway?—but there was a sort of prickly aura around Macey that suggested he keep his distance, even though only moments ago she'd been gasping for *more.*

Please, she'd whispered. *Oh, yes, please, Chas.*

Whatever she'd wanted, he'd given her. And it appeared, at least for now, that was all.

And he, at least, wasn't going to complain. It was a hell of a lot easier this way. And for the first time in far too long, he'd allowed himself pleasure without needing a pair of fangs jamming into his shoulder.

"I don't suppose you have a bathtub I could use," Macey said, rising from picking up her strewn clothing. She leaned against the counter and tossed back the rest of her whiskey.

"Yes, of course," he replied, a little taken aback by her matter-of-fact attitude.

For it was clear she wanted a soak—and he wouldn't be invited to join her.

This was going to be very interesting.

Fourteen

A Dawning of Hope

S EBASTIAN DRAGGED HIMSELF from the dream as though he were fighting out of a deep, dark pit. He was hot, sweaty, and hard with arousal, for the nocturnal visions had been dark and erotic and compelling. Dangerous.

He sat up, a shaking hand pushing away the hair plastered to his face. *No*, he told himself. *Not that. Never that.*

But the dream tried to lure him back, insistent and tempting as the images filtered through his sleep-fogged, weary mind: soft white skin, lush curves, full lips parted with pleasure and desire, glossy, dark hair, deep, velvet eyes…first it was his Giulia, then Victoria…and then their images had metamorphosed into Macey: the perfect combination of both of the women he'd loved and sacrificed for. She was twining with him, touching him, opening herself to him…and he took. Viciously, passionately.

That was what terrified him.

And there was blood—from him, *for* him—shiny and sleek, sliding down the long curve of her neck, tempting him even now in his memory. His nostrils flared as if he could scent her here… though she wasn't nearby.

He'd scented her tonight. Perhaps that was why this dream had come again—this time stronger, longer, more insidious and much clearer and more detailed than the ones that had previously tormented him. Harder to push away, more difficult to ignore. Terrifying.

He knew Macey had come to the Silver Chalice tonight, for though she hadn't even broached the threshold, Sebastian smelled her. When Chas rose suddenly from the bar and didn't return, he wondered…and when Ned brought him a message that they'd gone to Woodmore's, Sebastian's suspicions were confirmed.

Thank you for taking her away.

But they were at Woodmore's. The two of them. Surely the natural thing would occur…the tension between them, though subtle and dark, had leapt and sizzled—just like it had done with Victoria and Pesaro all those decades ago.

That must be why he'd dreamt so deeply tonight. It had to be.

Sebastian closed his eyes and touched his *vis bulla*. The sharp, pain-laced energy skittered along his hand, jolting through the rest of his body—a welcome shock, a necessary reminder. Then, following his habit, he found the ruby signet ring Wayren had given him long ago when she knew his intention. *It will give you strength*, she'd told him just before Sebastian embarked on the journey that took him to Lilith the Dark and set him on this path of the "long promise."

When the *hell* would this promise be finished, anyway, dammit?

The ruby ring was heavy and comforting—it was almost as steadying as Wayren's own presence was—and Sebastian felt the edge of his anxiety subside. *Thank you.*

And then, continuing on the rite of sorts, his routine to remind him of who he was, from where he'd come, and why he was here, Sebastian touched each of the five copper rings on his other hand. The Rings of Jubai hadn't moved for more than a hundred years, attached to his skin after he plunged his hand into the Pool in the mountains of Romania. It was then, as he knelt there with his hand in the horrible, cutting, thick waters, that Giulia had appeared to him the first time.

Help me.

Sebastian was never certain whether he'd actually heard her plea, seen her face…or merely desperately visualized it all in his mind, but she'd been there nevertheless. Freed to communicate with him, perhaps, when he donned the rings—or when he shoved his hand into the harsh waters of the Pool. He didn't know for certain whether the Pool and the rings were the impetus for Giulia appearing to him, giving him the chance to save her, but the two events would be forever connected in his mind.

And that was why he'd secretly gone back to the Pool, long after things had changed for him, long after he'd lost Victoria.

Now, he touched all five rings, out of habit attempting to twist or loosen each of them in turn…and then he froze. His eyes bolted wide in the darkness. His heart thudded sickeningly.

One of them moved.

Had it? Had one of them moved?

His fingers were suddenly slick and clumsy, but he managed to try it again…*yes*. The fourth one moved. It turned, shifted just a little, rotating the slightest bit. For the first time in a century.

Surely it was a sign.

He could hardly breathe, afraid he'd been mistaken…but when he tried it again, the ring moved once more.

A quick, hard shudder rushed over him. His hands turned to ice, his pulse surged and leapt, his lungs felt constricted.

Surely this meant the time was near.

At last.

Macey opened her eyes to find sun streaming into the room. Through the haphazardly drawn curtains, she could see the roof and spire of a church, with its cross sitting proudly on top of it.

Next to her, the bed sagged a little under Chas, who still appeared to be asleep—"appeared" being the key word. She was certain he could fake sleeping as well as he did most everything else.

Everything else. She gave a pleasant little shiver at the memory of last night.

She hadn't intended to end up here in his bed, but after her bath—and a long, steaming interlude of unpleasant thoughts— he'd poked his head in as she was wrapping up in a towel.

"Thought you might have drowned," he said. "You were in here so long."

"Takes more than a bath to get the best of a Venator," she told him…and found herself distracted by his dark, broad shoulders—still bare and now marked by her fingernails—and the rest of his nude torso. He was simply the most darkly attractive man she'd ever seen, and he tasted and felt as good as he looked.

"I'm going to bed," he said casually. It was neither an invitation nor a rebuff. Simply a statement.

"Alone?" The word popped out before she thought it through. Or maybe in the back of her mind Macey already knew she no longer wanted to be alone with her thoughts. She'd had plenty of time in the bath to relive those moments with Iscariot, to see the evidence of his power and malevolence in the slender red line down her sternum and around her breast, and to battle back reams of confusion and fury—and even guilt. To wonder and regret and stew.

Being with Chas would keep her from thinking about Iscariot and Capone, Sebastian and her father…and Grady.

"That's up to you, lulu." He made it clear he could go either way, and for that Macey was both grateful and insulted.

Nevertheless, she gave him a slow smile and dropped her towel. When his eyes narrowed with invitation, she lunged toward him. He staggered a little as she slammed him into the wall, and they almost slipped on the tile floor of the bathroom before he yanked her out into the hallway, muffling her mouth with his.

They took a little longer this second time, but their joining was no less rough and hot. She liked that, she realized, as she lay there damp and panting next to him afterward. She liked that it wasn't tender or sweet or sensual.

They—she and Chas—were people of violence. It seemed only right they should have sex the same way.

Still, though sated and loose and exhausted, Macey had a hard little knot of something in the center of her being—something sad and empty that kept her eyes wide open in the dark for far too long.

You'll get over it.

You'll get over him.

Now, it was the morning after and she looked over at her sleeping bed partner. His hard-planed face was soft and relaxed with slumber, and he had a lot of dark stubble—which had scraped and abraded her skin in several intimate places—and thick, tousled masses of hair brushing his shoulders and tumbling onto the white pillowcase. His shoulders and biceps were scratched by her, but they were also faintly scarred with fang marks.

Macey felt a little jolt of understanding when she looked at those scars. Some were perhaps a century old—perhaps even from the infamous Narcise, who'd apparently broken his heart—but most of the others were recent. Perhaps they were even from the night when she killed Alvisi last autumn. The memory of what she'd seen—Chas and some female undead, panting and writhing together—gave her both a flutter of arousal and a wave of repugnance.

And she'd seen precisely the same emotions on his face that night as well.

What a pair we are, the two of us.

The life of a Venator is a lonely one, lulu.

Perhaps they could be lonely—or less lonely—together. She looked at his face—blank and still and breathtakingly handsome with full, pursed lips and smooth olive skin dark with stubble, and all that black hair—and thought, *I could love him.*

Chas's eyes opened suddenly, and Macey caught her breath as their gazes locked. Heat rushed to her cheeks and she realized she was uncovered from the waist up, and that she'd been staring down at him like a lovestruck girl.

"Good morning." He spoke but didn't move; she got the sense that he felt as awkward as she did.

She supposed he rarely woke up with his lovers. After all, he generally staked them when they were finished having sex. Or perhaps during; she didn't really know. The thought made her belly shift unpleasantly and she licked her lips.

"I suppose this is a little unusual for you," she said, then immediately regretted her bluntness. Her cheeks burned hotter and she automatically pulled the blanket up over her breasts. "But…thank you." She added the last part quickly in an attempt to cover her blunder. "For last night. I was…"

"No thanks necessary, lulu," he replied smoothly. "Like you said…it's been brewing for a while."

She looked down and picked at the decorative knots in his quilted bedcover. "Do you think my father could really be alive?"

Chas propped his head up on one hand. "I truly don't know. And I'd tell you if I knew, Macey. I wouldn't lie to you."

"Oh, I believe you. When have you ever not spoken the bald, blunt truth?"

He gave a short laugh. "Never. Or not for a long time, anyway."

Silence for a moment as she picked at the coverlet threads. "Is she still alive?"

The bed gave a short, sharp tremor, he tensed up so sharply. "Narcise."

Macey nodded.

"No."

"Is that why you came here—moved ahead in time? What was it like? How did it happen? I can't…I can hardly believe it. But then again, I'm a vampire hunter, so I suppose anything is possible."

"She—Narcise—was very much alive when I left. And she was very happy. With someone other than me."

"But you weren't."

He shook his head, his lips twisting in a sad, pained manner. "No." He sat up abruptly, one powerful arm sweeping his pillow out of the way. "But I got over it."

Macey didn't think he'd really gotten over it. He still slept with vampires, didn't he? He still had a combination of pain and pleasure stamped on his face when they were having sex. Surely that wasn't "getting over" someone.

"And you'll do the same."

Her gaze bolted to his, and she saw cool comprehension there.

"Don't think I don't know what prompted all of this." His smile was wry and knowing. "Not that I'm complaining. But." He shrugged.

"I just don't want him to get hurt—any of them to get hurt—because of me," she added quickly.

It wasn't just about Grady. It really wasn't. She needed to protect all of them—Dr. Morgan at the library, Dottie, Sandy and her other friends. Even Flora.

"I can't have a normal life, with normal people around me. I can't have normal relationships. They'll get caught in the crossfire—just like my mother did. My father learned that the hard way, and so did Victoria Gardella. I'm not going to make the same mistake they did."

"I wish I disagreed with you." He laid a hand over hers. "But I don't."

I could learn to love him, Macey thought again, looking down at their hands. *I should.*

Because then it would be easier to forget Grady. It would be easier to face Iscariot and Capone. It would be easier to ignore her father—whether he was dead or alive.

If she had someone with her. A partner. Someone to touch and talk to and hold, and someone who understood. Someone who was as violent and dark and angry as she was.

Fifteen

Of French Grammar and Semantics

S EBASTIAN WAS ALONE in the pub, as he usually was just after dawn broke. It was a quiet time of day, and though the place tended to smell like stale spirits and body odor until he mopped the floor and wiped the counters, it was nevertheless quiet and provided welcome solitude. The simple tasks of cleaning and preparing for the night to come were a welcome routine for they were mindless and satisfying.

He had just returned from his almost-daily visit to St. Patrick's Church at four o'clock in the morning, leaving the sanctuary just before the sun was about to rise.

This schedule necessitated him wearing a heavy cloak when he ventured into the infant light of day, and required his driver Ned to be on the watch for enemies of either the mortal or undead type. After last autumn, when he'd been taken for that unexpected ride in Al Capone's limousine after one predawn visit, Sebastian took no chances.

Today he'd gone with a sense of expectation and hope. He sat in the church, basking in the silence as he twisted the loose ring on his right hand. But if he'd expected some great revelation or unexpected miracle now that one Ring of Jubai had begun to shift, he was disappointed.

Instead, he was alone but for a cloaked, veiled woman who knelt on a *prie-dieu* in front of the Blessed Virgin Mary and hardly moved the entire time he was present. She gave no indication she was aware of his presence, though she was here nearly every morning when he came. She rose to her feet just before Sebastian was about to leave himself, and he saw from her movements that she was very elderly, stooped, and took great care with each deliberate step.

It was a stark reminder that he'd lived as long as—likely longer, for surely she couldn't be 120 years old—this old woman, and yet he bore no outward sign of those many decades. A blessing and a curse.

Having made his sabbatical to the church, and having been disappointed that nothing seemed to have changed, Sebastian was in a foul mood when he returned to the pub. Surely it didn't help that the explicit, discomfiting dream still lingered in the back of his mind, and that he hadn't heard from Wayren for months.

Why was the bloody female never around when he wanted to talk to her? Wasn't that just like a—

The interior door opened across the room—the one attached to the hidden private entrance from Temple's aunt's millinery shop—and Sebastian stiffened. Before she even came into sight, he'd sensed, smelled, recognized Macey's presence.

Devil take it, not today.

But the minute she came through the door, he realized things were going to be even worse than he'd anticipated. She had fire in her eyes, and her entire being was a ball of fury and demanding. *And* the faint smell of coitus, of satisfaction and musk and sensuality, clung to her in a hot, red aura.

Sebastian kept his expression calm, even managing to show his normal, insouciant smile. He opened his mouth to greet her, too, but didn't have the chance.

"Is my father alive?"

She barreled across the room and didn't stop till she gripped the counter, leaning toward him, her chin thrust out and her eyes blazing.

Taken completely by surprise, Sebastian didn't respond immediately, and Macey's hand whipped out and grabbed the front of his shirt. Half up on the counter herself, she yanked him toward her so their faces were very close. Her energy, power, and essence enveloped him. "Tell me the damned truth, Sebastian."

He managed to keep his demeanor calm despite the riot of emotions charging through him, and firmly uncurled her fingers from his shirt. "Don't wrinkle the cotton, *cher*," he said with a mildness he didn't feel. "And to answer your question…is Max Denton alive? Not as far as I know."

He stepped away from the counter, ostensibly to retrieve a bottle of brandy and two glasses from beneath—but really to put a little distance between the two of them. His gums were swelling, threatening to push out his fangs, and the fact that he seemed to have as little control over them as a pubescent boy would have over an erection didn't help his mood.

The glasses made quiet, hard thunks as he set them on the counter. "Why are you asking?" He poured Macey a drink and filled his own halfway, then turned his back on her for a moment to add a generous dollop from the bottle of cow's blood he kept for his sustenance and sanity. Unfortunately, this particular morning he needed it more for the latter than the former. He turned back, taking a large gulp, as she spoke.

"I had an encounter with Nicholas Iscariot last night."

To Sebastian's continued consternation, she yanked open the top of her buttoned blouse to reveal a deep vee of cleavage, creamy white skin, the hint of a laced-up undergarment…and a bright red line that disappeared behind said undergarment. There were also two bites on the side of her throat.

Under normal circumstances, and with pretty much any other female who might have torn open her clothing, Sebastian would have thanked her for such a lovely sight…and would have taken full advantage of the gift.

Instead, he forced his attention from her exposed skin up to her eyes. "Tell me what happened." And, surreptitiously, he felt beneath his shirt to touch the *vis bulla*, pushing away the lingering temptation from his dream, the scent and sight of too much Macey, and focused on the grave matter at hand.

The shimmer of power from his amulet and the blood-saturated whiskey cleared Sebastian's head, for which he was immensely grateful. But when Macey told him what happened in the morgue between her and Iscariot, the tension returned—albeit for an entirely different reason. The entire altercation and its implications did not bode well. Nevertheless, he addressed the most pressing item first.

"If Max Denton is alive, I'm not aware of it. The last I knew, he'd died during the War. But I'm here in Chicago. Your father—and you—are from England, and he spent his time in Europe. I haven't had much communication from Bellitano—he is the acting *Summas* Gardella and stays in Rome. I am, so to speak, on my own."

Macey seemed to have calmed a little, though her dark Pesaro eyes were still a little wild. "So apparently the person I would need to ask is Wayren."

"Good luck with that," he said with a wry smile. "I haven't seen her since you received your *vis bulla*." He leaned on the counter, keeping a prudent space between them. "But, *petit*, it is mostly this that concerns me." He gestured to the red marks on her skin with a surprisingly steady hand. "You say Iscariot didn't even touch you, and yet you began to bleed from already healed marks? Marks he'd given you."

She nodded, yet he could sense the underlying terror she masked well. "It was as if my blood…my veins…stirred at his command. As if he had some sort of magnet or—or draw that made it ooze again. It wasn't a full rush of blood, as if he'd just cut me. But like whatever had begun to heal broke through. As if I were—or my lifeblood was—enthralled or hypnotized."

"And yet you ran him off." He felt a stab of pride. Macey was, despite the years between them and the complicated, horrifying dreams, the closest thing he would ever have to a daughter or a progeny.

"It was the cross that did it." She dug in her skirt pocket and extracted a chain and its palm-sized pendant.

Even though Sebastian regularly visited a church and wore his *vis bulla*—and prayed—he couldn't contain an unexpected shudder at the sight of the ornate silver cross. "Ah yes. Don't get that too close to me—wait." He peered at the relic, careful not to get too near. "What's this on there? This black residue."

To his relief, Macey brought the cross closer to her in order to examine it, and he was able to breathe more readily once again.

"It wasn't on here before," she said, frowning as she looked at the ashy substance clinging to the intricate design. "But I did shove it against his face. It probably burned him. Vampire flesh." She looked up, and now, instead of the terror beneath her gaze, there was satisfaction. "I wonder if he has a permanent mark."

"If so," Sebastian said—suddenly, fiercely grateful their conversation had evolved into something less strained and uncomfortable, "then you both have marked the other. That would be the first time I've heard of a Venator marking an undead."

Her expression sobered. "But he hasn't marked me in the same way Lilith the Dark marked Max Pesaro…has he? That permanent connection?"

Sebastian considered this unpleasant possibility for a moment, then replied, "If your bite marks healed originally, and you haven't felt him luring you when you weren't in his presence, then I don't believe it would be the same sort of connection. But recall, Macey, *petit*, I haven't seen you—other than briefly—since your first encounter with Iscariot. I don't know if your bites were healed properly or not. You have been a little absent." Bloody hell, he sounded and felt like a father. But that was a much-preferred role than the other portrayed in his nocturnal adventures.

She arched a brow and gave him a look that reminded Sebastian far too much of Victoria. "They healed. Only a faint scar remained until last night."

Before Sebastian could reply, the door from which Macey had entered opened once more and Temple came in. "Well, look who the cat dragged in again," she said when she saw Macey. "And a good thing you're here, too."

Sebastian saw she was holding a sheaf of papers and watched her long legs eat up the space as she strode across the pub. His usual niggle of minor awareness turned into a stronger sense of interest. Maybe it would help matters if he tapped into what she'd clearly been wanting for some time. At least with Temple, he wouldn't have to worry about losing his mind…or his soul.

"Since I haven't had anything else to do," Temple said with a pointed look at Macey, whom she was supposed to train and exercise in Venator fighting skills, "I've been researching Al Capone's prophecy."

She slid onto a stool, papers crackling as she did so, and caught Sebastian's eye. He gave her a smile a little warmer than usual, a little longer linger of his gaze, and then said, "And you've found something important, then, Temple, *cher*."

"I'll say." She caught his gaze and held it for a beat, and her fine brows lifted. Then she shuffled through her papers. "So our friend and colleague Capone thinks 'the dauntless one' named in the prophecy is referring to you, Macey. But I'm becoming more certain he's wrong. The prophecy says, 'From the deepest bowels of madness and grief shall the dauntless one root.'"

Temple looked up, stabbing the paper with a smooth, round fingernail. "That doesn't sound like you at all, sister, because from everything I've heard, you were 'rooted' in—born from—a solid, loving relationship between Max Denton and his wife Felicia. Neither of them were mad or aggrieved, and even if you look further and wonder if the phrase might be referring to the time after your mother was killed, and your father became grief-stricken and angry, I still don't believe it makes sense. You were, what, eight years old? Well rooted by that time, if you will. But aside from all of that, if you read further, after Mr. Capone's favorite foretelling, Rosamunde continues, 'Upon its unleashing, a root of malevolence shall marshal such power as never before known. It shall permeate far and deep, and only the dauntless one and his peer shall rise up to it.'"

Temple looked up again, triumph in her expression. "Did you hear that? It clearly says, 'only the dauntless one and *his* peer.'

Capone's got the gender wrong. The dauntless one is a male, not a female. And…" She yanked out a curling piece of paper, yellowed with age. "When I took a look at the original prophecy here—see, it's not written in Latin, but in old French—so I've no idea if it really is the original—"

"French would have been Rosamunde's spoken language, with her being in an abbey and of the nobility," Macey said, her eyes light with interest. "Only the serfs and peasants spoke English even in England during the Middle Ages." When Sebastian and Temple looked at her, she gave a self-deprecating smile. "Don't forget, I'm a librarian. We acquire all sorts of interesting trivia."

"Fascinating," Sebastian said, and meant every syllable. "Go on, Temple. This is quite enlightening."

She flashed him a brief smile. "I wondered why Capone would have believed Macey was the dauntless one anyway—or even why he would have thought this applied to our time and not, say, Isabella Gardella's or even Victoria's—and so I went back to look at the context and the original writing. Because, as I pointed out, I haven't had anything else to do but make damned hats with Aunt Cookie," she added, glaring at Macey again. "And I'm not a fan of needle pricks and discussions about lace and grosgrain. You're going to tell Al Capone to forget about this prophecy thing, sister, or I'm coming after to drag you home myself."

"It's not that simple," Macey began, her eyes beginning to flash once more. "It's not me I'm worried—"

"Ladies." Sebastian lifted his hands and gave them his most charming smile, with just a touch of thrall in his eyes. "Let's remain on topic. I find this all very interesting."

Temple grumbled something under her breath that sounded like "keep your damned fangs sheathed," but returned to the matter at hand. "Whatever you say, bossman. So I was looking at the original French writing and see—look here. The reference to what's translated as 'the dauntless one' is '*l'intrepid*,' so the article's gender isn't obvious—which is the correct way to write it if the noun begins with a vowel, as in this case. But if you look at the way it's written, that apostrophe hangs low and looks a little like a small 'a.'"

She looked up. "Apparently Capone—or whoever translated this prophecy for him—doesn't know his French, and made a big assumption, which would have been disproved later on, if he'd cared to read that far." Temple gathered up her papers with a satisfied smile. "Of course, you can argue that the gender is masculine for simplicity's sake, and it refers to either sex…but if you look at the prophecy that applied to Eustacia Gardella's death, you will see that isn't the case. It's clearly feminine."

Sebastian glanced at Macey, who seemed to be just as pleased and impressed with Temple's scholarship as he was. "Brilliant, *cher*," he said.

"Yes," Macey said. "Thank you, Temple. I admit I'm more than pleased to know I'm not the dauntless one, who's going to be facing—what did you say?—the 'root of malevolence…' How did the rest of the verse go?"

"'The root of malevolence shall marshal such power as never before known. It shall permeate far and deep, and only the dauntless one and his peer shall rise up to it.'"

"Yes. Right." Macey's voice was quiet and subdued, her eyes dark and wide. "And though it doesn't refer to me, we're now faced with the obvious question—if it's not me, who *is* the dauntless one? And the dauntless one's peer—which sounds just as ominous. And why does Al Capone believe he's even involved in the prophecy?"

"I'm not the dauntless one," Sebastian said immediately. "And though he stews with his own anger and fury, Woodmore's not actually mad." Macey must have heard the regret in his voice, for she choked back a laugh.

"Don't look at me, Vioget," said Temple. "I'm not the least bit dauntless."

"There are definitely other words to describe you," he muttered. "And you aren't a Venator, anyway."

"Praise God for small favors," she said with heartfelt emotion. "Look, I think Al Capone is all washed up. He's caught up in his own self-importance—but I didn't see anything in those pages that indicates the prophecy applies to now. He probably saw the writ somewhere and seized on it without really understanding it. The man might run a bootlegging empire, but he ain't the sharpest tack in the box."

Perhaps Temple was correct…though if anyone were to embody the definition of a root of malevolence, it was Nicholas Iscariot.

Sixteen

The Web is Spun More Thoroughly

W HERE DA HELL have you been?" Al Capone's voice was low, shaking with fury and power. His porcine features seemed more puffy than usual—maybe a little too much pasta— and his eyes, though they sparked with anger, were half hidden by fleshy cheeks. His fingers were curled into fists on his cluttered desk and he was half out of his chair. "These disappearances of yours are a habit that stops *now*, or I'll put you under house arrest and you won't be able to take a damned *piss* without me knowing."

Macey wasn't cowed. She'd faced down a damned vampire prince last night. A mere mortal—no matter how strong—couldn't beat that. Standing in the center of his office, she put her hands on her hips and fixed him with a cold gaze of her own. "I took care of Danny Fanalucci at the morgue, and at the same time, I had a little run-in with Nicholas Iscariot. It wasn't a good night and I was in no mood to deal with you, Snorky, so I went and expended my energy elsewhere. I suggest you keep your temper tantrums to yourself."

Her pronouncement about Iscariot seemed to have little effect on Capone, but his Brooklyn accent became thicker. "I don't give a rat's ass how bad a night you had, toots. You finish a job, you come back here, you report to me by dawn, and you wait for your next assignment. Dat's how it goes."

"I don't think so. Not anymore." She stalked across the room to his desk, bracing her hands on top to face him over it just as she had done to Sebastian a few hours ago. "Iscariot says my father is alive. Do you know anything about this?"

Capone jolted a little, surprise blanching his features. "No, and I wouldn't believe any damned thing that creature says."

She eased back a little, gritting her teeth. "I didn't think you'd be any help. You can't even get the damned prophecy correct," she added under her breath, resisting the urge to throw that in his face.

Not yet. I'll save that little fact for later.

"I'm only here to resign, Al. I'm done being on your payroll. You're going to have to find another chump to protect you—or get off your fat ass and do it yourself. I've got Iscariot to deal with and you're weighing me down like a big, cumbersome anchor."

He didn't look up at her. Instead, he seemed interested in a newspaper on the desk. "Oh, look here, doll. There's a big exhibit—some Japanese artist, I can't even say his name—opening at the Art Institute tomorrow night. Fancy party, they're calling it a gala. I think I'd better attend." He shoved the paper toward her. "Read the article. It looks very interesting."

"I'm not interested in—" Macey stopped as her gaze landed on the paper. *Hiroshige Exhibit to Open with Gala Hosted by Institute Director.* But it wasn't the headline that caught her attention and had her world slowing into something ugly and murky. It was the byline accompanying the article: *J. Grady.*

"The *Tribune* will probably be covering the event," Capone said lazily, and slid the paper away from Macey's side of the desk as he settled back into his seat for the first time since she'd entered. He still wasn't looking at her, but there was a softness to his plump lips that was very close to a satisfied smile.

Macey turned away, her hands clenched so tightly she felt her fingernails denting her skin.

"Does that mean you ain't resigning, then, doll?"

Her jaw hurt and her insides were in turmoil. Macey was truly caught between the Scylla and Charybdis. She gave him a look over her shoulder filled with loathing. "No, I'm not resigning."

His low, complacent chuckle followed her as she stalked from the room.

Macey stared listlessly at the closet filled with all the clothing Al Capone had given her. In direct contrast to her mood, everything seemed to sparkle or shimmer. The fabrics were silk, gossamer, velour, and wool. The rich colors varied from blues and violets to reds and burgundies. There were black and white frocks too, but every shade for each article of clothing complemented her coloring.

A sour bile taste rose in the back of her throat as she yanked out a crimson dress. *Might as well dress like the whore I am.* The handkerchief-hemmed frock was the color of blood, and it sparkled with tiny red and silver beads in a flamelike pattern over the bodice.

She was digging ruthlessly through racks of scarves and headpieces when someone knocked on the door of her apartment. With a muttered curse, she glanced at the clock and saw that it was too early for Gus to be calling for her…and at the same moment, she recognized that an ugly tendril of cold had settled over the back of her neck.

Macey spun, snatching up her nearest stake, and approached the door. She looked through the peephole and her eyes widened with shock.

Still holding her weapon, she opened the door to one of Capone's security team, who was standing next to Flora. He had a dull, glazed look in his eyes.

"Macey, let me in."

"Release him first," she told Flora, gesturing to the security guard, who, thankfully, showed no signs of fang marks.

Her friend—could she even call her a friend?—did as Macey requested, and as the man stumbled off toward the elevator, Flora stepped into the apartment.

"Whoa. Nice digs you got here, Macey." There was admiration tinged with envy in Flora's voice as she turned in a slow circle, taking in the luxurious surroundings. "Look at all those clothes!"

"What are you doing here?" Macey glanced at the door. Capone might sense the presence of an undead, and who knew what he would do then? "What do you want?"

"This cloche, for one!" Flora tugged the tight boiled-wool hat down over her head and admired herself in the mirror. It was one of Cookie's creations, a mustard color with bright orange and red flowers and a swirl of aubergine feathers on one side. "This looks much better on me than it would on you, Mace. Can I have it?"

"Why are you here?" Macey said from between clenched teeth. She considered setting down her stake, but thought better of it. The brick of ice at the back of her neck reminded her to stay on her guard.

Flora snatched off the hat and gave her a venomous side-eye look. Macey was taken aback by the expression there, but then it disappeared so quickly she wondered if it had just been a natural part of Flora's undeadness or a trick of the light.

"What did you do to Iscariot?" She flounced over and sat on the bed, disregarding the blood-red gown Macey had just laid out.

"Why do you ask?"

Flora huffed, and her eyes flashed red for a moment. "He was determined to get you before, but now he's really got a bang on for you. I've never—well, no one's ever seen him so furious. His face is all marked up too. So what did you do?"

Her emotions warring between satisfaction and apprehension, Macey walked over to the window and looked out over Chicago. Somewhere he was out there…waiting for her. Would she be as lucky the next time they met? Would *he* be as lucky the next time?

She set her jaw grimly. No, he wouldn't. Not if she had anything to say about it. She tightened her grip on the stake.

"Why are you really here, Flora? You said you wanted me to help you, but then you attacked a man that night and left him for dead in the alley. You fed on him—and who knows how many other innocent people."

"A gal has to eat. Even a vampire gal!"

Macey turned to stare down her friend. "Sebastian Vioget is a vampire and he hasn't ever—in more than a century—fed on a mortal. If you truly wanted my help, you can start by doing that—and by not *killing* people." Macey kept her voice calm with effort.

Flora's expression turned from petulant to hopeful. "Can you help me, then? Do you know how? Can you reverse this—this thing?" She waved a hand at herself.

"Definitely not unless you change your ways. And even then I don't know."

"Then what's the point?" Flora stood suddenly, and her fangs shot out. Her eyes blazed red. "Why should I even try to change if there's no reason to?"

"Why?" Macey felt a stab of pain deep inside. Flora didn't understand, and whether it was the real Flora speaking—the friend she'd loved—or the undead one, she didn't know. It didn't matter. Hopelessness washed over her. "Because it's the right thing to do. Not to kill people. Not to hurt them."

"But *you* do it." Flora sashayed across the room and began to flick through the dresses hanging in Macey's closet. "You slay vampires, you beat them up, you burn their faces—yes, I can tell that's what happened to Nicholas—and you get to dress like a rich woman to boot!" She spun, her eyes like fire-pit coals. Her fangs shone, lethal and longer than Macey had ever seen them. "You stake a vampire and you send him or her to hell. Every time, Macey. You are judging and sentencing them to damnation whenever you use that stake. So what makes you so much better, so much different than me? I at least *chose* to be this way. You— well, your abilities were *given* to you. Just like all these clothes, and all of this."

Macey could hardly breathe. The back of her throat burned and the fingers clasping her stake suddenly felt large and clumsy. Black shadows threatened to obliterate her vision. "Get out of here."

Flora looked as if she were about to argue, perhaps even to attack…but then she changed. Her eyes returned to their normal cornflower color, her fangs retracted, and the fury ceased rolling off her. "Aw, Macey…"

"Leave. And never come here again." Macey thrust a hand out, pointing to the door. She had to work very hard to keep it from shaking, but she managed it for the most part.

Flora gave her one last inscrutable look. It was not angry nor regretful nor pleading. It was as if she were trying to read Macey's mind. "Whatever you say."

Flora clomped to the door and went through, slamming it behind her. Macey hurried over to watch through the peephole and make certain she left…and once Flora entered the elevator, Macey drew in a long, deep breath. She was shaking a little, from fury as well as regret. Then suddenly, she bolted to her feet and snatched up the telephone.

"Watch for a tall, slender, redheaded woman with lots of freckles. She's coming off the north elevator in a few minutes. Don't talk to her or say anything to her; I just want to make sure she leaves," Macey said once she was put through to the security team in the main lobby. "And look to see where she goes. What direction."

"She's here, Miss Denton," replied the guard, Joey. "Just comin' off the elevator. I seen her come in earlier, too, all huddled under an umbrella, though it ain't even raining out. I'll see where the broad goes and call you back."

Macey hung up the phone and sank onto the bed next to her mussed-up red frock. Flora's accusations rang in her mind.

You are judging and sentencing them to damnation whenever you use that stake.

It was true.

But it was her calling. Her family legacy.

The telephone rang, its shrill *brringg-brringg* cutting through the stillness. Macey answered it and listened while Joey told her that Flora left the way she'd come: covered in a long coat and beneath an umbrella. Alone, and without any sort of transportation waiting nearby.

Something shimmered deep inside Macey as she set the telephone receiver back on its cradle. Her eyes were damp and she blinked hard, then scrubbed at them to keep the tears at bay.

Macey turned back to the bed and picked up the glitzy red dress. At any other time, she would have swooned over its beauty. The fabric and its beading fairly burned like light shining through one of Capone's beloved Chiantis. But tonight, the frock represented an ugly compromise of her beliefs. A scarlet letter of her own making, so to speak.

She pulled on an opaque satin slip that covered her from breasts to mid-thigh and hugged her curves like a second skin. Then her garters and stockings—tonight, shimmery black ones that rolled up over her knees. And finally the frock itself, that sheer, lightweight bit of fabric that floated around her body like a breeze. The weight of beaded cuffs and the flame designs over the front of the bodice as well as along the handkerchief hem helped the flimsy tunic hang properly.

Macey was just finishing with last-minute accessories—a bejeweled headband, gloves, stakes, and her silver cross—when her escort knocked on the door.

She flung it open without checking the peephole, and there stood Chas.

Seventeen

An Evening of Glitter and Glitz

WHAT THE HELL are you doing here?" Chas demanded as he pushed his way into the apartment. And just as Flora had done only a short while earlier, he stopped and stared, as his gaze swept the place.

"I live here," Macey snapped. "What's your excuse?" She grabbed her pocketbook. *Just what I don't need. What is he doing here? How did he even get in?* "I'm going to be late. I don't have time to—"

He grabbed her by the arm and swung her around roughly. "What is going on, Macey? What are you doing back here?"

"Leave your hands off me."

"That's not what you said last night." He bared his teeth in a humorless grin, still holding her by the arm.

"Is that why you're here?" she retorted, ignoring the heat that rushed to her cheeks. She didn't try to pull away; she wouldn't give him the satisfaction. "Can't get on without me, Chas?"

"I can get on without you fine, lulu. It's the rest of the world, God help them, who needs you. Not the bastard who's giving you all *this.*" He swept an arm around in an angry motion. "You have a job to do—or have you forgotten, now that you're living in the lap of luxury?"

"How many times do we have to have this conversation? And let go of me," she said, considering using the big square heel on her black-and-red shoes to make her point…right on top of his toes. "How did you get in here, anyway? Capone's got the place guarded like Fort Knox."

Chas shrugged and released her none too gently. Macey resisted the urge to rub her arm, which smarted from his obnoxious grip.

"I didn't have any weapons on me, and I was delivering a hat to you. They searched the hatbox—thorough blokes, they are. I left it in the hall, by the way. But from the looks of it, you don't need any more hats." His tone was filled with sarcasm and fury.

"Fine. Thanks. Well, gotta run. I'm leaving now."

"I need you tonight—"

"What? Look, Chas, what happened last night was—"

"I don't mean that, dammit," he said. "I need you to *do your job*. Tonight. There's something brewing out there—something's going on—and I can't keep up with all the undead in this town on my own."

It was on the tip of her tongue to make a sharp comment about if he didn't feel the need to sleep with every vampire he staked, he probably could—but she thought better of it. *No need to hurt him too.* So, instead of lashing out like part of her wanted to, Macey calmed herself a little and said, "I can't tonight, Chas. I have to go to the Art Institute."

Maybe it was her tone, for his response was more controlled as well. "With Capone?" Nevertheless, his teeth were gritted and his Gypsy eyes flashed with anger. "You have to be on his arm while there's work to be done, protecting his fat ass—when he could do it himself if he tried."

Macey shook her head, curling her fingers, then relaxed them and exhaled. She might as well tell him the truth. "Grady's going to be there. Capone made it clear if I didn't come, something would happen…to him. To Grady. I actually tried to resign today, to leave him for good, and that's when he pulled this out of his hat."

There was a beat of silence. Chas's lips pursed and he shook his head. His expression was black. "You can't keep allowing him to do this to you. There are too many vampires in Chicago, and too many deaths because of them. Haven't you been reading the papers?"

"What am I supposed to do, Chas? Let Capone kill an innocent man?"

"There are a helluva lot more than *one* innocent person who are dying every night at the hands and fangs of the undead. You need to do your job."

She clenched her jaw. "Not tonight, Chas. I'll figure something out. But not tonight."

His face set like stone, he turned away. "You're a fool, Macey. You're making a big mistake." Those were the last words he said before he slammed the door behind him.

She swore, blinked back tears of anger and frustration, and grabbed her pocketbook. *Just one more night. I'll figure out something tomorrow.*

Resolved and resigned, Macey left her rooms. She rode the elevator down to the lobby of the Lexington and arrived only moments before Capone did.

He gave her a smooth smile, which she returned with a cold glare.

This is it. This is the last night I walk by your side.

Now that she knew the prophecy didn't apply to Capone, there really was no reason to hang around, being pinned by his mobster thumb. She just had to extricate herself from him without putting Grady at risk.

The Art Institute was closed to the public at this time of night, but open to those who had the social cachet—or the means to buy a ticket—to attend the gala. As such, the affair was a formal one, with top hats and tailcoats everywhere, snowy white bib shirts, waistcoats, pristine bow ties, and glittering evening gowns of every hue. Jewels shone everywhere: affixed to headbands, combs, wrists, throats, and even on long necklaces that hung nearly to the navel of its wearer. The men wore gems and other shiny accessories in their cufflinks, chunky rings, and in jet, silver, or gold beads on the spats covering their shoes.

Macey could safely say she'd never been in the company of so much wealth and power, nor so much net worth of jewelry and fashion. She wasn't an expert by any means, but at least two of the gowns she saw were likely Worth originals, imported from Paris.

If she hadn't been struggling with a riot of emotions—guilt, anger, and impatience—she might have enjoyed the sights and experience.

The bright flashbulbs from the press blinded her as she and Capone climbed the short side steps to the Art Institute in the company of other well-dressed attendees. Did that mean she'd be gracing the front of the papers again tomorrow, on the arm of the most feared man in Chicago? *Damn.*

That made her even more determined this would be the last time she was photographed with him. She firmly extricated herself from his grip in her arm, easing back to place a comfortable distance from him as he jovially greeted everyone from the institute director to the mayor to a Vanderbilt to Washington Porter—the man responsible for supplying most of Chicago's fresh fruit.

Capone's glad-handing gave Macey the opportunity to stroll along and admire some of the woodcut prints of spring landscapes in Japan, and to observe the layout of the gala.

In keeping with the theme of the evening, the high-ceilinged, windowless gallery in which the exhibit was displayed had been decorated in a minimalist Japanese fashion. Single fresh branches from cherry trees, likely cut today in the prime of their blooming season, stood in tall, elegant black vases and released a lovely fragrance to each passerby. Plain tapestries in the blues and violets often mirrored in Utagawa Hiroshige's landscapes hung on the walls behind some of the framed prints. Silks of blue were draped over tables, cascading in smooth swaths like waterfalls to end in elegant pools on the floor. The servers were dressed in traditional Japanese kimonos, and each wore an ink-black wig sporting the gender-appropriate hairstyle. They carried trays with shrimp cocktails on tiny picks, small seaweed rolls, and rice balls, as well as small fried dumplings.

Instead of spirits and wine, the official beverage being served was hot tea in small, handle-less cups. The waiters lifted short, flat iron-cast pots to pour the fragrant green tea in an elegant stream before offering a steaming cup to each guest.

Though the tea was the official drink, there were plenty of dim corners where the furtive glint of bottle or flask could be seen.

Despite noticing all of these details with interest, Macey simply couldn't relax and partake of the festivities. She was too busy waiting for the back of her neck to get cold—which would actually be a relief, she freely admitted, for she knew how to deal with that—and both dreading and anticipating the possibility that she would encounter Grady.

When it happened, however, she wasn't expecting it.

She was at *Hakone*, admiring the vibrant hues of the elegant, arched green mountains overlooking the subtle shades of blue ocean, when the back of her bare neck prickled with awareness. Not with undead awareness, but with something far more potent.

She didn't have to turn to know it was Grady standing behind her. But when she did turn, her palms damp and her insides a basket of butterflies, she wasn't prepared to encounter Grady *and* the young blond woman standing there with him.

"Miss Denton," he said in a detached voice. "I thought that was you. I noticed your companion's arrival, and assumed that would be you on his arm, though there were so many cameramen taking photographs I couldn't see your face. But it appears I was correct."

His voice was cool and detached, but his eyes…they were not. Oh, not by a long shot. They were a dark, wild blue, hot and probing as they caught her gaze. She found it difficult to look away, even more difficult to form words. What was that storming through his eyes? Anger? Accusation? Disgust?

Relief?

When she finally broke the connection, her attention bounced around to take in Grady's whole person: his unruly cocoa-brown hair, combed back neatly except for a tiny curl flipping up behind his ear; the crisp black tuxedo jacket that made his shoulders look broader than ever; the pristine white bowtie, shirt, and textured white-on-white waistcoat; the faint ink stain on his hand that indicated he'd recently been taking notes—even here, during this formal occasion.

Macey dragged her eyes away and was doing her best to find something to say when Grady rescued her—so to speak. "Pardon me for my lapse. Miss McCormick, meet Miss Denton. She's an *associate* of Mr. Capone's."

The venom in his voice when he said "associate" took Macey by surprise. It felt as if someone had punched her in the stomach; painful and as if she couldn't snatch in a good breath.

Grady continued, "Miss Denton, please meet Miss Carol McCormick. The Colonel—er, my boss—is her cousin, in case you hadn't guessed." He smiled at his companion, whose hand was linked to his arm, and she smiled up in return. How cozy. Macey couldn't help but notice there wasn't a trace of the Irish in his tone tonight. Instead, they were stilted and formal, as if he were taking care with each word or syllable.

"The pleasure is mine," replied Miss McCormick, bestowing the same warm, open smile on Macey. Apparently, she was oblivious to the undercurrents between her escort and Macey—or she was simply gracious enough to be able to ignore them.

Or perhaps there weren't any undercurrents at all and Macey was exaggerating them in her own mind.

Which, really, would be the very best thing that could happen, she realized suddenly.

In fact…determination and relief took hold of her. This *was* the best thing that could happen. Capone could no longer use Grady as a threat to Macey if she didn't care a fig for him—and vice versa.

And tonight would be her chance to demonstrate that to Big Al. To finally sever the ties, so to speak.

"And mine," Macey managed to say. Now her smile was genuine, but when she transferred her attention to Grady, she made her expression turn cool and remote.

"Since he's obviously not giving up the details, allow me to ask how you know Jameson," said Miss McCormick, looking up at him as if he were a moving pictures star. "Obviously, I know him because he's my cousin's star reporter—you did hear about the counterfeit gang he busted up, didn't you, Miss Denton? What a hero he was, nearly getting burned up in that warehouse fire!"

Several reactions pinged in Macey's brain during Miss McCormick's enthusiastic speech, but the one that settled right in the front of her mind was "*Jameson.*" So the J was for Jameson.

Quickly following that tidbit of information was shock that he'd nearly died. And she'd had no idea any of it had happened.

And the irony was…his near-death hadn't been at the hands of Capone *or* the undead.

"Miss Denton don't get around to reading the newspapers all that often."

Macey's heart lurched as Capone's hard Brooklyn tones cut into the conversation. She shot a look at Grady, who'd gone rigid and stone-faced, then turned as Big Al continued, "It's a pleasure to meet you, Mr. Grady. I want to personally thank you for your work exposing the counterfeiting scheme." He offered his hand.

"Thank you." Grady didn't sound as if he meant it. In fact, he did very little to hide his loathing for the crime boss, though he didn't go as far as ignoring the proffered handshake.

Capone wasn't the powerful man he was without being aware of his effect on people, but he didn't seem to mind. "Those scumbags took me for over a hundred thousand bucks with their fake tenners," he continued. He held one of the small teacups in his hand and gestured a little, sloshing the liquid over his French-cuffed sleeve. "I got a lotta hands in a lotta pies, but there's one thing I ain't interested in, and it's fake money." He leaned closer to Grady. His voice dropped lower, but Macey could still hear him when he said, "You ever want a job't pays better than sniffing out news stories, you come see me."

"I don't think so, Mr. Capone," Grady replied. "You and I operate on different sides of the law—and I have no interest in crossing that river. Excuse me." Without another look at Macey, he turned smoothly, taking Carol McCormick with him. They strolled off through the crowd of glittering jewels, black evening jackets, and rainbows of silk and satin: a tall, confident figure partnered with a slender, elegant, glittering blond one.

That left Capone and Macey alone, and she steeled her expression into a cold, emotionless mask. "And there he goes—your last bit of leverage over me, Scarface. You wouldn't take the risk of hurting someone you admire so much—and quite frankly, after the way he spoke to me tonight, I wouldn't care if you did."

"I'm not so certain about that, doll." Capone waved at one of the Japanese-garbed waiters and gestured sharply with his empty teacup. The waiter produced a flask and covertly filled the mobster's glass, neatly replacing the contraband bottle back into the pocket of his loose kimono in mere seconds.

She leaned closer, dropping her voice. "Well, you can be certain about this, Mr. Capone: as of tonight, I'm no longer in your employ. And as of tonight, if anything happens to any of my friends or anyone with a connection to me, I'm placing the blame squarely on *you*."

"That oughta be interesting."

It was Capone's sly, dismissive comment that sent her over the edge. "Just try me, Alphonsus."

He laughed. "You don't frighten me, you dumb broad. You're—"

Macey stepped closer, right up to him so she brushed against his belly. "I should frighten the hell out of you. I know far too much about you—and I'm certain Nicholas Iscariot would be delighted to know that you wear the *vis bulla*. More than that, he'd be even more pleased to foil the 'dauntless one's' prophecy by ridding the earth of you and your Chianti-swilling ass. You've already indicated how incapable you are of protecting yourself from the undead without a woman to protect you," she said from between her teeth.

"Why, you little *bitch*. You know what happened to da last person who made vague threats at me? He ended up in the goddamn *morgue* wid a bullet through his head." His Brooklyn accent came through like a thick and chunky pasta sauce.

"Then let me clear up any *vagueness*. This is not a threat, Alphonsus. This is *fact*. If any harm comes to Grady or any other of my friends or associates, I'll make certain the undead know *exactly* where to find you…and precisely how to get to you. And I can guarantee that if anything happens to *me*, every single Venator on this earth—including my father, if he happens to be alive— will be out for you before you can load your gun."

She fixed him with one last hard, steady look. Then, as if she were a queen, Macey turned deliberately and gracefully—and blundered off into the crowd, hardly noticing where she was going.

Her lungs were heaving, and, admittedly, her knees were more than a little trembly, but she was liberated. The line in the sand had been drawn.

Capone had a lot more to lose than she did.

It was her own damned fault she had taken so long to realize it.

Eighteen

Miss McCormick Becomes a Topic

MACEY WALKED AWAY as if she had a destination, even though she had nowhere in mind except to get as far from Capone and Grady as possible. Then—yes. *There.*

She pushed open the door to the ladies' lounge with relief, aware that her heart was pounding with what doctors called adrenaline.

I'm free.

She stopped in front of the nearest stretch of mirror and stared at herself. Other than bright red patches of emotion on each cheek, she had to admit, she looked pretty good. Strong. Bold. Fearsome. And put together just as beautifully as the lovely Miss McCormick—thanks to her now-former employer.

But now that she was done with Capone, she wouldn't be dressing like this anymore. Except for the hats she'd get from Temple's Aunt Cookie, which were quite exquisite.

Macey fixed an awkward curl, pinning it above her ear with a jet-and-ruby-beaded hairpin with a hand that was now steady. She also made certain the long jet-black earrings were still screwed tightly in place, adjusting them slightly because her earlobes were beginning to ache. Then, realizing she had no reason to stay here—in the lounge or at the Art Institute—she went through the door and found herself back in the midst of the glittering gala. Not wanting to be noticed, however, she slipped behind one of the big columns near a corner and took a look around to get her bearings.

From her safe corner out of sight of the party attendees, she scanned the crowd for a glimpse of Grady (she told herself it was simply because she didn't want to run into him again), but she didn't see him—or the beacon-haired Miss McCormick.

Had they ducked out for a bit of privacy? Were they walking through one of the deserted galleries, searching for a private corner—like the one in which she was lingering?

She scowled a little at the reminder of how good Grady was at taking advantage of private corners—or high-walled booth tables, for that matter—sliding closer and pulling a gal near for a thorough bit of kissing and hugging while he looked into her eyes and called her "lass" in that delicious brogue. A little shiver of memory caught her by surprise and she shoved it away, forcibly replacing the memory of his face with that of Chas.

"Hey there, doll," came a smooth voice behind her. "You look a little lost."

Macey turned. The man behind her was tall and wide, and he edged far too close to her with his powerful body. She didn't recognize him—nor was he an undead—but his demeanor wasn't one that instilled comfort or pleasure; in fact, the barely veiled lasciviousness in his eyes made her frown.

"I'm not," she said. "Lost. Thank you for your concern." She would have brushed past him, but he caught her arm.

"What's the hurry, tootsie?" His fingers were tight and he quickly and neatly pivoted her back into the shadows, following with his bulky body. "Pretty girl like you shouldn't be walking around by yourself in a place like this."

"In a place like what?" she asked calmly. The fury, guilt, and other unpleasant emotions she'd tamped down and away throughout the evening were bubbling nicely to the surface— and the lout in front of her had no idea he was about to be the recipient of their explosion. "And I wasn't walking. Let go of me."

"Come on now, tootsie roll," he said, pushing her back toward the wall. His eyes were dark and hungry and he brushed a finger over the bare skin of her throat. "You look lonely."

"I won't say it again. Take your hands off me." She kept her voice pleasant, but her eyes were steely and hard. Inside, she was smiling. What was that old saying? The bigger they were…

"Now don't be shy, dollface. I know how to make a gal—"

A loud *pop!* followed by a flash of light had Macey's assailant spinning around in shock.

"That's a great shot there, Mr. Badgley. How about a nice smile now, while I get another one of the woman you're accosting in the corner, still cowering away from you as you hold her in place." Grady stood there, speaking through a cold, humorless smile. "Would you care to finish your statement about you know how to make a gal…what was it you were going to say? Cringe? I'm sure Mrs. Badgley will appreciate it when the story hits the front page tomorrow." He let the heavy camera hang from its strap around his neck and pulled out a notebook and pencil.

Badgley growled something and took a threatening step toward Grady, but the other man didn't back down. "Is that a 'no comment'?" His voice was hard, and Macey noticed his pencil hand gripped the camera as if it were a weapon.

"Give me that damned film," snarled Badgley.

"Just try and take it." Grady met him, glare for glare, steady and calm. When Badgley eased back, the news hawk growled, "Now get the hell away from here. And if I see you with your hands on any other woman who's not your wife, I'll print these pictures. Or better yet—I'll send copies of them to your wife. I suspect her rich daddy won't appreciate it at all. Now get your arse away from here."

Apparently, Badgley was smart enough to know when he was out of choices, and he stalked off into the glitz and glamour of the gala. That left Macey and Grady alone in the dimly lit alcove.

"I didn't need your help," she said, suddenly furious and unsettled at being alone with him—and being the recipient of his unnecessary gallantry. "I was just about to take care of him when you interrupted. Thanks for nothing." She had to keep her distance and her ire up, but she didn't find it difficult. She *was* irritated that Grady had ruined the perfect chance for her to blow off some steam.

"Though Badgley would have deserved flying across the room and landing in the middle of the marble floor, I didn't think it was prudent for you to draw attention to yourself." He wasn't smiling, but he wasn't exactly glowering at her anymore either. "A little difficult to explain that sort of strength."

"How did you know that's what—" Macey felt a rush of heat bloom over her cheeks.

Their eyes met and she knew he remembered too…that moment in his bedroom when he'd undressed her and discovered the elegant little *vis bulla* dangling from her navel.

How strong? he'd asked, sifting it gently between his fingers, watching her with deep blue eyes.

I could throw you across the room if I wanted. Want to try me?

Ah, no, Macey, lass. I've got other things on my mind…

"So," she said, quickly marshaling her thoughts, reengaging her protective shield, ignoring the memory that was making her insides turn into a hot mush, "dating the boss's younger cousin, are you? And star investigative reporter now. Moving up in the world, aren't you, Grady."

He stepped back a little, a gesture for which she was supremely grateful. For it was becoming difficult to ignore the familiarity of him—the smell of his skin, the sight of the hair through which she'd run her fingers, the lips she'd kissed, the eyes that had looked at her with love. His entire being.

"Carol's a nice gal," he said, glancing up as the lights flickered. "But—"

The lights went out. Everything was pitch black.

Nineteen

Standoff in the Gallery

G RADY WASN'T SURPRISED WHEN, unlike every other
woman in the vicinity, Macey didn't scream or even gasp when
the lights went out.

In fact, she pushed past him, brushing against his jacket sleeve
with her quick, compact body. He reacted smoothly enough to
grab her arm as she went by. Her gossamer sleeve felt rich and
sensuous under his fingers. He remembered the tiny red and black
beads glinting in the dark curls at her temple.

"Vampires?" he asked in the vicinity of where her ear should
be. He felt the soft brush of her hair against his cheek and caught
a good whiff of her—floral and lightly sweet—and closed his eyes
as a pang of regret and pain twinged in his belly.

She paused long enough to answer his question—"Not this
time"—then was off into the pitch black of the art gallery.

Grady resisted the urge to go after her for a number of reasons;
the most relevant being that she didn't need his help or protection.
She, clearly, didn't want anything from him—something he
needed to remind himself. Daily.

He'd been hanging around vampire hunters and counterfeiters
too much lately. Just because the lights had gone out didn't mean
anything was wrong—even though, from the number of nervous,
high-pitched giggles that still penetrated the darkness, along with
low-voiced conversation tinged with concern, no one else seemed
to agree.

But before he could move out of the shadowy alcove and make his way back to the main galley, the lights overhead sizzled and popped, then came back on. There was a soft wave of voices lifting with relief and excitement as the party went back into full swing as if nothing had happened. If Grady didn't know any better, he would have thought Macey planned it all as a way to escape from him. Hell, for all he knew, she had.

He frowned and took the opportunity to unhook the camera strap from around his neck, tucking the pencil and notebook back in his pocket…and it was then he realized the chattering and the undercurrent of uncomfortable chuckles had suddenly turned to silence.

Something was wrong.

Grady heard a soft scuffling sound and absolutely nothing else. He silently put the heavy camera onto the floor deep in the corner and listened, keeping himself tucked behind the large pillar that had hidden Badgley and Macey from passersby.

Then there was a voice. It wasn't terribly loud, but it carried and it had authority. Or, rather, its words had authority.

"Thank you for your attention, ladies and gentlemen. If everyone will do just as I say, this young lady here won't get hurt."

The silence tightened and Grady was desperate to look around the pillar, but he knew he had to make certain he wasn't seen. Yet his palms had gone damp and his insides swirled because he was certain the "young lady" was Macey. It had to be Macey.

Whatever was going on, she would surely be in the middle of it.

He put that fear roughly from his mind and looked up at the tall, round pillar, tried to tell his heart she knew how to take care of herself. And if he could climb high enough up the column, no one would see him and he could look down and see what was going on.

He considered his options. There was a decorative base at knee height, and then another flourish—like a small platform— just above his head. That would be a good start if he could get there without being noticed.

"Everyone into the center here where I can see you," came the authoritative voice. "All of you. Move slowly and carefully and keep your hands held high—right where I can see them. Remember, this young woman's life—and your own—is at stake."

Swiftly, Grady pulled off his shiny black shoes then stockings, taking care to remain out of sight and soundless. When a shadow carrying a long, ominous shape fell on the floor just beyond his hiding place, Grady froze and flattened himself against the column. He edged around the pillar, matching the speed of the approaching gunman in order to stay out of sight, but taking care not to go too far around the column so he was seen on the other side.

But it was when he was halfway around the column that he was able to catch a glimpse of what was happening. The sight of four men holding Tommy guns pointed at the crowd of people made his insides freeze, but it was a fifth man—presumably the speaker—who was holding a woman up against him, his arm around her throat, and a bent elbow indicating some sort of weapon pointed at her.

The woman was wearing red—like Macey—but that was all Grady could see of her.

The sound of approaching footfalls jolted his attention away from the scenario. He shifted around the column just in time to remain out of sight of the man who'd just passed by. Now he wasn't alone, however, and was using the slender barrel of his gun to direct two partygoers ahead of him. They too had their hands held high.

"I've got two more," called the gunman as he prodded his captives toward the main gathering. "They were cowering in the toilets."

Grady didn't have any time to waste; these bandits—or whoever they were—were clearly going to be thorough about rounding up everyone. He'd already whipped off his tuxedo jacket, tie, and waistcoat, and now he bundled them into the corner with his shoes and stockings.

After removing his suspenders and hanging them around his neck, he climbed on top of the decorative base around the column. It was barely wide enough for him to perch on it tiptoe. He curled his feet down and around the smooth edges, and that little boost in height was all he needed to be able to fully grasp the upper ledge that was now at the level of his forehead. The ledge was hardly any wider than the base, but Grady was able to grip using the column's vertical grooves for his flexible toes, and the power of his hands and arms to pull himself up to—and then, carefully but quickly, past—the small platform.

The platform was square against the rounded sides of the pillar, leaving small triangles of space for his toes to balance as he wrapped the suspenders around the column, wrapping one end around each hand as leverage to help him climb. After that, everything became a lot easier, but he'd resisted using the suspenders to ascend at the lower level for fear someone would see the black braces moving up the column.

Now, his feet planted solidly against the column, holding himself in place with the suspenders, he was well above the heads of anyone below. And as the covered light bulbs that lit the galley hung from long wires from the high ceiling to bring the illumination close to the ground, he was above them and their shades. This left a good bit of darkness in which he could hide.

By this time, the gunmen had made everyone line up and they were going down the line, two by two, with Tommy guns still trained on the crowd, and divesting each person of any jewelry, money, or firearms they might have.

The jewels and money went into two large canvas sacks, and the weapons were piled in the center of the marble floor. Grady saw that Al Capone was not immune from being frisked, nor was Colonel McCormick, nor even Mr. Vanderbilt.

"Well done," said the authoritative voice once all of the weapons had been removed and the valuables collected. "And not one casualty. What a well-behaved group you are." He was still holding the woman in the red dress, but now, all at once, he released her, shoving her roughly toward the other victims. "I'm finished with you for now."

She stumbled but caught herself and staggered into the crowd, sobbing softly. That was when Grady realized it wasn't Macey who'd been the hostage, and he found himself scanning the cluster of people in hopes of catching sight of her.

Maybe she'd escaped notice as well, and had gone to contact the authorities. Or—and this he hoped wasn't the case—she was lurking in the shadows as he was, looking for an opportunity to put a stop to this robbery. For bullets were just as deadly to a vampire hunter as they were to any mortal. While she might be brilliant with a stake—though he'd never seen her in action—this wasn't Macey's area of expertise.

"Now, everyone—this way." The leader made a gesture to the right, and his gunmen lined up on either side to direct the crowd toward one end of the long, narrow exhibition.

It only took Grady a moment to see what was going to happen. The hostages were being herded past the tall metal security gates that reached from floor to ceiling and barricaded that end of the gallery. Thus he wasn't surprised when, once all sixty or so of Chicago's elite—and a few of the not so wealthy and powerful— were hustled through, the gunman pulled the gates shut with a loud clang.

"This should keep you all nicely put," said the leader as one of his men stood aside, holding a slew of heavy chains. Three other gunmen trained their weapons on the crowd so as to keep them from rushing the doors as it became clear the chains were meant to lock them inside.

But it was the last thief who'd caught Grady's attention. He was dragging in a large black object about the size of a travel trunk. Grady couldn't see what it was from his vantage point, but it looked like some sort of engine or machine.

Something very unpleasant trickled down his spine. Up until now, Grady had felt confident things would end nonviolently. Clearly, these men were thieves and were taking advantage of the exclusive gathering of the rich and powerful to relieve them of their valuables…at least, that was what he thought until he saw the black machine.

He'd figured, being on this side of the metal gate, he'd easily be able to free everyone quickly and readily, and perhaps even contact the authorities before the thieves made their escape.

But this big black machine…this changed everything.

Because it looked an awful lot like a bomb.

Twenty

In Which We Meet Betsy

MACEY HAD HAD TO KEEP herself from searching for Grady during the entire jewelry heist. Though she caught sight of Carol McCormick ("*nice gal*"), her uncle the "Colonel," Capone, Mr. Washington, and even the odious Mr. Badgley, Grady was nowhere to be seen.

She'd left him behind when the lights went out, relieved to have the opportunity to escape the rest of that conversation—whatever it might have been. She wondered what he'd been about to say…and where he was now.

She gave a mental head shake. *Focus, Mace.* She had much more important things to think about now—like an opportunity to keep these bold jewel thieves—all of whom had been acting as waiters until they simultaneously threw off their kimonos and pulled out their weapons—from making off with all their valuables, whether she knew where Grady was or not.

At first—when the lights came on and the partygoers had, one by one, noticed the terrifying tableau before them and gone silent—she'd been consumed with somehow keeping the young female hostage from being injured. But with armed gunmen everywhere keeping strict eyes on all of them, Macey hadn't had the opportunity to do anything yet.

Thank goodness the young woman had been released unharmed. And now that she'd joined the rest of the crowd, Macey's current biggest concern was stopping the criminals before they escaped with their loot. Yet having been taken completely by surprise—at least with vampires, she would have sensed their presence—and having no weapons, Macey was nearly as helpless as the rest of the hostages.

And the last thing she wanted to do was cause a disruption that would get herself or someone else killed. Still…she felt as if she should be doing *something*. And from the sidelong look Capone was giving her, he felt the same way too. Perhaps he was right—who would think of a slender, petite young woman doing anything to challenge these thieves? It was the mobsters like Capone and his ilk that needed to be more carefully watched.

Which was clearly why each person had been searched from head to toe, with the men's hands thankfully being impersonal but thorough. Even Capone's second pistol, tucked into his stocking behind the knee, had been removed.

When the stake Macey had slipped into her garter was discovered, the man searching her held it up and looked at her as if she were mad. "What da hell is this for? A wooden stake? Ya growin' tomatoes?" He tossed it away without a second look.

Clearly, the man had never read *Dracula*.

Now, having been corralled into a smaller portion of the galley, it appeared the hostages would be locked up and left there until the next morning, when someone would come to free them, unless Macey could break them out sooner.

She was strong enough…maybe, she thought as one of the gang began wrapping heavy chains around the opening of the gate. Looking up, she saw that the gates went all the way to the ceiling—so there would be no climbing over them once they were locked in, even if someone could manage to scale the tall brass spikes.

A sudden stillness fell over her fellow hostages, who had been whispering and muttering among themselves, and Macey jolted around to look at the gunmen beyond the gates around which they crowded.

"Now that I have your attention once again," said the leader, "I would like to bid all of you a wonderful evening. And a fond farewell." He gestured to a large black machinelike object that sat on the floor several feet from the gate. "I'd like to introduce you to Betsy."

Macey's belly lurched. There was something ominous about Betsy, about the way she looked, and the way the man smiled affectionately at it.

He walked over to it and, with a flourish, produced a finger-sized brass key from his pocket. The entire room held its collective breath—even the gunman wrapping the chains around the gate paused—as he fit the key into something on the top of the mechanism. He turned it and the machine began to *tick…tick… tick.*

With another dramatic flourish, he withdrew the key and tucked it back into his pocket. "Just in case," he said with a jaunty wink at the crowd of people behind the gate. "You won't be able to get out, but in the unlikely event someone makes their way in here—"

"What da hell is it?" demanded Capone. He was standing at the front of the gate, face thrust against the bars, his powerful fists gripping them.

"Betsy? Why, she's a little present from me. An explosive— heh heh—gift. She's going to make sure none of you are around to identify us, or the fact that we've acquired all of your valuable possessions. That would be very unpleasant for us, you know."

He spread his hands regretfully. "I'd love to chat further, but the fellas and I must be leaving right away. We have five minutes less—oh let me see…" The man leaned over the top of the machine and looked at a small white clock set into it. "Five minutes, less twenty seconds. No, twenty-one…no, twenty-two—well, you get the idea. *Tick, tick, tick.*" He smiled widely at the crowd of captives, then looked at his companions. "Which means it's time for us to finish—"

"Heyyyy…where'd everybody go?" came a loud voice.

Someone gasped and the gunmen spun to look at a disheveled figure staggering from the shadows. From the looks of it, he was either injured or drunk. His white shirt hung half untucked from his trousers, which sagged without the help of their suspenders.

Drunk. Clearly drunk. And very confused.

Seemingly oblivious to everything going on around him, he staggered across the marble floor, his bare feet—*bare feet?*—making soft flopping sounds with every step.

Then Macey saw his face. *It was Grady.*

Her heart stopped. Literally. And a cold wash of something rushed over her as her pulse started up again.

"Whashhh thish?" Grady asked, looking at Betsy, then spinning unsteadily around, bumping into the leader as he did so. Macey froze, unable to breathe.

"Get the hell away from me," said the thief, giving Grady a good shove. The force sent him sprawling onto the floor, his hands landing with loud smacks on the marble.

"What in da hell is wrong with you?" Grady cried, his words thick and slurred as he pulled himself gracelessly to his feet.

"Get him in there with the rest of 'em," ordered the leader, clearly rattled. "We've got to get out of here before that thing goes off."

Macey realized her fingers were clenched into her palms. The bandits could just as easily decide to put a bullet into Grady to get him out of the way as unravel the chains and add him to the group—but for whatever the reason, they didn't.

Maybe they were afraid the sounds of gunshots would bring help. There were probably some guards or night watchmen still stationed outside or around the museum. Capone himself had men waiting in the car just outside…

The chains were unraveled, ticking against the bars in their own darker, duller way than Betsy's more demure countdown clock, and the gates were opened just far enough for their captors to shove Grady inside with the rest of the hostages.

Macey exchanged glances with Capone and she felt him tense next to her—obviously ready to try to barge his way through the ajar gates.

But the nose of a Tommy gun poked between the bars, prodding Al back from where he stood, and he and the rest of the crowd had no recourse but to step back or get blown to pieces.

"Let's go," said the leader sharply as one henchman slipped the padlock into place while the other held the chains.

The decisive click of the lock closing seemed to be an underscore to the ticking of their sealed fate.

The leader, clearly relieved that all had gone as planned despite the intrusion of Grady, cast one last friendly wave. Ignoring the sudden pleas for release, the demands to be set free—even offers of money—he led his gang quickly from the galley without a backward glance.

All was silent for a long moment except for the *tick-tick-tick*. Someone was sobbing quietly, but no one else seemed to move, as if frozen in shock.

Why hadn't Grady done something when he was outside the gate? Macey thought desperately. Surely he wasn't truly drunk… he'd been perfectly sober when she saw him less than an hour ago.

Hell, why hadn't *Macey* herself done something?

Aw, and what could Grady have done anyway—inebriated or not?

He could have gone for help…but by the time anyone arrived, the bomb would have gone off—killing the hostages, as well as anyone who'd responded to the emergency call.

She felt cold and empty. They were well and truly done for.

They were really going to die.

There was simply no way out unless she could use her brute strength to bend the bars of the gate. And even then…there wasn't enough time for everyone to get out.

All of these thoughts ran through her head as the gang of thieves hurried out. Macey looked for a place where the bars seemed a little further apart. But they all seemed perfectly positioned, and immeasurably strong.

Nevertheless, she gripped two of them and began to pull even as several people began to shake the metal gates with desperation and violence. This made it more difficult for her to do what she was trying to do, and the bars weren't moving apart anyway.

"I need a hairpin. Now." A sharp, familiar voice cut through the crowd, but before anyone could respond, someone was there, pulling at Macey's hair.

"Grady?" She spun, clapping a hand to the side of her head where he'd just yanked a hairpin—and several strands of hair— free.

Their eyes met and she saw at once that he definitely wasn't drunk. He smelled of spirits, but he was sober as the day was long.

"Move," he said. "Out of my damned way!" Grady wasn't talking to her; he was shouting at the people gathered around the opening of the gate, which was chained closed.

"What's he going to do?" someone whispered.

"Does anyone have a gun? We could put a hole through the padlock."

"He's picking the lock!"

"Give the man some space," snapped Colonel McCormick. "Grady knows what he's doing. Move back—and that's an order!"

"Hurry!" someone whimpered. "Please hurry."

"How much time do we have left?" whispered someone else in a quavering voice.

"Three minutes."

"*Less* than three minutes by my watch," argued a different voice.

"Shut up and let the man work!" Capone snapped.

Silence fell and Macey felt the entire room breathing together: in and out, trying to keep from panicking as the incessant *tick, tick, tick* filled their ears…counting down the moment till their death.

Yet, despite this hopeful moment, she recognized they were fighting a losing battle. Even if he got the lock open and the gates unchained, the bomb was going to go off in a little more than two minutes. There was simply not enough time for everyone to get through the gates and out of the museum—or even away from the explosion.

But at least he was doing something. Trying something—which was more than Macey could say for herself.

She had forgotten what it was like to feel helpless—but now the feeling came back in a rush of terror…and, surprisingly, acceptance.

A soft click echoed through the dead silent chamber and a wave of soft, hopeful gasps and whispers filtered through—and then everyone started to move.

"Let me out!"

"Get the gates open!"

"Stop!" cried Macey and Colonel McCormick together as Grady rose from his bent position. Already, the crowd surged forward, slamming Grady, Macey, and several others into the metal bars.

"We've got less than a minute!" cried someone. "*Let us out of here!*"

"Let us out!" shouted another voice, and the cries echoed in the high-ceilinged galley. The desperate surge of the crowd became stronger as Grady worked rapidly to unravel the chains, his work being hampered by the pushing and shoving.

"Give him room to open the gates," the Colonel boomed, but his voice was strained. He had clearly come to the same conclusion Macey had.

They'd made progress, but few of them would clear the bomb in time. Yet Macey stood next to McCormick, and, surprisingly, Capone joined them, and they made a sort of barrier to try and keep the rest of the crowd back, protecting Grady from getting smashed against the gate.

Just before Grady dropped the last part of the chain, he looked up and over his shoulder at Macey and McCormick. "I have the key to the bomb. Hold them back, just in case—"

Those were his last startling words as he yanked the last bit of chain through and quickly bolted through the open gates.

A roar went up from the crowd and they surged again, sharp and hard, desperate and wild. Macey, light of weight and small of stature, was thrown into the metal bars. She crashed into them, hitting her head with a sharp clang as McCormick shouted over the chaos: "Hold! Hold back! He's turning off the bomb! Hold *back*, I say! Move *back*!"

Somehow, his words penetrated the mob, and though a good portion of the group continued to shove their way up to the opening and wormed through, many of them heard the Colonel and edged back—and still others saw Grady as he turned and rose from next to Betsy, holding a brass key in his hand.

There was a calm smile on his face and the ticking had stopped.

They were saved.

"I picked his pocket," Grady explained. For about the hundredth time. "When I bumped into him. I saw where he'd put the key, and I retrieved it."

Everyone was lauding him as a hero—an appellation he knew he deserved, but it still felt uncomfortable wearing it.

In a surprisingly overt display, Carol had flung her arms around his neck in the midst of all the backslapping and hand-shaking of congratulations, and now she'd attached herself to his arm as if she were going to take him home with her.

The Colonel was standing off to the side, looking as proud as a parent. Probably not so much because of Grady's actions, but because of the exclusive story his paper was going to print in tomorrow's first edition. He'd already muttered, "Meet me at the office as soon as you can," when he leaned forward to embrace Grady in congratulations.

That was no problem; he couldn't wait to get to the typewriter. This bloody story better be above the damned fold.

Big Al Capone had shaken his hand again, thanked him once more—this time for saving his life instead of saving his cash—and reiterated his offer of a job. Grady's decline was less abrupt than previously, simply because he was feeling slightly more benevolent.

After all, he'd just extended his life—and that of sixty other people. Including Macey, who, by the way, he hadn't seen since the moment their eyes met as he bolted to his feet next to Betsy, holding aloft the key that had saved the day.

Admiration, gratitude, and something else had snapped between them in that moment before he was swarmed and swallowed by a mob of hysterically relieved women and gruffly ecstatic men.

But he hadn't seen her since.

Curiously enough…she wasn't with Capone when the mobster left.

He retrieved his shoes, stockings, and tuxedo coat, evaded a few more hearty blackslaps and handshakes, and made his exit as quickly as possible. He'd already asked McCormick to arrange a car home for Carol so he could get to work.

"I'm going to the office," he told her when she didn't seem inclined to release his arm, even once they were outside the Art Institute and waiting for her ride to be brought around. She opened her mouth to speak, but he continued with a smile and a shake of the head, "It's your uncle's orders—take it up with him. I've got a story to write."

Grady knew he was safe saying that, for the Colonel would never let his niece stand in the way of a good story—no matter how prettily she begged.

She did look very pretty, out here with the moonlight gilding her blond hair into something even lighter and more ethereal. And she was gazing up at him with parted lips and soft, admiring eyes, still holding on to his arm.

So he kissed her. He was a hero, after all. And she clearly wanted to be kissed.

And he wanted to kiss her. Not so much because she was lovely Carol McCormick gilded in the moonlight, but because of who she *wasn't*.

And when she pushed up close and slipped him a bit of tongue, he was not only surprised but also receptive, kissing her a little more thoroughly, moving his arms a little more tightly around her.

A shadow moved in his peripheral vision accompanied by a small beam of light. Someone was coming from around the corner, carrying an electric torch. Probably the night watchman. Loath to put Miss McCormick in a compromising position—especially in case her aunt or uncle happened to come upon them, or worse, to hear about it—Grady released her and stepped back, his hand sliding along a bare arm to clasp her fingers.

The figure with the handheld beacon had become fully visible now, and with a lurch of his belly, he recognized it. Her. Macey.

She was walking straight toward them, calmly and in a businesslike fashion, directing the torch around on the ground and along the walkway that circumnavigated the building. Of course she had to have seen them kissing, and Grady wasn't certain what sort of reaction she—or Carol, for that matter—might have in this situation. Proper ladies didn't generally kiss in public, and there was the whole awkwardness of the fact that he'd been kissing Carol instead of who he really wanted to kiss.

Ah, dammit to hell.

But Macey didn't seem put off at all. "I was looking for clues as to where the thieves went," she said as she approached. "Thought I might be able to tell which direction they went; I couldn't have come out more than a few minutes after them."

"Good thinking," he somehow managed to reply. Everyone else seemed to have been more interested in congratulating him or enjoying the fact that they were still alive rather than attempting to chase down the perps. "Er…did you find anything helpful? And I would probably call them would-be murderers instead of merely thieves."

She gave him a wry smile. "Quite true. And possibly." She gave Carol a nod. "Have a nice rest of your evening. The moon is lovely." And then she moved off into the darkness, clearly continuing on a circuit around the museum.

Grady didn't realize he was staring after her until Carol spoke. "Should she be going off by herself like that? In the dark, with would-be murderers around? And why is *she* looking for clues?

Isn't that something the police should do? Who *is* that woman anyway?"

As if to answer her question, the sound of approaching sirens cut through the distance. And just then, Carol's ride—the Colonel's private auto—pulled up to the drive below, giving Grady a neat exit from that conversation.

"I'm off to the Trib," he said, escorting her down the long flight of narrow steps.

"Will I see you soon, Jameson?" she asked, looking up at him with an arch smile.

"I'm sure you will," he replied, wincing a little at her use of his full name, which always felt so clunky to him, and managed a crooked smile.

"You were such a hero tonight," she said—for about the dozenth time. "I'm so proud to know you."

He tucked her into the auto, pressed a quick kiss to her forehead, and escaped. An all-nighter would be a welcome distraction.

And he damned well better get a big byline and a headline above the fold.

Grady was just finishing his final draft of the story when a shadow fell across his desk.

"It's coming, it's coming," he said without looking up. The Colonel had been breathing down his neck for over an hour, determined to get the story to the typesetters in time for the first edition.

"Grady, it's your uncle."

He stopped, his body dropping several degrees colder, and looked up. McCormick stood there, a grave look on his face. "Officer Montrose just called. They've been looking for you everywhere. You need to go to the hospital immediately."

Suddenly feeling as if he'd been submerged in deep, dark, cold water, Grady rose slowly. "What happened?" he managed to say as he looked around dully for his hat and coat, then realized he was still wearing his tuxedo jacket and didn't have anything else.

"Some sort of attack; they didn't give any details except that you needed to come right away. I've already called for my car. You shouldn't be driving in this state and you won't want to take time to park."

"Thank you." Grady ignored the roaring in his ears long enough to add, "It's finished." He gestured to the article, still in the typewriter, then ran from the room.

He didn't wait for the elevator, but instead bolted down the stairs, terror swelling in his chest.

Not you too, Linwood. Don't die.

Twenty-One

A Pile of Consequences

DESPITE A CLOSE, careful circuit around the Art Institute, Macey didn't find anything that would help track down the direction in which the thieves went. She spent more than an hour poking around in the dark, with only her flashlight and some iffy streetlights to help look for clues. Maybe there'd be something to see in the daylight.

And all the while, she couldn't help but think of how brave and clever and skillful Grady had been. Without him, they surely would have been blown to bits. Her heart squeezed and she wished desperately to be able to thank him herself—for saving her, and the rest of them.

It was nearly one o'clock when she gave up her search for clues, and that was when Macey realized belatedly she wasn't certain where to go now that she had left Capone's employ. It also occurred to her that she did have a few things she wanted to retrieve from her rooms at the Lexington, but she didn't know whether she'd even be allowed entrance.

Still, as she walked down deserted, moonlit Lake Shore Drive, still dressed in her glitzy red frock and chunky-heeled shoes, she decided to make the attempt. Maybe she'd beat Capone back to the hotel, or maybe he wouldn't try to stop her. Perhaps she'd put the fear of God into him, as her foster mother Melissa used to say.

Focusing on that small problem was so much better than remembering Grady and Miss Carol McCormick necking in the moonlight.

Unexpected and dismaying as the sight had been, it was a good thing, she told herself. A good thing he'd moved on to greener pastures—or, at least, a lot less *dangerous* pastures. (Macey didn't necessarily think Carol McCormick's so-called pasture was greener…although it certainly was richer.)

Because even though she'd drawn the line with Big Al, that didn't mean it would be any less risky for Grady to socialize with Macey. Just as they'd done to her father, the vampires would do the same to her: destroy anyone or anything she cared for.

And now that she had Nicholas Iscariot looking for vengeance… She shuddered. Flora's warning, and the information that Iscariot hadn't escaped Macey unscathed, only made her more of a target for the master of the undead. She would have to be terribly careful, extremely brave, and very strong.

And then, all at once, Macey suddenly felt lighter of heart. She had Chas and Sebastian. And now that she'd left Capone, she'd be working with them more, planning and strategizing with them, training with Temple, even visiting with Aunt Cookie in her millinery. She was back where she needed to be.

And she could forget about Grady, move on and see what developed with Chas…

Macey smiled a little in the waning moonlight, though deep inside that heavy little stone of sadness and guilt still sat there. It would eventually dissolve, she knew, and at least she wouldn't make the same mistake as her father. She wouldn't be responsible for the death of someone she loved.

She'd been walking for a few blocks when she realized her feet hadn't taken her to the Lexington, but instead toward Old St. Patrick's Church, where she'd encountered the elderly woman. The elegant steeple, which was so old it hardly stood half as high as the newer buildings that surrounded it, cast a cross-topped shadow over the pavement.

As she looked at it, considering whether to walk closer and perhaps even go in, Macey remembered what the old woman had said to her.

Do you still have the rosary? The one I gave you? Keep the rosary near. You will be in need of it.

She stopped suddenly on the pavement. Those words, that warning, settled sharply in her mind and sent urgent prickles along her arms. She didn't know where it was, but she knew where she'd last had it. At her old apartment above Mrs. Gutchinson's.

Forget the Lexington. Her old flat—that was where she'd go for the rest of the night—it was probably only another two hours until dawn. Many of her things were still there, and the place was deserted. No one would bother her or look for her there.

She could search for the rosary. After her experience with Nicholas Iscariot, burning his face with the large cross, Macey realized she needed all the help she could get.

Macey couldn't find it.

There was no electricity at the house anymore, but she had her flashlight. Nevertheless, she didn't find the rosary, and though the piece had no real meaning for her—not being Catholic or even particularly religious—she felt guilty and unsettled that it was missing.

Weary and a little heartsick, she watched the dawn through her bedroom window—the window on which she'd laid that rosary the first night she'd ever encountered a vampire. After managing to stake him, she'd placed the holy article there on the sill in hopes of warding off any other undead intruders.

Grady had seen it and remarked on it too, and that was the beginning of him learning about her secret life.

She'd not realized how amazing it was that she'd been given the rosary on the very same day she encountered her first vampire.

That could not be a coincidence. Nor could it be one that the old woman wanted her to have it.

Perhaps Macey should go back and talk to her. Find out more. Find out what to do if she didn't locate the prayer beads.

She shook her head and stood, restless, discomfited, and impatient. It was dawn. Time to leave, to return to The Silver Chalice and the secret room beneath Cookie's Smart Millinery, and to put her life—such as it was—back together.

She chose to walk instead of trying to find a cab, and as it turned out, that was the best decision. For standing on the busiest street corners were newsboys, hawking their first editions.

Macey couldn't stop herself from buying a copy of the *Tribune*, and sure enough, splashed on the top of the front page was the headline *Explosive Event For Gala Attendees: Would-be Bombers Still at Large*. The byline was, of course, J. Grady.

But before she could examine the photograph of a cluster of the movers and shakers of Chicago, surrounding Grady and Rob McCormick next to the defused Betsy, Macey caught sight of another headline further down the page. *Brutal Attack Leaves Police Officer Near Death.*

As she scanned the article, all feeling drained from her body, leaving her cold and shaky. And nauseated.

What have I done?

"Taxi!" she shrieked, suddenly spinning toward busy Michigan Avenue. "Taxi!"

Miraculously, one pulled up and she scrambled in, heart pounding, stomach churning. "St. Joe's Hospital. Quickly."

Oh God, oh God...please don't let him die. Please don't let him die.

Twenty-Two

Of Blame and Recriminations

MACEY WAS OUT OF BREATH by the time she got to the correct floor at the hospital. She rushed down the hall of the critical unit ward, ignoring the startled looks from nurses and patients alike, jolting to a stop outside Room 340.

Heart thudding, insides in turmoil, she drew a deep breath and peeked around the corner and into the room.

Grady sat, head bowed, in a chair pulled up close to the bed. Macey released her suspended breath when she saw that the patient was not—as she'd feared—shrouded from head to toe by a sheet.

She stepped into the room and Grady's head snapped up, swiveling in her direction. Shock widened his eyes—weary eyes, with dark circles beneath them, gilded with pain and anxiety. He was overdue for a shave, and—as with Macey—he was still dressed in his formal clothing from the gala. He hadn't even taken off his tuxedo jacket; it hung crooked and wrinkled from his shoulders, and would probably never be the same. His hair was rumpled and disorderly, and his cheeks were hollow with grief.

There was no one else in the room except for Linwood, whose rough, labored breathing also made the only noise. His eyes were closed, his skin sickly white. Macey could see yards of bandages around the parts of his neck, throat, and shoulders exposed by the half-drawn sheet. Grady held one of his uncle's hands, his deft, lock-picking fingers wrapped around a paw that was just as large as his own, but too pale and limp to be powerful.

"What are you doing here?" The question wasn't challenging or angry—but by all means, it should have been. It should have been filled with blame and fury. Instead, he sounded surprised and perhaps even relieved.

She moved closer, looking down at Linwood's inert body. His breathing rasped loudly in the momentary silence. "I saw the newspaper. As soon as I read the article, I knew what had happened." She didn't need to say the words—that Detective Linwood and his companions, two other police officers, had been attacked by vampires.

It was an attack that could have been prevented if she had been fulfilling her duty instead of allowing Big Al Capone to manipulate and control her. Her stomach lurched again, and she spared a moment of thanks that she'd had nothing to eat since last night—or else everything would probably come up.

"He hasn't been conscious since they brought him in. We're just hoping he wakes up." Grady's voice was low and steady, and he was looking at his uncle again as Macey moved to the foot of the bed. "I wanted him to come to the gala last night. He wasn't even supposed to be working. But he wanted to follow up on a lead about those counterfeiters…"

"The ring you broke up?" Macey asked, recognizing guilt and self-recrimination in Grady's voice. "Don't you blame yourself for that," she added sharply, allowing her own fury and guilt to come through in her tone. "*This*," she said, stabbing a finger at Linwood, "is not your fault in any way."

"He's all I have. And if he hadn't been trying to help me, he—"

"*No*," she whispered fiercely, trying to hold back tears of frustration and grief and guilt. Her hands trembled. "No, Grady, don't you even *say* that. It's my fault. If I'd been…if I'd been doing what I should have been doing, this wouldn't have happened. I should have been out there last night. I should have been…" She stopped, everything suddenly making terrible, awful, horrible sense.

It was Nicholas Iscariot.

It had to have been.

She felt lightheaded with horror and fear. What better way to get to Macey—to torture and then destroy her—than to destroy someone she lo—someone she *cared* about. Not by killing or attacking him, but by attacking and mutilating someone *he* loved. Thereby extending the pain and anguish of both Grady *and* Macey…until Iscariot actually got to the final destruction of Grady himself.

And anyone else Macey had an attachment to.

"Are you all right?" Grady stood. He towered over her, his shadow falling across the white sheets of the bed.

Distance yawned between them as he faced her—a gulf, Lake Michigan, the Rockies; some nameless, vast expanse—and yet she felt him: his warmth, his presence, his energy.

He didn't reach for her, but she felt him as if he had. They looked at each other, gazes meeting: anguish to guilt, weariness to regret. Something bumped deep inside her, nudging that hard little stone still lodged in her heart.

"I'm so sorry," Macey whispered. He nodded and she saw him swallow hard. "What are the doctors saying?"

The damage had been done. Her lesson learned. Perhaps Linwood would recover…but with those sorts of wounds, the brutal laying open of throat and torso—that assault had been much more than a feeding. It was an attack. A message.

Just as had been laid upon Mrs. Gutchinson. And Chelle. Macey's jaw tightened and her fingers curled, reminding her of their power—of the strength that flowed through them. Now she had more reason to confront Iscariot, to face him again and finish this.

"They don't know. They've done everything they can for him," Grady replied. "Now we wait. And pray he wakes up."

Macey nodded. Then…*pray.* Her eyes widened. The rosary! Grady might know where it was, for he'd been the one to pack up some of Macey's things after they found Mrs. Gutchinson in her apartment. Maybe he'd seen it then. She didn't remember much about that horrible hour...

"Grady," she said softly, "do you happen to remember that rosary I had? The one with the pink bead and the extra tiny cross?"

He nodded, seemingly unsurprised at her random question. "I have it. I—packed it up with your things. That day. It's all still at my place." How he managed not to sound filled with recrimination, she didn't know—considering she'd slept with him, then fled his house after Chas punched him in the jaw to keep him there...and she never went back. Never saw him again after that for months except to tell him goodbye.

Oh, *damn*, this was hard.

She struggled to keep her emotions out of the way and focused on the matter at hand. "I need to get it—the rosary. Please," she added belatedly. "It's important—in all this."

He looked away, back down at Linwood, and she said quickly, "Just tell me where it is. I don't...you don't need to leave him." That would be much better anyway. Much, much better.

Before he could reply, the door opened and they turned as a nurse and doctor stepped in.

"You're still here, are you?" said the doctor as he moved to examine his patient.

"You really ought to get some rest, Mr. Grady. You've been here all night." The nurse, who couldn't be more than twenty, patted his arm. When she looked over and noticed Macey, the warm smile froze into something stiffer.

Grady exchanged a few murmured words with the physician as Macey stepped back to give them privacy. Then he took her arm and led her from the small room.

"I need to go home and get out of these clothes anyway. The doc said Linwood's stable. Not improving, but not declining either." His expression was tight, his eyes so worried.

The last thing—well, nearly the last thing—Macey wanted to do was go back to his place with Grady...but she didn't see any way out of the situation. She needed the rosary—according to the old woman, anyway.

Maybe it could wait.

She didn't have to get it today, right this minute.

"Good God, what the hell are you afraid of, Macey?" Grady's low, furious voice cut into her thoughts. She realized he still gripped her arm.

"I just don't want to impose," she said lamely.

He muttered something clearly unfit for polite company. "Are you coming or not?" His eyes flashed stormy blue and his jaw moved.

"Yes." She didn't see how she had any choice in the matter.

Grady's ethnicity was firmly displayed by the location of his residence, for it was on a street filled with signs identifying businesses owned by O'Briens and Garricks, as well as not one but two Catholic churches within a five-block radius. He lived in a single-family brick home with a small upstairs—with which Macey was intimately familiar—and a neat but cluttered first floor.

She suspected, but didn't know for certain, the small brick bungalow had been his aunt and uncle's home. If that was the case, where Detective Linwood now lived since his wife had been killed in gangster crossfire, Macey didn't know. And she didn't ask.

She hoped and prayed that Linwood would be returning to wherever it was, regardless.

"I'll be back down in a minute." Grady gestured for her to sit on the worn brown tweed sofa. She ignored him, instead wandering the room to look at the bookshelves that lined one wall as he climbed the stairs to presumably change his clothes. As before when she visited, the bibliophile in her appreciated not only the vast number of tomes on the shelves, but the variety of topics they covered—everything from fiction (including vampire stories) to books on chemistry, anatomy, physics, engineering, history, and a multitude of other subjects.

Next to the sofa was a square table, scratched and bumped at the corners. Beneath were stacks of newspapers, and on top of it was a jumble of padlocks, wires, chains, keys, and lock picks. Well, that answered at least one question…

Which put her in mind of another, and she walked over to the fireplace mantel to examine the collection of photographs crowded there. Almost immediately, she found the picture she remembered—of Grady standing next to the amazing Harry Houdini. No, she hadn't imagined it, and when she realized Grady was dressed in a British soldier uniform, it began to answer even more questions.

She was looking at the photo that could only be Linwood and his wife when the stairs creaked and groaned with Grady's descent. Macey turned as he came into view. He looked much better, now clothed in more casual trousers and a light blue shirt buttoned all the way except for the top one. His hair was damp, making his curls tighten up and appear more the color of coal than cocoa. He hadn't shaved, however, and the dark stubble made him look much more disreputable than normal.

He gave her a quick smile, then passed over her small valise. "You look as if you could stand for a little freshening up yourself. Those shoes can't be comfortable."

Oh no. No, no, no. She wasn't going to fall for that. She had to get out of here, away from him and this place as quickly as she could. "I'm fine. Is the rosary in here?" She unfastened the bag, but before she could begin to dig through, he replied.

"No. I have it here." He didn't press her about changing clothes; perhaps he was merely being polite and as desirous of getting rid of her as she was of leaving. For all she knew, Miss McCormick could be expected.

The thought soured her belly, but she ignored it. This was the last time she ever need—or dared—see Grady, and if he wanted to gawk at Miss McCormick's legs and squire her to the moving pictures, then that was better for everyone involved.

He'd gone over to the open window that overlooked the house next door—so close the sounds of young children playing filtered from across the way—and picked up something that had been lying along the windowsill. It was the rosary.

"I figured it wouldn't hurt to have it there." He didn't look sheepish at all about taking practical steps to protect himself; instead, he appeared determined and pragmatic about the fact that the undead actually did exist, and they could potentially attack him.

Little did he know how probable it would be.

Macey walked over to take the rosary, then reached to trace a finger over one of the three crosses that had been engraved in the wooden windowsill. He'd filled them—and ones at every other entrance of his home—with silver that had been blessed in a church and then melted down so he could pour it into the grooves. He'd done that after reading a portion of *The Venators*—which was written by someone who only knew some of the secrets of their legacy. But the part about silver crosses was accurate, along with the information that an undead couldn't cross a threshold without being invited in.

Still, vampires were tricky and smart, and had more than once managed to get into a house. Including Mrs. Gutchinson's.

"Thank you," she said, and realized in her evening frock she didn't have a pocket into which she could slip the rosary. So she pulled it on like a necklace and tucked the long end beneath the glittering red gown.

Grady looked as if he were about to say something, but she forestalled him, turning back toward the sofa. "Someone's been practicing." She gestured to the jumble of locks and picks. "And thank God for that."

"I learned a lot from Houdini. He's been a great mentor to me."

"I saw the photograph. You were in the British army? But how did you meet him?"

"Not many people are aware that Houdini trained over a thousand American and British troops during the War. He kept it hush-hush for obvious reasons. He showed us some of his escape artist techniques, including ways to pick locks and what to do if we were ever in a struck, sinking submarine—which, thank the Blessed Virgin, never happened to me. He thought if we ever got caught by the Germans, this knowledge would give us a good chance to escape. Some of us even had shoes outfitted with hollow heels that held lock picks and other tools." He gave a wry smile. "I didn't have mine on last night—they didn't go with the tux—hence my borrowing your hairpin."

"You saved a lot of lives last night. Including mine. Thank you. What you did was clever and very brave."

A reserved expression erased his smile. "Not so very different from what you do."

"No. It's a lot different from what I do."

"Is it?" He fixed her with intense blue eyes. "I want revenge on those bastards, Macey. On those vampires who did that to my uncle—and all the other innocent people who've been killed. Including Jennie Fallon—remember her? You know I've been following this for months."

Now she nodded. "I promise. I'll take care of it."

"Ah, no," he said, his voice hard. "I'm not going to sit back and wait and be watching for you to 'take care of it.'"

A stab of fear caught her by surprise. "No, Grady, that's not how it's going to be. You can't. You don't have the skills, the knowledge, the—"

He moved toward her, eyes flashing. "I can wield a stake and a cross just as easily as anyone. And as you saw last night, I am not at all helpless. In fact, I'm pretty damned able to take care of myself. I've been doing it since my miserable mother left me on the street in Dublin when I was ten. I am not going to sit back and let you put yourself at risk—"

"Let me? It's my *job*. It's my *legacy*. I've been *chosen* to do this. I have abilities and skills you can't even begin to dream of. I am *trained* and *equipped* to hunt and kill vampires, and you aren't. Grady, you *aren't*." Her voice caught, dammit, and she furiously swallowed back the terror.

"I have skills of my own. And I'm a bloody damned quick study."

"You have no idea what the undead are capable of." Desperation and fear tightened her voice. Her hands were curled into fists.

"I've seen firsthand what they're capable of, Macey."

She'd never seen him this way before: this determined, this angry, this cold and hard and closed off. And not a hint of the Irish in his voice. "You have no idea what *I'm* capable of," she said furiously.

"I'm not afraid of you, or the undead. After how I lived on the streets, and what I saw in the War—"

The last bit of her control snapped and Macey reacted. She hardly realized what she was doing, but the next thing she knew, she'd lifted, flung, and slammed Grady up against the wall, holding him there several inches above the floor, half a foot above her face.

He looked down at her, eyes stunned, as her hands—curled into his shirt just below his shoulders—pinned him in place. She wasn't even breathing hard; she'd barely used any effort—and she met his gaze to prove it to him. Holding him there, with the strength of several men.

"*Holy Christ,*" he murmured.

And then he kissed her.

Macey was so shocked when he grabbed her shoulders and tipped his head down to hers, she lost her grip on him. Grady's feet slid to the floor, and, still pulling her to him, he covered her mouth with hard, demanding lips.

She lost her mind at that moment—everything fell away but the taste of him, the familiar scent of his skin, the feel of his body, pulling her against his. He gathered her close with strong arms— not the superhuman arms of a Venator, not with extraordinary strength—but with a power of his own that went beyond mere physicality.

She found his damp hair, felt the warmth of his skin as she slid her hands around the back of his neck to pull him close, to taste him. Their tongues tangled, slipped and slid, thrusting and sweeping as pleasure and heat roared up through her, and down past her belly. Her knees buckled a little, her eyes closed, and when he slid his mouth away to press soft kisses on her cheek, he whispered something in Irish against her skin.

Macey shivered with pleasure as his miraculous mouth moved along the side of her neck to the sensitive part of her throat, while a hand cupped the back of her head, gently stroking the soft skin there. But it was when she felt him shift the chain of the rosary out of the way, pulling it from beneath her dress, that she remembered.

She froze.

"No. *No.*" She pulled away—an easy task, due not only to her strength, but from catching him off guard.

Her mind was reeling, her thoughts exploding, her body hot and damp and trembling—and terrified. "I can't—we can't—look, Grady, you have to understand, I live in a world you can't be part of." The words tumbled from her lips faster than she could think them or even make sense of them. "You might be a good pickpocket, and a brilliant lock-picker, but that's not the same as hunting and fighting and staking the undead."

Stubbornness sketched across his face. He was breathing hard too, and his eyes—which had been heavy-lidded with desire—now narrowed with frustration and anger. "You can't keep me away, Macey. From you—or from the damned vampires. This," he said, gesturing to her, to them, to the hot, passionate kiss they'd just shared, the heat throbbing between them, "is proof you can't deny."

She grappled for a way to make him understand, because the fear…the fear was simply too much for her to bear. It was bad enough that he was a target because of her, but now he wanted to hunt them down? Fight them on his own? Go out and *search* for them?

And he wanted to be with her too. He had some sort of crazy notion they could be fighting together. Like a team? Not on her life.

She had to make him understand. He wasn't going to be a Felicia. She wasn't going to be her father.

"I can't," she said harshly. "Do this. Be here. And—and—I'm with Chas now. You were right—he's more than just a friend." She kept her expression blank and cold because, by God, she had to make him understand. She had to *repel* him. "I got what I came for, thank you." She flipped up the end of the rosary, then tucked it back inside her neckline. "I promise you, I'll take care of the ones who did that to your uncle. But you stay the hell out of it, Grady. You stay the hell away from me and them."

"Or what?" he said. His eyes blazed and he was in her face again, close enough to grab her. "You'll sic your boyfriend on me?"

Oh, bitter. Oh, yes, the bitterness, the hurt was there.

Good. She was sorry for it, but it was necessary. She managed to keep the tears from coming, managed to keep her voice steady as a rock. "Just let us handle this, Grady. We know what we're doing. You stick with picking locks and capturing—you know, mortal criminals—and writing newspaper stories."

He jolted as if she'd struck him, but she wasn't stopping, wasn't allowing any moment for remorse. But when she got to the door—this time, he didn't try to stop her—she paused and looked back at him. "About Linwood…use salted holy water on his wounds. That should help."

And then, no longer able to keep up her facade, she ducked out the door and fled down the street.

Macey didn't know where to go, so she went to Chas's.

After all, she was "with Chas" now. Might as well make it true.

That sort of gritty anger and a dull reality fueled her now. She ignored the option of going to the front door—if Chas was there, he was probably sleeping, as it was late morning.

Instead, she went around to the back alley side of the building and jumped high enough to pull down the rickety metal fire escape that led to his window. It clanged and creaked as she wrestled it into place, glad to have something physical to do to expend her pent-up emotions.

She was exhausted, having not slept, and with every bit of the roller coaster of emotions she'd been on—like the amusement park ride she'd read about on Coney Island in New York—Macey felt as if she were about to explode.

When the fire escape ladder was in place, she clambered up quickly, pulled it up after her, and peered through the window into the living room. No sign of life; no surprise. The window was stuck, but she was strong enough to yank the damn thing up—apparently he normally used the door—and she climbed in. As she turned to close the window, she noticed that a small silver cross had been nailed above it. And then, feeling the stuffy heat of the apartment, she decided not to close it after all.

And that was when she smelled blood.

Lots of blood.

Twenty-Three

A Severe Miscalculation

MACEY'S HEART SURGED into her throat. And then she saw the trail…smears along the floor and the short hall to the back of the apartment.

"Chas?" she called, dashing through the empty living room to the single, small bedroom in the back. "Chas?"

The smell of blood was stronger back here, and suddenly terrified by what she'd find, Macey paused for a brief prayer before she pushed the door open.

He was there, huddled, curled up on the bed. Blood stained the sheets and what part of his clothes she could see. He was breathing—hard, heavily; she could see his torso lurching as she rushed over to him.

"Oh, God, Chas!" Macey turned him carefully onto his back, tensing when he groaned with pain, and sucked in a horrified breath. *Oh my God.* "Chas!"

He was…a mess. Fresh blood, dried blood, jagged wounds, neat slices. But he moaned, and his eyes fluttered.

"Fuck…you…" he managed to say. His gaze was glazed and feverish, but there was no mistaking the fury in his expression and in the two syllables he managed to breathe.

I should have gone with him last night. Oh God, what have I done?

She had no time to waste. And who cared if he was angry with her—he had a right to be—she had to help him. And quickly.

Macey stumbled away and out into the kitchenette. She tore through the cupboards and found two large Mason jars, still smelling slightly of whiskey. Collecting them under her arm, she pulled out a canister of salt—thank God he kept it on hand in quantity—and dropped it on the table.

Bolting out the door, she slammed it shut behind her and dashed across the courtyard to St. Anselm's, all the while thankful that Chas had chosen a home right next to a church.

Noon mass was going on as she slipped inside—at least, she guessed that was what it was; people were in the pews and singing as the priest walked down the aisle—but Macey ignored the few people who turned back to look at her.

Instead, she found a large basin of holy water in the vestibule of the church and filled the Mason jars, then ran back to Chas's apartment. Less than a minute later, she was back in his room with the jars of salted holy water.

"I'm sorry, Chas," she said as she began to pour it generously over him, soaking his skin, clothes, and sheets.

He screamed, arching and twisting with agony as the water sizzled and steamed whenever it hit an open wound. He cursed her and cried, huddling into a ball in spite of himself—which required Macey to readjust him onto his back, tears of anguish spilling from her eyes as she forced him to continue the terrible pain. It was the only way—the only hope. He was so far gone, so injured and depleted of blood, that only a miracle could save him.

Chas shuddered, shook, even sobbed and cursed when she came back with the Mason jars refilled and dumped them on him a second time. He cried, *Just let me goddamned die*"—but she ignored him and kept pouring, kept sobbing, kept her teeth gritted as she did one of the hardest things she'd ever had to do.

Finally, after dousing him the second time, she tottered into the living room and located his telephone. She called The Silver Chalice.

No sooner had she identified herself than Temple—who'd answered the phone—lit into her. "Where the hell are you? Where have you *been*?"

Macey finally got her to listen, and the woman calmed down enough to comprehend the seriousness of Chas's situation. "You're at his house? I'm coming there right away." Though that was the only thing Temple said, Macey could hear the underlying fury and blame in her words.

This was all her fault. All of it—Linwood, Chas, and whatever else had happened.

Blind with unshed tears, shaky with uncertainty and exhaustion, Macey found clean towels and blankets and brought them, along with warm-water-soaked cloths to clean him up as well as she could. She cut away his clothes, dabbing at his injuries as carefully as possible without moving him. He was panting, still curled on his side in agony, rigid against the torture.

But when she tried to roll him onto his back again to get the front, he cried out. His eyes bolted open, blazing with pain.

"My…god…damned…arm," he said furiously. "*Stop!*" Then his eyes rolled back in his head and he went limp.

Choking back tears—for she'd never seen such agony in his face—she took a better look at the arm he seemed to favor. Her empty stomach pitched, for the jagged edge of his humerus partially protruded from the skin of his bicep. Until she began washing away the blood, she hadn't realized the extent of the injury.

"Oh my God," she breathed. Venator or no, it was no wonder he wanted to die. How long had he been lying here like this? And how in the *hell* had he gotten himself here anyway? And why— why oh why—had he not gone to the hospital?

"I'm calling an ambulance. You need a doctor," she said, even though he was unconscious and couldn't hear her.

Except he could. A hand closed tightly over her thigh. It was clearly a negative response, and his grip *hurt*.

"Chas," she said, pulling away, and felt worse when he forced his eyes open. They were bloodshot, his face was gray, and his lips were peeled back in a furious expression. "You're going to die if I don't get you help." Her voice rose in a desperate plea. *I need you.*

"Don't…fucking…care. Long…past…time." Perhaps it was easier for him to be distracted, dragging out those words instead of focused on the pain. His hand moved and somehow curled around her arm. It was like an iron band, and he slowly, deliberately pulled her down onto the bed. "Stay. Here. Let… me…go."

"Please, Chas." *I can't lose you too.* Macey struggled, trying to peel his fingers away, but somehow he was too strong—or she was too exhausted and heartsick—and the next thing she knew, she'd collapsed onto the bed next to him, sobbing silently.

What have I done?

Finally, Macey felt the heavy grip ease. His breathing was rough and unsteady, but he didn't awaken as she slipped free and looked down at him. His arm lay useless next to him.

You're a Venator. You're strong. Fix it.

Fix it, or he won't fight again.

He'll probably die.

Oh God.

Macey touched his face. It burned her hand, and he didn't move. He was completely out of it. But…did the wounds on his chest and throat look slightly better? A little less ugly and raw? Had the bleeding slowed? Perhaps.

All right. Next thing. Could she put the bone back into place? She was strong enough…

Trying not to think too hard about what had to be done, and whether she was doing the right thing, she swiftly cut away what was left of his sleeve to bare Chas's muscular arm. Once his arm was uncovered and she could see where things had to go, she grasped his forearm with two hands that barely fit around it and drew in another deep, steadying breath.

And she gave a sharp, hard pull.

Chas shrieked, bucked awake and half upright…then, mercifully, collapsed back onto the bed. Silent but for his panting, and otherwise unmoving. He was obviously unconscious once more, or he would have been cursing her. Or worse.

Shaking, Macey looked down at what she'd done—the bone was no longer protruding, and things looked more "in place" despite the ugly black, purple, and raw red laceration. Then she bolted from the room to puke—but nothing came from her empty belly. After that, she found the telephone and called an ambulance. Then she went next door to St. Anselm's to fill the Mason jars one more time.

Where was Temple?

Whether salted holy water would work on a compound fracture or its laceration, she had no idea, but at this point, Macey was out of ideas. All she knew was the bone was in place, and now they had to worry about infection.

She couldn't lose Chas. Good God, what would she do without him? Alone in Chicago, facing vampires on her own?

Well, hell. Hadn't he been doing just that while Macey was messing around with Al Capone?

I need you to do your job. Tonight. There's something brewing out there—something's going on—and I can't keep up with all the undead in this town on my own.

He'd been right. And now he and Macey—and all of them—were paying the price for her blindness.

She touched the rosary around her neck, offered up a quick prayer, then dumped two full jars of the salted holy water over Chas's leg, and splashed a little more on the rest of his wounds for good measure. He jolted and moaned in his sleep. His breathing sharpened, but he didn't awaken.

She didn't know whether that was a good thing or not.

Macey heard a noise from the living room. The back of her neck felt normal, so she snatched up a stake along with the pistol Chas kept on his bureau and hurried out of the bedroom. It was too soon for the ambulance.

"Temple!" she cried with relief. "What took you so long? I was worried."

The cool and collected woman still had every one of her short, sleek hairs in place, and her skirt and blouse were perfectly straight and pressed, but her expression was more taut than a bowstring.

"It's only been an hour, sister, and there was a traffic jam. And if anyone is asking anyone where they been, it should be me asking you."

"I know," Macey said, glancing at the clock for the first time. It *had* been only an hour—but she'd felt like it was half a day. A look outside told her why, for she'd not even noticed the heavy rain clouds that made it dark, seeming later in the day than it was. "Look, I'm done with Capone for good. I'm not going back."

"Long overdue," snapped Temple, brushing past Macey to stalk down the hall to the bedroom. "Is he going to live?" She paused to flip a thumb in the direction of Chas.

"I hope so." Macey filled her in on Chas's condition. "I don't know how he even got back here, he's so weak—and why he didn't go to you or Sebastian instead. I don't know where or when he was attacked, but I'd sure as hell like to find out."

"What the hell you been doing anyway?" Temple muttered sourly. "Well, it's probably that old theater, the Iroquois—now they're calling it the Oriental Theatre. They're done fixing it up, and isn't the grand opening tonight? That's why there was such a traffic jam."

Even newcomers to Chicago like Temple knew the story of the original Iroquois Theatre—when hundreds of people had been trapped inside during a fire in 1903. No one had touched the property for more than twenty years because of the bad memories and reputation. But the new owners had been working diligently on it, and something about the reopening had been mentioned in the papers nearly every week.

"So what do you know about the theater?"

"There was an incident there last night—several cops were hurt. One died. The papers aren't saying what it was, and the owners are trying to push it off as an accident. But I don't think so."

By now they were in Chas's bedroom and Temple was digging in the small satchel she brought even as she looked at his unmoving figure. "He don't look too good."

"I've got to go," Macey said after she answered a few more questions about Chas's condition.

"Yes you do. And forget the damned ambulance. I'll get Aunt Cookie here and we'll do what we can. Good thing we got a church nearby. That water's probably the only thing that could save him." Temple stepped back and eyeballed Macey. "You're going to want to clean up a little."

She began to protest, but swallowed it. Right. She couldn't go on a vampire-hunting rampage dressed in an evening frock. And maybe something to eat would be in order.

And then she'd be off to visit Sebastian and beg his forgiveness.

Then they could figure out what to do next.

Sebastian had awakened late that afternoon (which, with him being a nocturnal, was more like his morning) in a glorious mood. Truly, he hadn't felt so upbeat and happy in decades…possibly centuries.

The fact that Temple, with her long, strong legs and full, sensual lips—along with several other delicious assets—had joined him in bed for the first time might have had something to do with it. He stretched lazily, smiling to himself. It had been a delightful interlude—and in a bed instead of some cramped mode of transport.

And he hadn't dreamed about Macey—or Victoria or Giulia, for that matter. He'd slept well. He felt invigorated and revived.

He'd told no one about the loose ring, which had now become even looser. In fact, he was able to work it up and over his knuckle, which meant he could pull it off his finger. He didn't know what it meant, but surely it had to be a good sign.

This morning—figuratively speaking, for it was nearly four in the afternoon—he sat up in bed with a smile on his face and went through the routine of twisting his ruby ring, and then each of the copper rings.

His heart skipped when he felt a different one turn. It wiggled a little on his pinkie finger, sending him bolting from the bed.

Temple was long gone—he'd felt her slip away sometime during his sleep, for she was on a completely different schedule than he—and Sebastian was alone with the cautious hope that shuttled through him.

Two loose rings. Something was definitely happening.

And today…yes, today was the 25th of April, 1926.

On the 26th of April, 1821, Wayren had given Sebastian the ruby signet ring in a dream. *This will help you get through this. It will give you strength.*

That was the day he'd left Victoria for good and set out for the raw mountainside cave of Munţii Fârâgaş.

That was the day he made the long promise—to himself and to Giulia.

One hundred and five years ago.

He flung the sheets away, washed, dressed, cleaned his teeth, and went from his private apartments to the pub. He saw a scrawled note from Temple on the desk in the back room, but before he got to it, he heard the door from the exterior stairs leading from the street open.

It was Macey.

She looked different somehow. Softer. A little blurry, perhaps. Blurry was a strange word, but—

"Sebastian…I'm back. May I…may I come in?"

"Macey!" Relief burst over him. "Of course. You're back."

She smiled with shyness and obvious regret, even a little bashfulness. "I wasn't sure if you'd ever want to see me again," she said, closing the door before she strode across the wood-planked floor to him. Her eyes were large and luminous in her face, and his heart creaked a little when he saw Giulia there yet again.

"I've missed you," she said, still holding him with her gaze, as if afraid he'd banish her. "I shouldn't have left." Her voice trailed off. "Can you forgive me?"

"You're here," he said. "You're here, *cher*, you're here now."

"Sebastian." She looked as if she were about to cry. "I…"

He came around from behind the counter, hardly thinking about what he was doing. He gathered her into his arms, pulling her close in a fatherly—definitely fatherly—embrace. "Macey," he whispered into her curls. "It's all right." His chin rested on top of her head; her hair smelled clean and fresh, and her body was warm against him—compact and lithe, just as Giulia's had been.

He suddenly became aware of her...very aware.

Sebastian stilled, trembling a deep inside as he battled grief and curiosity. The memory of those dark, lascivious dreams rushed into the forefront of his mind, swamping his thoughts as he held her. He pushed them back, clearing away the temptation, banishing the tease filtering through his mind.

No.

Macey lifted her head from his shoulder and looked up at him. She was right there: her lovely face so very close, her eyes incredibly soft and beautiful...and there was something else there... Interest? Curiosity? Heat?

A warning bell rang in the back of his mind, and Sebastian began to push her away, but she gripped his arms.

"What is it?" she asked, and he was suddenly aware of her thighs pressing against his. A hip nestled into his leg. She licked her lips nervously and his mouth went dry, his attention focused there.

"You're curious too, aren't you, Sebastian?" she whispered. Her little tongue came out, darting along the seam of her lush pink mouth, sending a stab of lust down through his torso. "You want to know what it's like to kiss me."

"No," he made himself say firmly. Her mouth was close. So close. He could *feel* the warmth of her lips. If he drew in a deep breath, they'd brush against his. "No," he said again. "I'm not. I never have been."

But his fangs were in the way, filling his mouth with their sharp, bold lengths. His breathing grew rougher, and desire blazed through him. She pressed against his body; surely she could feel his cock beginning to harden between his legs, the subtle tremors beneath his skin.

"Kiss me, Sebastian. I want to taste you." She lifted her face, and her mouth brushed his—warm and soft and moist.

Her tongue slipped out, sliding over his parted lips, leaving hot, adulterous tingles radiating through his body. Her eyes—Giulia's eyes; always Giulia's eyes—captured his, dark and heady and fathomless. "*Please*, Sebastian."

With a groan of effort, he shoved her away, hard enough to break her grip—and to give him some much-needed space.

She caught herself from stumbling, and when she turned back around to look up at him, her soft, lovely face was melting…and it was no longer Macey's.

And the back of his neck had gone abruptly cold.

With a tight curse, Sebastian leapt over the bar counter and grabbed a stake, but the creature—it had metamorphosed into some anonymous vampiress or demon who slightly resembled Macey, but was no longer her mirror image—bolted to the door through which she'd come.

He stared after her—it—whatever it was, chest heaving, ever so thankful he'd resisted, that he'd pushed her away and kept himself clean. He knew he should follow her—it—but he was still reeling, still incredibly grateful he'd been strong.

Hands trembling more than they should, considering what he'd lived through in more than 120 years, Sebastian pulled out his favorite liquor bottle—the dark glass one with the black prism-like stopper that fit in his palm. The one even Chas Woodmore didn't know about.

He poured a generous bit of the special rosy-amber drink into a glass and swigged it down. The exuberance of the day was gone… and yet it had been replaced by something like determination. Relief.

What he'd always feared would happen—in a manner of speaking—had occurred, and he'd fought his way through it. He'd been strong.

"Is this the fulfillment of the long promise, then?" he demanded of the universe at large. Where the hell was Wayren? He could really use her about now… His hand covered the top of the pyramidal bottle stopper, gripping it tightly as he felt its heat and power seep into his skin.

The back of his neck went sharply cold again.

Much too cold.

Sebastian shoved the bottle under the counter and launched himself toward the door through which the faux Macey had just exited, but it burst open before he got there. The tempting vampiress stood there on the threshold, now with her own fangs gleaming and her eyes bold and burning. She wore a hot, knowing smile.

Sebastian had already somersaulted backward, snatching up a chair and a stake as the creature stepped aside to allow her companions to pour in.

Three, four, no, seven, no, *ten*... He lost count as the undead streamed into his pub, with glowing red or Guardian-pink eyes and all with fangs at the ready. There was no subtlety, no dancing around the situation—they were there, and they were there for him.

All thanks to the faux Macey, whom he'd invited in and who had, in turn, thus been liberated to invite her own crew inside...

And then, there in front of him, the faux Macey shimmered, lengthened, broadened in a sort of swirling metamorphosis...and became Nicholas Iscariot.

"Well, well. I had no idea you were so talented, Nicky," Sebastian said coolly. He counted twelve undead, not including the Macey-turned-vampiress-turned-Iscariot. He eased along the counter, keeping his hands out of sight from the intruders. "What's next on the agenda...Carole Lombard?"

"Sebastian Vioget. It's a pleasure to finally meet you— although your reputation does precede you."

The son of Judas Iscariot was tall, lean, and cold in his male beauty. His hair shone dark, and though slicked back on the sides and back, it rose like a high, smooth wave over his equally tall white forehead. He wore a well-cut suit, red tie, and white spats, with a crimson handkerchief bursting from the breast pocket of his jacket. Sebastian couldn't fault the creature for his sense of style. Iscariot's handsome face was smooth as white marble, with a

square chin, hollow cheeks, protruding eyes, and strong brows…
except for the diagonal cross marking his left cheek and jaw.

Sebastian's own fangs were long and ready, and he felt the
heat of his eyes burning with fury. And even then, as he faced the
most powerful and fearsome of the world's undead—along with
a mob of his goons—he slipped his fingers beneath the cotton of
his shirt to touch the *vis bulla*…and then to twist the ruby ring on
his finger. Strength and comfort rushed through him.

Now. There. He was ready.

Ready to see this to the end.

Sebastian smiled coolly. "I see my Macey has left her mark,
Scarface."

Iscariot's eyes flared wider and redder, and yet he lifted one
slender white finger to keep his minions from surging forward.
"I'm not particularly pleased with her, as you might imagine. But,
of course, that's why I'm here." He bared his fangs in a polite
smile. "Though that isn't the only reason I've paid you a visit at
last. As I'm certain you can surmise."

"The Rings of Jubai. Of course." Sebastian sounded bored
as he extended the hand with the copper bands, pretending to
admire his fingers. "How unoriginal of you, Nicky."

"Well, one can only plan so many surprises. Speaking of
which, I could tell you *greatly* enjoyed the one I cooked up for
you a moment ago. It was very much worth the effort it cost me
to mask myself, even for that short while…" Iscariot twirled his
finger and spun into Macey once again, writhing his curvy body
and parting his lips in a seductive manner. "To see you panting
and lusting after me."

"I didn't realize you enjoyed that sort of attention from men."
Sebastian whipped a stake across the room like a knife-thrower. It
spun through the air, nailing a nearby undead in the heart with a
delicious *splat*.

The vampire hadn't even poofed into dust before Sebastian
winged a second pike from behind, sending it revolving in the
other direction—directly toward the heart of Iscariot's sinuous
Macey body.

Iscariot-Macey dodged just in time, and the stake plunged into an unfortunate undead just behind him. There was so much fury and power in the stake meant for Iscariot that the unlucky victim was pinned against the wall for a brief instant before he poofed into dust.

Under attack, Iscariot had popped back into himself, and his eyes were surely hotter than the fires of hell. Loathing rolled off him like beads of sweat. "That wasn't very hospitable of you, Vioget. Not at all."

"Oh, so sorry…I slipped." Sebastian grinned. He had several other stakes at his disposal, but he figured he'd showed off enough. He didn't need anyone comparing him to Max Pesaro. "Now, though I suspect it'll be futile, I'm going to have to ask you and your mollies—at least, the ones you have left—to leave. The place doesn't open till sundown and I've got work to do."

Iscariot didn't bother to speak. He gave some sort of silent command and the vampires attacked.

But Sebastian was ready for them. He was still behind the counter, and as the undead surged toward him, he withdrew the silver-gilt sword tucked beneath the long expanse and swung around, brandishing it in both hands.

Power roared through him as the blade sliced through one, then a second undead throat before being halted in midair by the meaty hand of a third creature. Sebastian released the sword's hilt and grabbed a stake as he vaulted over the counter, his feet smashing into the shoulder and torso of a startled vampire.

He tumbled to the ground and came up swinging, stabbing one, then a second undead as he dove into the legs of a third, upending the creature. He dusted the first vamp, missed the second, devil it, and then suddenly, as he came back up onto his feet, he was surrounded. Trapped, gripped, held.

Numerous fists pummeled him in the torso, arms, shoulders, back…nails raked down his face and limbs…someone kicked him in the belly, knocking every bit of breath from him. He coughed and doubled over, trying to find his breath as fangs penetrated his arm…his shoulder…a thigh…

Blood flowed from him, blood and power and consciousness. The world wavered, black and red, swimming silently…

Then everything quieted. Stilled.

Sebastian opened his eyes—one was already swelling from a well-placed blow—and found himself face to face with Iscariot. The heat of the creature's breath warmed his face. It smelled of death.

The rough beams of the pub's ceiling rose high behind the master vampire as strong hands held Sebastian immobile on the ground. So he was still here, lying in a pool of his own tainted blood.

Sebastian relaxed. So this was how it would end.

He managed his trademark smile—crooked, insouciant, and charming, and more difficult than usual, given the fact that his lips were also swelling, and perhaps he'd even lost a tooth because something throbbed terribly in there—and waited eagerly for the final pain. For surely Iscariot wouldn't let it be as simple as a stake…yet it would finally end. It would all be over. The denouement, the story climaxed, the long promise fulfilled.

"Take care with the rings." Sebastian heaved the words out, managing to twitch his numb, copper-ringed hand beneath the foot that smashed it into the ground. "I wouldn't want you to… lose them after all this effort."

Iscariot smiled and eased back. "I have no intention of relieving you of those rings. Not yet, anyway. In fact, I think I'll let you keep them a little longer."

Something struck Sebastian in the face—hard and heavy— and that was the last he knew.

Twenty-Four

An Eerie Stillness Portends Nothing Positive

B Y THE TIME MACEY ARRIVED at The Silver Chalice, it was
past six o'clock. A heavy rainstorm with thick, gray clouds and
a terrible downpour—not to mention lightning and thunder—
wreaked havoc on the traffic, and made it impossible to find a taxi.

The delay did, however, allow her to grab a copy of the
afternoon edition of the *Tribune* from a corner newsstand. While
she sat impatiently in the back of an unmoving cab, she scanned
the headlines with her heart in her throat.

If Linwood died, it would be in the paper.

And so far, there was nothing. Not even, she noticed sadly, an
afternoon byline by J. Grady.

When the cab pulled up on the street by The Silver Chalice,
Macey tossed the fare and a generous tip into the front seat and
scrambled out into pouring rain. She was soaked by the time she
got to the silver finial at the top of the wrought iron gate that led
below street level to the pub's door.

She flung it open, bursting inside in a torrent of rain and
cyclonic wind caught up in the stairwell, and slammed the door
behind her. Expecting to find Sebastian behind the counter,
Macey was mildly surprised that the place was empty and silent.

The chairs were still upended neatly over the tables, ready to
be put down at seven, when the joint opened—which was only a
half-hour from now. The counter was clear except for a single glass
partly filled with some sort of spirits.

She sniffed. Was that the faint scent of undead ash? She wasn't certain.

She sniffed again. Blood? Did she smell blood?

Skin prickling slightly, she poked her head into the back office. Empty. "Sebastian?" She went into the hall leading to his private apartments.

Silence, stillness.

Nothing seemed out of place, but something felt off.

She opened a door she'd never breached before and found herself in Sebastian's bedroom. Curious and apprehensive, she went inside, noticing the wooden valet stand that held his robe. On one wall was a massive wardrobe, neat as a pin, with hangers of tailored clothing and rows of polished shoes. He was a dapper man, Sebastian Vioget.

Telling herself it was in the interest of his safety—for she knew something wasn't quite right—Macey opened the drawer of the table next to his neatly made bed. Stakes. A pistol. Vials of presumably holy water.

And a copper ring.

She plunged her hand into the drawer and pulled out the simple band of braided copper.

Was this one of the Rings of Jubai?

If so, for how long had Sebastian been able to remove it?

What did it mean that it was here, and he was not?

Macey looked down at it, holding it in the palm of her hand. The five rings had been forged by Lilith the Dark centuries ago and given to five of her Guardian vampires. Did that mean it was malevolent and evil on its own?

What would happen if she slid it onto her finger? Would it adhere to her skin, as it had done to Sebastian's, a hundred years ago?

She decided not to tempt fate. Instead, still apprehensive, she returned it to its place and closed the drawer.

Now she really needed to find Sebastian.

I wish I could talk to Chas.

Back out into the pub moments later, Macey looked around one last time…and that was when she saw it.

A stake. On the floor at the seam of the wall in the rear of the bar, hidden by shadows unless one looked closely.

There was no reason a stake would be on the floor over here unless it had been used, and if it had…it should have been returned to its rightful place. The apprehensive prickles grew stronger as she picked it up and examined the tip beneath one of the lamps.

It was gritty with vampire dust.

It was well past seven o'clock in the evening and still stormy by the time Macey was able to get back to Chas's house.

"Lordy Moses, what're you doing here?" Temple said when she came in. "Don't you have something to *do*?"

Macey didn't really have an answer for that reasonable question. She wanted quite desperately to talk to Chas, but dared not even put that desire into words; he'd been in such a bad way when she left. Instead, she fumbled for an explanation for her detour back to the house in the shadow of St. Anselm's.

"Sebastian's not at the pub," she told Temple. "And it looks like vampires were there—maybe they took him. Maybe he just disappeared on his own, for his own reasons. Maybe he went after them himself. I don't know. I came to get supplies and weapons— and to see if you knew where he could be." Macey had decided not to mention anything about the copper ring. "And…to see if there's been any change." She glanced down the hall.

Temple's jaw tightened. "No, and no. Sebastian was sleeping when I left to come here. And Chas—there's no change there. Except…"

"What?"

"He's called for Narcise a few times." Temple shrugged, and Macey noticed she wouldn't quite meet her eyes. Did the other woman know about the two of them already?

"Poor sot," was all Macey said, surprised by the pang in her heart. She'd think about what that meant later.

"Auntie thinks he should go to the hospital."

"Then take him. I'm going to the Oriental Theatre." If that was where Linwood and his companions had been attacked, that was as good a place as any to begin her hunt for Nicholas Iscariot.

And if she was going alone, she was going well armed and fully prepared.

Temple nodded, her expression grave. "I'll come with you. I may not be a Venator, but you know I've got some good moves."

Macey hesitated, then shook her head. "Much as I would love to have you watching my back, I don't think it's a good idea. If Sebastian comes back, or if I don't—well, someone has to be here to—to…" She shrugged. "Someone has to take care of things."

Temple looked as if she were about to argue, but her words were forestalled when Aunt Cookie appeared. "That man's gotta see a doctor. His fever's gone bad. I'm calling an ambulance."

Fear seized Macey by the throat. "Do it. Don't waste any more time." She turned to her friend. "Take care of him, Temple."

"You shouldn't go alone."

Macey looked at her, and for the first time, the reality of her situation became clear. She was completely alone. "There's no one else."

✝

Despite the horrible fate of the Iroquois twenty-some years ago, the luxe decor of the Oriental Theatre seemed to have wiped away any of the lingering negativity of its predecessor. Throngs of people filled the sidewalk in front of it, and the street was backed up in both directions as attendees climbed out of private automobiles and taxis to line up for admission.

Jaunty, carnival-like music rolled out from inside the open doors like an aural red carpet. Every few minutes, streamers and confetti exploded from a cannon-like device, showering laughing and talking patrons as they made their way inside. As soon as they stepped over the threshold, each attendee was given a small paper cone of honey-toasted almonds.

Unlike the previous night's gala at the Art Institute, this was not a formal occasion. There were many fewer jewels and a severe lack of tuxedos and tailcoats. Macey didn't mind that, for she'd chosen to dress much more casually herself tonight—in loose sailor pants and a simple cotton blouse, along with sturdy, low-heeled shoes.

But as soon as she stepped through the brass-and-glass revolving door, she recognized another, more disturbing difference.

The back of her neck and all along the tops of her shoulders went frigid. The sudden, nauseating chill was accompanied by a wave of malevolence that staggered her. It was almost as if she'd walked into—no, through—a wall of evil incarnate.

Feeling dizzy from the intensity, Macey stopped in the midst of the incoming flow of people and slipped off to the side to get her bearings. Her hands had gone cold. Whatever percolated inside this building was terrifying and strong.

Upon its unleashing, a root of malevolence shall marshal such power as never before known. The second part of Rosamunde's prophecy flashed through her mind. If anything felt like a "root of malevolence," it was the sensation in this place.

…And only the dauntless one and his peer shall rise up to it.

The dauntless one and his peer…

But Macey wasn't the dauntless one. And she was alone.

Someone bumped into her—an oblivious young man, speaking and gesturing enthusiastically to a group of friends as they brushed by—jarring her back to the moment. She stepped back even further from the crowd, now pressing her back flush against the wall.

What am I going to do?

She watched the hordes of people streaming into the building, her anxiety growing. Whatever was here, whatever Nicholas Iscariot had planned, wherever he was…every single person who crossed this threshold was in mortal danger.

I have to get them out.

The answer flashed into her mind with bell-like clarity.

"Fire!" she cried. "*Fire!*"

The reaction was instantaneous. Whether it was because of the history of this location and the terrible fire that had killed hundreds, or simply the normal response to such a warning, it didn't matter. All that mattered was that people were leaving.

Shouts, screams, panic...

A stampede could be dangerous...but was it more dangerous than being trapped by the malevolent undead?

No.

She hoped.

The crowd had already reversed itself, spinning and pouring back out onto the street. More people took up the cries of "Fire!" and Macey helped, hurrying deeper into the theater like a fish swimming upstream. People pushed past her, the vast majority of them taller and broader than she, bumping her with shoulders and arms, stepping on her toes, making her stumble from side to side. All through this maelstrom of activity, Macey was utterly, terribly aware of the ugly chill leaching into the back of her neck.

Whatever the malignancy was, it remained.

She pushed through the lobby, navigating along the walls so as not to be swept out with the mob while doing her best to make sure everyone got out safely. To her relief, the exodus was surprisingly orderly—helped in part by the ticket-takers at the doors, and the fact that many extra exits had been added to the new structure. A few people pushed harder than necessary, but no one seemed to be panicked, and the patrons filed out quickly from all sides of the building.

By now, the crowd was coming out of the viewing auditorium, and even though there were some comments like "I don't smell any smoke!" and "Where's the fire?" no one was taking a chance on remaining inside.

The last thing anyone wanted was for a repeat of history.

Macey began to breathe a little easier as the crowd thinned, and then she heard sirens in the distance. Someone had taken the warning seriously; the firemen were on their way.

What would happen when they saw there was no blaze?

Would everyone come back in?

She was standing at the top of one of the side aisles, which sloped gently down toward the stage above which the moving picture screen was mounted. The sense of evil fairly pressed down upon her in this smaller, quieter space. Macey reached for her stake, extracting it from a deep pocket. She found comfort in the solid, round pike as she held it alongside her trouser-clad thigh.

By now more half the auditorium was empty. The patrons who remained seemed uninterested in the warning cries of "fire!" and were meandering about in a surprisingly relaxed manner, chatting and laughing as if they hadn't a care in the world.

Why weren't they leaving? They didn't even seem to notice the activity going on around them, even when she shouted, "Fire!" to a cluster of people standing in the aisle.

When she noticed their clothing, Macey froze. Her hand strayed onto the edge of a velvet-upholstered seat and gripped hard. They were dressed in the fashions of twenty years ago…not today.

She looked around, and it was true: all of them. Everyone who was here, everyone who remained…they were all dressed in the attire of 1903, when the Iroquois had burned down in this very location.

A dull thud drew her attention toward the door up the aisle behind her. It was closed. It had been open just a moment earlier—but now her ears were filled with the cacophony of the rest of the doors thudding closed around the top of the auditorium.

She wasn't going to be able to open them. The hair on her arms stood on end and she turned slowly to look around the theater. Its occupants—people? spirits? vampires?—there were too many mixed sensations assaulting her to be certain—continued to interact as if Macey wasn't there, as if they hadn't died in a fire twenty years ago, as if they were unaware of the eerie, creeping malevolence that seemed to filter through the air.

As she turned slowly, watching, waiting, expectant, Macey noticed one of the stragglers from across the theater. She was reminded of Flora, for the woman had bright penny-colored hair and long, gangly limbs—

It *was* Flora.

But she was dressed normally, in today's fashion. And she had her hand tucked through the elbow of a dark-haired companion in a suit. They were making their way up the aisle toward an exit on the opposite side of the auditorium. He looked at Flora, smiling and exuding charm, and that was when Macey saw his profile.

Her heart stuttered…and then stopped dead. *No.*

God, no, not Grady.

Not Grady with Flora.

A warning shriek clogged in her throat as Macey lunged, vaulting over a row of seats toward them.

Flora turned and smiled over her shoulder at Macey—as if she'd known she was there all along. Then, with a grin, she tightened her grip on Grady's arm and leaned in to speak to him.

Macey scrambled over another seat—and then all at once, a swarm of people surrounded her. Everyone was in her way, blocking her movements, her view, her desperate attempt to catch up to Flora and Grady, who were now nearly at the exit.

"Grady!" she cried…and wasn't really sure whether the syllables came out or whether she was merely screaming inside her head. *Nooo…*

She pushed and shoved, realizing dully that these people, these beings, were insubstantial. Not quite real, not quite phantoms… certainly not undead.

But they were cold and sharp and raw as she pushed at them, sort of *through* them, using stake, arm, and hip. Macey felt as if she were battling upstream in an icy river filled with great swaths of fabric—silk, cotton, wool—and they clung to her, wrapping around her as she fought through them, stabbing ineffectively, marching through people-shaped entities, of ice and cold and evil and dankness…

Suddenly she slammed into someone strong and solid. Hard. Cold. She struck out with her stake as powerful hands grabbed her, pulling at her. The stake hit something, someone; she felt the give and the subsequent *pop.*

More hands, clawing at her, pulling…no longer ghostlike, but terribly strong, holding her back as she fought and writhed, kicked, bucked, stabbed…

There was a poof, an explosion of dust. A blow to her side. A yank in one direction as she flailed out one more thrust with her stake at another creature. The chill, the cold enveloped her. Glowing red eyes and eerie shadows filled her vision.

And then all at once everything stilled. She was free.

Everything fell away, except…

Nicholas Iscariot stood in front of her.

Twenty-Five

Two Unbearable Tasks

G OING SOMEWHERE?" asked Iscariot. He was impeccably dressed in a well-cut suit with a silky handkerchief in the pocket and a perfect tie. "So soon? When I haven't had the chance to properly thank you for *this*?" His expression turned dark as he turned his head so Macey could see the livid red cross-shaped scar on his face.

She jolted at the sight of it, shocked at its raw, red ferocity, and yet pleased that he hadn't left their battle in the morgue unscathed.

"I think it's rather appropriate," she replied, still panting and trembling from the aftershocks of her recent battle. Blood streamed from a wound on her arm, and she saw Iscariot's eyes stray there, saw the way his mouth tightened. "All things considered."

Somehow, she still held her stake. She took comfort in its smooth familiarity. One unexpected lunge, one well-placed thrust, and he was done. The confusion and dreaminess from swimming upstream through the ghostlike people had faded, but the presence of undead lingered as Iscariot's minions surrounded both of them. Watching.

And as she faced him, every other distraction disappeared into the periphery. She tightened her grip on the stake.

"Don't bother with that," said Iscariot, focusing his glowing eyes on her weapon. "You won't need it…yet."

Macey looked away a heartbeat too late as he swung his gaze sharply up and to hers. Instantly, she felt the shimmering waver of their gazes locking, his eyes immediately tugging at her and luring her into the muzzy-headed lull that would lead to her demise. She kept her fingers tight on her weapon, her feet planted solidly on the ground, and fought to tear her eyes from his.

"Vioget tried to do it himself," said Iscariot. He sounded a long way away. "Earlier this evening. But, of course, he didn't succeed…"

Dreamlike, Macey found herself reaching toward her abdomen, her fingers crawling slowly over her belly. It was a battle for even the scarcest bit of movement, curbed as she was by Iscariot's thrall. But when she got there at last and touched her *vis bulla*, even through the thin linen of her blouse, there was an answering surge of power. It shuttled through her, and, energized, she tore her gaze from Iscariot's. Without hesitation, she leapt toward him, arm raised in a vicious thrust.

She slammed into the vampire, full body against his tall, slender, muscular one…but he twisted at the last minute and her stake plunged into his shoulder as their bodies collided. They tumbled to the ground, falling onto a row of plush seats, grasping and grappling with the other.

Macey's stake was knocked from her hand, and she dimly heard it rolling toward the stage as Iscariot raked his sharp nails down along her arm. The linen split and so did her skin in a searing hot pain. Her blood burst forth as she twisted away, somersaulting over one of the seats, her arm burning.

By the time she landed on her feet, she had a second stake in hand and was half crouched, waiting for the next attack.

"Oh, don't let's belabor all of this," said Iscariot. He stood near the stage, looking up at where Macey stood, halfway up the aisle. To her satisfaction, she saw that his clothing was askew and he'd lost the pocket handkerchief. He was a little out of breath, and a dark blossom was spreading over the front of his shirt and coat. "I see no reason to play around with you. It's a waste of time and effort, and the result will be the same. Still, I expect you to provide me with a good bit of entertainment."

"Isn't that just like you, Nicholas," she panted, swiping at the blood streaming from her arm. "Always walking away from a fight. I must frighten the hell out of you."

The verbal mark clearly struck home, for his eyes flared richly hot and red, and even from her distance, Macey could see the telltale ring of blue around his irises. Only Judas Iscariot's children had that eerie blue glow. It was evidence of their great and terrible power.

"And you aren't brave enough to take me on all by yourself, either," she said, gesturing to the hulking figures of his undead companions. They stood and sat about in the theater as if about to watch the feature. "You can't handle me."

"I don't have the time or inclination to waste matching wits or stakes with you, my lovely Venator. But I did promise some amusement for my people—and since you managed to set free their meals and entertainment already, it's up to you to provide the show. The others," he said, flicking his wrist—and suddenly a few of the silvery-gray spirits dressed in twenty-year-old fashion were back, hovering around him as if they'd been summoned. "They were just a little experiment of mine. I quite liked how it turned out, but perhaps they need a little refining. They do have a rather chilly ambience, don't they?" He moved his hand again, and the phantoms evaporated into small wisps of smoke.

From the corner of her eye, Macey saw an undead moving stealthily toward her from behind. Without turning her head, she grabbed the nearest seat and used the height to pivot toward the vampire. *Poof!* The stake met its mark and the curiosity seeker was gone.

Iscariot didn't seem to mind. Instead, he was looking out into the darkness, beckoning with a slender white hand. "Now, don't be concerned I'm expecting you to carry the show all on your own, Macey Gardella. That wouldn't be fair now, would it?"

He'd stepped onto the stage, and a spotlight blinked on, shining down on him. Something moved in the shadows, and as Macey watched with growing apprehension, a long rope descended from the catwalk above. Something—no, *someone*—dangled from the end of the rope. Another light came on, but even before it illuminated the figure, Macey had recognized it.

Him. Grady.

It took every bit of control she had to keep still and quiet, to not react—although everything inside her screamed *Nooooo.* Her very muscles, her thoughts, her limbs and digits—everything shrieked at her to leap down there, to vault over the chairs and launch herself onto the stage in a blaze of fury and horror and protect him. Save him.

But she didn't. Instead, she stood there. Waiting. Observing. Forcing herself to keep her mind clear and open and ready. Because surely that was precisely what Iscariot wanted her to do: to attack. To protect. To spin into action without thinking.

She couldn't tell whether Grady was conscious. She did see blood…staining his throat and the open front of his shirt, which was coatless, untucked, and torn. He hung from his wrists, which were tied together with thick ropes. His head sagged forward a little, and his feet didn't quite touch the ground.

He didn't move. There was no sign of breathing or struggle from him.

Macey turned her attention to Iscariot, careful not to meet his eyes directly but with enough boldness that he knew she was not cowed.

"Is that it?" she asked. "You've got a single, measly mortal man that, presumably, you want me to save? *If* he isn't past saving already. That's all you've got to offer in the form of entertainment, Nicholas? Why don't you and I go a few rounds instead—you and me, without your goons to protect you? *That* would be a sell-out performance."

She was walking toward him down the aisle, toward the stage where her stake had rolled, figuring that the closer she got to Grady, the easier it would be to help him…whenever the opportunity arose. "Why should I even try to free him?" She nodded to Grady.

"For all I know, you've already turned him undead…which means there's no sense in my exerting myself anyway. He's already lost."

She was five, maybe six rows from the stage now. She didn't see her other stake, but it had to be nearby.

A few vampires had moved closer to her, but none of them appeared ready to pounce. Some even chose seats, as if to watch the outcome. That made her a little nervous.

Iscariot smiled, and the pure glee in his expression was what frightened Macey more than anything else. "Never fear, my sweet Venator. He's quite alive, and still very mortal." He walked over to Grady. "Let the lovely Venator bitch know you're still alive," Iscariot said, grabbing a handful of hair to lift Grady's head. "So she knows you're worth fighting for."

Grady shifted and moaned, and Macey saw his eyes fluttering. She also watched carefully, for, thanks to her wayward stake, Iscariot was bleeding profusely from the shoulder. Grady didn't seem to notice or be attracted to the fresh blood, which she took as a good sign.

So far.

"Now," said Iscariot. "Perhaps a bit of an *hors d'oeuvre* is in order?" He bared his fangs and plunged them viciously into the outside of Grady's upthrust arm.

Macey's insides surged as Grady jolted, and his eyes flew open, wide with shock and pain. She resisted the desire to rush forward and tear Iscariot away, for surely that was what he wanted. Surely there was some sort of threat or trap waiting for her. Surely that was what he hoped for…what he'd planned.

But Grady… *Oh, Grady.* Oh, God, oh, God…

She had to hold herself rigid and still and unmoving, watching and waiting even as her insides churned and wept as Grady jolted and struggled, trembling and groaning as Iscariot drew from his veins.

Even when the master vampire, clearly annoyed, beckoned another vampire to join him on the stage and drive his fangs into Grady's other arm, she remained still, waiting, terrified she would make the wrong decision.

But when Iscariot gestured for a third undead to join them, Macey couldn't hold back any longer. "Stop! All right, *stop!*"

She was onstage—damn the risk, whatever it was—slamming her stake into a nearby vampire on the way in a moment of frustration. "Let him go. I'll do whatever you want. Just let him go." Furious at the sob that caught in her throat, Macey bared her teeth like a feral cat and lunged recklessly at Iscariot once more.

She was halted in mid-leap, thrown to the ground in a violent sweep from behind. Her head slammed into the wooden stage, bouncing twice before strong hands dragged her upright.

Three of them—there were three of them needed to subdue her, so wildly did she fight them.

"It's always a pleasure to watch a Venator in action," Iscariot said playfully. "Did I not promise you some fine entertainment?" he added, speaking to his audience of undead. There was a smattering of applause and a few catcalls.

"I'm here. You have me. What is it you want?" Macey said. Her head throbbed and her whole body ached. The scent of blood and undead ash filled her nostrils.

"I have a little task for you. Actually, two of them. And then after that…well, I see no reason you can't go about your business." He smiled lazily. "But first, we must set the stage, so to speak. I must prepare the…er…warrior, shall we say?"

He approached her with raw heat in his eyes. "Hold her."

The vampires complied, brutal and fierce, pinning her into place: one behind, gripping her wrists in a numbing vise that forced her to drop the stake, and one on either side, holding her at the ankles. Macey couldn't move except for the heaving of her torso.

Iscariot took his time unbuttoning her shirt as she panted in front of him. "I hate to ruin a good blouse," he explained.

One button, two, then three. Four.

"Ah!" Iscariot stepped back sharply at the sight of the large silver cross—the one that had marked his cheek—she'd tucked down inside her blouse. She shifted her shoulders suddenly and the cross swung around, bumping into one of the vampires who stood next to her.

He shrieked and fell back, holding his arm. The other two kept their grip, but barely, easing back from her and the holy relic while still holding her by the ankles. Her arms were free, but she remained unmoving, conscious that Grady's safety was still at risk.

"We can't do with this, now, can we." Iscariot's brow furrowed, then relaxed as he turned to Grady. "Release the mortal."

Macey felt a surge of hope as Grady's bound wrists were unfastened from the hanging rope, but Iscariot was taking no chances in releasing him, for he instructed that they were to stay tied.

"Remove the cross."

Macey didn't know whether Grady had the strength to comply, or whether he even comprehended the instructions. But when he drew nearer, walking unsteadily and slowly, he lifted his face slightly. Their eyes met and she felt a rush of…something. It shocked her, burrowing deep inside. And she let out her breath because though there was pain, real, deep pain, in his sea-blue eyes—pain and horror—there was also lucidity and determination and strength.

Please let him be all right.

"Grady," she whispered when he was close enough to hear. "Keep it. Use it." She wanted to say something more…much more…but she dared not.

He gave a bare nod, then had to step around behind her to unclasp the necklace, for his hands were still bound at the wrists. For a moment, as he stood there behind her, tall and so very near, his fingers working slowly to unseat the cross's hook, she closed her eyes and reveled in his presence…and then hated herself for wanting his comfort. *I'm sorry. I'm so sorry.*

She wished to sag backward, just enough to touch him, just enough that he could feel her and she could feel him.

The weight of the cross sagged lower as the chain loosened, then Grady came back around to face her as he gathered up the pendant. He said something, muttered something she couldn't understand, and before he could repeat it or she could respond or tell him she was sorry, the vampires were back at her in full force, dragging her away from him.

She struggled. But she no longer had any weapon she could get to, nothing that would help except the small, delicate rosary she'd tucked deep inside her corset simply to have it with her.

Grady, go, she thought fiercely. *Get out of here.* In the dark melee that was her world, she could no longer see him, but she sent the thoughts with every bit of her being.

"Now, where were we?" Iscariot approached again as she was once more forced into immobility. He yanked at her blouse so it bared one shoulder. The shirt hung open now, exposing her flimsy laced-up undergarment…and the stripe of a scar disappearing down behind it, along her sternum.

"I can see how incredibly pleased you—or at least your lovely body is—to see me," said Iscariot, tracing a finger over the fresh blood. With rough hands, he tore open the top two inches of the corset, revealing more of the scar and a swell of breast. His fangs were long and ready, seeming to vibrate with need as he leaned closer. "Your blood—it knows me, doesn't it?"

"What do you—*argh*." Macey gasped as he plunged his fangs into her shoulder. She stifled a scream and twisted, trying in vain to free herself from the brutality. The pain was intense— dark and red and searing; somehow different from anything she'd experienced before.

Her veins leapt and blood surged and she sank into darkness, dark splotches of nothing, sagging and writhing in the grip of the creatures who held her.

When Iscariot withdrew, he was panting and his eyes were lit with an unholy emotion. A delicate trickle of blood oozed from the corner of his mouth. "If only I didn't have other plans for you, my sweet…" His finger was unsteady as he reached up to wipe it away. Then he smeared the blood—Macey's blood—over her parted lips. It was rich and hot, tasting of iron and life.

"But," he said, turning away reluctantly, "I do have other plans for you. And now that the stage has been set, it's time to get down to business."

Macey tried to get her bearings, for now all was coming to a head. But her vision tilted and spun. Her legs no longer had the strength to support her body; the guards were doing all of the work to hold her upright. How could a single bite have affected her so violently?

Was he marking her this time?

"I have two tasks for you to accomplish, Macey Gardella," said Iscariot, stepping upstage, away from her. "Please, if you will?" He gestured for her to follow him, and when her three vampire assailants released her, Macey complied on unsteady feet.

She looked around for Grady, but he was no longer in sight. With the spotlights flaring onto the stage, and no illumination out in the house, she could see nothing but vague silhouettes of undead…and their pairs of red or pink eyes. If Grady was out there, she couldn't detect him.

Please, let him have left. Let him be gone.

A mechanized grinding attracted her attention, and Macey looked over to see the floor opening in front of her… No, it wasn't the entire floor. It was the front third of the stage, folding down and in on itself in the manner of an accordion, leaving a large open hole.

The orchestra pit.

Iscariot came to stand next to her, and she saw he was holding a wooden stake. His eyes gleamed and he gestured for her to look down into the pit. She couldn't see the entire space, for part of it was hidden beneath the stage. What she could see, however, appeared empty and shadowed.

"There are two things I want, Macey Gardella. Succeed in them, and I'll set you and your friend free. I'll never bother you again."

An awful, cold dread settled over her, and she resisted taking the two steps forward that would give her more of a view inside the hole.

"What?" she managed to say.

"I want the Rings of Jubai," he said, grasping her arm. "And I want Sebastian Vioget's soul."

He flung her into the pit.

Twenty-Six

Wherein Our Hero Plays the Role of a Buffet

GRADY WAS NO FOOL.

When the tall, redheaded gal had arrived at his house, knocking vehemently on the door—but wouldn't step over the threshold even when he opened it and stepped back—he knew something was not right.

He recognized the redhead as Macey's friend—he'd seen them together the first night he really got to talk to her, at the club called The Gyro. The night the vampires attacked.

"It's Macey," exclaimed the woman, whose name he couldn't remember right away. She stood on the doorstep in pouring rain, beneath an umbrella. Her light blue eyes were wild and filled with concern, and he had a moment of appreciation for what were surely excellent acting skills. "She needs help. I don't know where else to go. Or what to do. You're her boyfriend, right? You can help!"

Grady played along with the lass, though the idea of him being Macey's boyfriend was not only laughable but painful. No, it wasn't he who was waking up next to her, smelling the sweet, musky scent of her skin, teasing her about which vampire literature she'd been reading, debating with her about pretty much everything, seeing her dark eyes glow with humor...

"What's wrong? Where is she?" He pretended to be as naive as the gal—Flora was her name; that was it—thought he was. He started to ask her to come in and caught himself in time. She hadn't put even a toe over the threshold and its embedded silver crosses the whole time they stood there talking. His suspicions grew.

"There's no time," she replied, dancing about impatiently—but still not allowing any part of her body to break the "plane" of the doorway. "Hurry! We have to leave now!"

"All right. Just give me one minute. Wait out there," he added for good measure, just in case she thought he was inviting her inside.

Grady dashed up the stairs, his mind reeling. It only took him a few minutes to gather up what he needed, change his shoes, and then scrawl a quick note for his housekeeper to give to Uncle Linwood…just in case. He only hoped Linwood would be around to read it.

His latest contact with the hospital had given him no news—nothing had changed. But at last Grady would have the chance to do *something* other than wait around and worry.

When he came bounding back down the stairs, Flora hadn't moved, but the freckles stood out in sharp relief on her white face. She was still standing in the downpour, dry beneath her umbrella. "Let's go."

"Where are we going?" he asked, steeling himself and stepping outside. He braced himself for attack, curling his fingers around the stake he'd slipped in his pocket just in case…but Flora only grabbed his arm and bullied him through the rain to a waiting vehicle.

Grady hesitated before climbing into the automobile—once he was in there, he would be completely at the mercy of the undead. But he hadn't been reading, studying, preparing, and investigating for almost a year now for nothing—though the seeds had been planted long before.

A quick look through the windows told him there was only the driver inside, which gave him a modicum of relief when Flora gestured for him to climb in the back. At least he wasn't sliding into a complete ambush.

Still, his fingers remained around the stake, and he was careful not to look directly into the eyes of either vampire. He settled into a seat in the corner, keeping a distance from Flora, and prepared himself for whatever was to come.

"Where are we going? Where is she?" Grady wasn't certain whether Macey was actually at the location Flora was taking him, or whether he was the bait for the vampire hunter.

While upstairs, gathering up everything he thought he might need, Grady had considered all of his options. If Macey was wherever he was going, she obviously needed some sort of help. It was possible Flora really was trying to help her—though why she'd come for Grady, that was the question.

If Macey wasn't there, and he was going to be the lure—so to speak—Grady figured it was better for him to be the bait rather than someone who had no idea what he or she was getting into.

He wished he had a way to contact that bloke Chas Woodmore, but other than the name of the dark, angry man— and the knowledge that it was he and not Grady who was the "boyfriend"—he knew nothing about the guy.

There'd been something mentioned once about a placed called The Silver Chalice, which Grady had put in his note to Linwood—but even that could be a dead end. And he'd never been able to find the place anyway.

So all he had with him were his wits and his two decades of experience escaping an infinite number of dangerous, impossible situations. If they didn't serve him well, Grady thought grimly, he didn't bloody deserve to be trying to help anyone.

"You ever hear of the Oriental Theatre? The new place?" Flora said. She was examining him with the interest of a cat with a mouse. Grady was too careful to look directly at her, so it was hard for him to tell whether her eyes were glowing red.

"Yes, as a matter of fact. My uncle was attacked there last night. Is that where we're going?"

"Right the first time." She smiled, and now her fangs showed. "You're a good-looking guy, Mr. Grady. I can see why Macey's sweet on you."

He reared back a little in spite of himself, and she moved closer, attempting to enthrall him with her gaze. When she reached for him, he closed his eyes and curled his fingers into fists. He didn't fight it as her fangs slid into his skin.

Grady wasn't certain how much time had passed since he'd arrived at the Oriental Theatre. But now, he was in possession of Macey's heavy silver cross, having just removed it from her trembling, abused body.

He'd taken his time with the task, fumbling purposely with the clasp at the back of her warm, slender neck in order to be close for a moment. He wanted to say something to her, but he didn't know what. He wanted to tell her it would be all right, that *he* would be all right...but he couldn't.

Because he didn't have any idea how it would come true.

He was still stunned, remembering the battle she'd fought in vain: the beating and vicious feeding...the kicking and fighting and stabbing... He'd witnessed the melee with horror, sitting next to Flora in the wings of the stage until they'd hung him by the wrists from the catwalk.

The vampires had foolishly bound his hands with thick rope—one of the easiest bonds to loosen because of its rigidity and inflexibility—and left his legs unencumbered, though they had removed the stake from his pocket. But their examination hadn't been thorough enough, and he still had several tricks up his sleeve—or in his heels, to be more specific.

Despite his preparations and expectations, Grady'd been more than a little unsteady when they arrived at the theater. Flora seemed enamored with him, and though she'd fed on him briefly in the auto and forced a few blood-tinged kisses from his mouth, he was aware how much more thorough and vicious she could have been. Linwood was an example of that, and now so was Macey.

Therefore, they must have other plans for him, and they surely involved Macey. When he emerged from the automobile, the continuing trickle of blood pumping from his throat had made him lightheaded and weak as he followed Flora though the rain, into the back door of the theater.

Once inside, things happened quickly and in a dizzying manner, and the next thing he knew, he was watching Macey fight her way through a horde of undead as he hung from his wrists in a spotlight.

He could have escaped from the fetters quite easily, but that would be tipping his hand too soon—and too overtly. He was right onstage in front of everyone. So Grady had more than one reason to be thankful when they unfastened him from the hanging rope and commanded him to remove the cross from Macey's throat.

Apparently, the undead weren't terribly concerned with him retaining the pendant—or maybe they were simply distracted by the threat of Macey—for when he was finished, he was able to stuff the powerful pendant into his pocket, and no one seemed to notice.

Wrists still bound, Grady casually moved out of the limelight, keeping an eye on the man who was clearly the leader of the vampires. Nicholas, Macey had called him. Grady admitted the creature was the most terrifying being he'd ever encountered.

It would be to his best interest to remain beneath the vampire's notice—which didn't seem to be difficult, for Nicholas had barely looked at him. All of his attention was on Macey.

No one seemed to notice when Grady eased further into the shadows then off the stage. His foot landed on something that shifted. It was round and slender, and he crouched to the ground and snatched up the stake. Even with bound wrists, he was still able to slip it up one sleeve, then returned his attention to the stage. Now that he was armed, and relatively free of notice, perhaps there was something he could do to change the game in their direction.

Perhaps now was the time to use the small packet of powder tucked inside his sock.

He looked up in time to see the lean, pale-skinned vampire Iscariot slam his fangs into Macey's shoulder. Horrified, Grady jolted along with her, and he found he couldn't tear his eyes away from the sight of the creature penetrating her flesh while his long-fingered, lethal hands dug into her skin.

Tears of rage and horror filled his eyes as he watched her fighting in vain, gasping and shuddering, writhing and bucking as the torture went on and on. His heart beat so fast and hard that Grady's vision turned red and throbbing, and he had to actually curl his hands around the edge of the stage to keep himself from leaping up there to stop it.

"It's delicious, isn't it?" said a voice through the roaring in his ears. "Watching it."

He barely heard the words, hardly registered her presence before Flora sank her awful fangs into the curve of his neck.

TWENTY-SEVEN

A Desperate Battle

MACEY HIT THE GROUND HARD, with the breath knocked out of her. Just after she thumped onto the floor, she heard the hollow sound of a wooden stake landing next to her.

Everything was quiet in the space—an empty, unused orchestra pit. The edges were shadowed and dark, and the only light came from the opening in the stage above.

Macey picked up the stake, heart pounding…for by know, she thought she knew what Iscariot had planned.

And just as she rose to her feet, something shifted at the edge of darkness…then moved slowly into the light.

"Sebastian," she breathed. Though she'd prepared herself, the sight of him—battered, bloody, and wild-eyed—knocked the breath from her. Anguish and hunger burned in his eyes as she moved closer to him, still holding the stake. She could see he'd been fed on, that so much blood had been taken from him…

"Get away," he said. "What the hell are you thinking…" His eyes burned hotter, and his nostrils flared as if he'd caught her scent.

Macey stopped, fully aware of her predicament.

I want the Rings of Jubai. And Sebastian Vioget's soul.

Iscariot's desire was clear: she was to battle Sebastian to the death. Killing him would release the rings, but by marking her, drawing her blood so viciously and thoroughly, Iscariot had ensured Sebastian would be unable to fight the temptation to taste mortal blood for the first time—thus losing his soul.

He should be weak and helpless, with such a loss of blood… but it had only made him desperately hungry. The scent of her own fresh blood would be filling his nostrils, and he would go for her—inhumanly strong in his weakness and need.

Her rough breathing filled her ears—no, that was Sebastian's. He was breathing, and his heart was beating…Macey felt its thudding, the power of it trapped inside the pit with her. His immortal pulse throbbed, pounding like an insistent drum, determined to capture her own heartbeat. To control it. To subdue her.

She saw, now, that Sebastian was crouched on the floor, his arms wrapped around his bent knees, each hand gripping the opposite wrist. Blood oozed from the imprint of his fingernails into his own flesh. He was holding himself back.

"Go," he groaned, burying his face in his knees. His body shook visibly. "Get out of here."

Macey didn't bother to look too closely for an exit—not only would Iscariot have ensured there wasn't one, but she was not about to leave Sebastian here. Never.

She *would* kill him first.

She would kill him, and take the rings if she needed to.

Then Macey remembered, somehow in the midst of this turmoil, the copper ring she'd found in his bedside table. *If it was one of the Rings of Jubai, Iscariot wouldn't have them all even if Sebastian dies.*

"Sebastian," she whispered, moving as close as she dared, while wiping away as much of her blood as possible with the flap of her shirt. "Are you wearing all the rings?"

He lifted his face and she nearly fell backward. That was when she knew there was no hope.

His eyes…they blazed with hunger and pain and lust. She didn't know whether he'd even heard her…whether he even cared. Whether he even knew it was she, Macey.

His fangs: they were long and sharp and lethal, desperate for their first taste of mortal blood. His fingers had slipped and were digging viciously into the backs of his hands now. But even in the faulty light she could see how he trembled with desire, and how desperately he fought the need to lunge for her.

Macey felt cold and empty. So it would come to this. It was the only way. If Victoria Gardella could slay her husband…

She gripped the stake. No matter what, she'd kill Sebastian before he tasted her. That was the only way possible to save his soul, and—perhaps, if he'd somehow fulfilled his long promise—Giulia Pesaro's as well.

Sebastian was starved and beaten, and he was weak—not so much physically as emotionally and mentally. Whatever Iscariot had done to him, it had made the Venator-turned-vampire into the most vulnerable of men.

And it was Macey he wanted. Only Macey that could cause him to lose control, to succumb to the desire that had festered and been controlled for more than a century.

Not just any mortal, but she: the manifestation of the two women for whom he'd made his sacrifice.

"That's not much of an entertainment." Iscariot's impatient voice traveled down into the darkness. His shadow moved around near the rim of the stage. "Shall we spice things up a bit?"

Macey had no chance to react or respond, for all at once, there were more dark figures struggling over the top of the pit, and then someone was flung down inside.

Grady.

He landed so close to Sebastian that Macey actually heard the Venator-vampire groan with desperation.

But Sebastian could resist Grady. This was merely Iscariot's way of upping the ante, of bringing more temptation to Sebastian, to overwhelm him with the scent and sight and proximity of fresh blood.

Macey grabbed Grady by the shirt and yanked him away from Sebastian while whispering in his ear, "Find us a way out of this place."

She couldn't see his face, but she felt him tighten, as if to argue—but then he nodded. He squeezed her arm with his bound hands before he crawled off…just as Sebastian let out a tortuous, keening cry—and lunged.

Macey vaulted to her feet and slammed into him as hard as possible, forestalling his attack on her. They crashed into the wooden wall of the pit, which in the back of her mind gave her hope that they could somehow find their way out of this place. At least it wasn't brick.

His hands grabbed for her, wild and furious. His eyes were no longer Sebastian's, but that of a desperate demon. His beautiful, chiseled features were stretched into madness and starvation. He knocked her onto her back, his full weight slamming her onto the concrete floor, her head whipping back once again as he knocked the breath from her lungs.

Light and dark flashed in her eyes, and pain radiated like an explosion in the back of her skull, but she still had the stake gripped fiercely in her hand. Ready. *One thrust…that's it. One—*

No, she thought. *No.*

Sebastian was on top of her in a horrible mockery of lovemaking, the skill for which he was so well known: his powerful arms and legs wrapped around her, his hips and torso molding against hers. His face was a mask of darkness as it sank down toward her as if prepared to devour her with a kiss.

"Do it," he said from between clenched teeth. His mouth was next to her throat. She felt the heat of his lips moving against her, the smooth sensation of fang as they slid along her skin. "God, Macey, *do it*." He vibrated against her, struggling with the demon inside him.

"No," she cried, and slammed her head sharply into the side of his temple, then shoved him off with a strength she didn't know she still had.

She staggered to her feet, bumping against the wall, and saw Grady a few inches away. He turned and something glinted as it flew through the air toward her.

Macey caught it: the silver cross he'd just removed from her throat. Panting, heaving, she held up the cross in front of her as Sebastian pulled to his feet, also gasping desperately.

"Listen to me," she said, moving closer so he could hear her and Iscariot could not—for the vampire master and his cohorts continued to watch from above. "Just stay back, Sebastian. We're going to get out of here. I'm not going to—"

He laughed. It was not Sebastian Vioget's laugh, but that of someone else. It sent dark, insidious shivers through her body, and she realized: this was no longer Sebastian.

"Do you think that would stop me now?" he said, lashing out with a powerful hand. "One who's worn the like for a hundred years?"

He snatched the cross from her and flung it away into the darkness as he grabbed her wrist and pulled her toward him. She slammed up against his body once more, her stake trapped uselessly between them.

"There's nothing that can save me," he said from behind compressed teeth. "Nothing any longer." He had her pushed back against the wall before she was over the shock at the theft of her cross. She saw the truth in his unfamiliar eyes.

"I'm not strong enough. I'm not *strong enough to do this anymore*. Not even for *her*." Tears streamed from his eyes—red, glistening tears—as she saw one last hint of the man he'd been. She had to use the stake. There was no other choice.

He bared his fangs and plunged toward her throat.

TWENTY-EIGHT

The Effect of One Small Bead

"NOOOO!" Macey cried, and ripped aside just far enough that he barely nicked her, a light, superficial scratch. "Sebastian," she panted, trying one last time. "You *are* strong enough. For *her*, for Giulia—you can fight this! *Please*, Sebastian!"

But he wasn't listening. He swung back toward her again, grabbing the front of her torn corset. It ripped, and as she stumbled away she felt something move, shifting and spilling delicately inside the side-lacer.

The rosary.

You will need it someday.

If she ever needed anything, any extra help, it was now.

Sebastian lunged toward her again, strong and vampire fast, and Macey caught him with her hand, holding him off, pushing him away desperately. She dropped the stake in her other hand and fished down inside her corset, dragging the rosary out just as Sebastian yanked her arm away, twisting it brutally down and aside.

She cried out in pain and triumph, whipping out the rosary at the very last moment.

"Stop!" she cried, hoping and praying that somehow this delicate string of beads would somehow miraculously do what the massive silver cross did not. She dangled it in front of his face. "You can't do this. You don't want to do this, Sebastian, you have to be strong—"

Sebastian froze. He stilled—and it was the strangest, eeriest thing the way he stopped there, a sudden calm in the midst of a mindless, demonic storm.

"No," he whispered, his chest heaving, his eyes wild…but no longer glowing. He reached to touch it with a trembling hand. "How…"

"Sebastian?" Macey panted, still waiting for something to change. She didn't release the miraculous object, even as she sagged against the wall behind her. She held it in front of her, and the object seemed almost to hypnotize Sebastian.

"Macey." Grady was there. Even here, in the shadows she could see he was weak, blood-soaked, and had an expression of horror etched on his face. He was holding a stake at the ready, and he looked at Sebastian, then at her. "Is it…is he…?"

"Macey," Sebastian whispered at the same time. And, blessedly, his eyes were his own again, his voice normal.

"Have you completed your tasks already, then?" came an insistent voice as Iscariot's shadow loomed over the opening.

He couldn't see them now—they'd edged off to the side in the shadows, and the master vampire was shining a light down in an attempt to illuminate the pit.

"Here," Grady said, grabbing Macey's arm—and he put himself between her and Sebastian, giving the blond man a wary, measured look. "This way. Now." He gestured to the wall as he brandished the stake in his hand. He'd found a way out.

"But they'll see us leave," she muttered, stopping to look up at Iscariot. "You take Sebastian through there—they think I've done what they asked."

"Are you bloody insane?" Grady said, just as Sebastian growled, "Don't be a damned fool."

"But they'll—"

Grady held out his hand and there was a small paper packet in his palm. "I've got this. It'll hide us for a minute."

She didn't know what it was, but she didn't have to know. She trusted him. But could she trust Sebastian now? Macey looked at him, still uncertain about his sudden change. He just seemed so back to normal, other than the extreme exhaustion and pain he was experiencing.

Then she turned her attention to where the vampires were all leaning over the rim of the pit looking down into the space, then she nodded to Grady.

"Whatever it is, do it now." She tottered to the edge of the circle of light, exaggerating her panting while staggering as if she were mortally injured. She looked up at Iscariot, speaking as if she were completely destroyed, "Sebastian…he's… I can't…he…he…"

From the corner of her eye, she saw Grady as he moved his arm sharply. There was a *snick*, then the faint, pungent smell of tinder.

"*Now*," he said, and Macey staggered out of the light into the shadows, moving toward the opening that yawned like a black hole in one side of the pit. Just as she passed by, Grady tossed something toward the middle of the space.

Macey stumbled through the opening—which she noticed vaguely was a doorway—with Sebastian on her heels. There was a soft *boom*, and suddenly dark smoke filled the air, smothering the pit. But they'd already burst through the exit, and Grady slammed it closed behind them.

"What the hell was that?" Macey asked Grady, even as she glanced worriedly at Sebastian. He was still weak and still needed to feed—how much longer until he succumbed to the weakness again? They had to get him back to The Silver Chalice.

They.

She and Grady?

What an odd thought.

"I don't know which way to go," she muttered as Grady bumped into her from behind.

"This way," he said, taking her arm and directing her through a warren of low-ceilinged rooms and corridors used for moving props, stage equipment, and actors.

Not far behind them were the sounds of angry exclamations—it would only be moments before Iscariot and the others were on their trail. Macey pushed Sebastian ahead of her, placing him between herself and Grady as the reporter led them quickly through the underground of the theater.

Get out now, figure the rest of this out later, she told herself.

Finally, somehow, they came to a heavy door marked EXIT. With a rough push, Grady opened it to the dark, stormy night and Macey and Sebastian stumbled out into a slick, shadowy alley.

They slammed the door closed behind them. "They're right behind us," Macey gasped. "Let's run!"

"Wait—let's block the door. It'll give us a head start."

She and Grady looked around, but the only moveable object was an automobile parked a few feet away.

"That'll do," said Sebastian, speaking for the first time since they'd left. "Macey."

The two of them—with help from Grady, who reached inside and unfastened the brake and then steered—pushed the vehicle until it was up against the theater door. No sooner had they put in place than the door swung open…only to be stopped cold by the heavy metal automobile. The opening was barely wide enough for a hand to protrude.

They were safe—for now.

"Let's get out of here," said Macey, glancing at Grady, who was as out of breath from excitement and exertion as she was. "And thank you."

"This way," said Sebastian, and took off at a fast, certain pace.

They hadn't gone far—only a block or so—before Sebastian suddenly stopped, and turned to face them. They were in a narrow alley, made more eerie and shadowy by the storm clouds and rain. He seemed to block their way, his eyes suddenly burning red.

Macey stopped up short, quickly thrusting Grady behind her, but he yanked her by the arm and tried to pull her back, and she saw Grady was holding a stake.

"Where did you get this?" Sebastian lunged toward Macey, grabbing her by the arm and spinning her around. His hand was in an upraised fist, as if ready to strike a blow.

Grady gave an exclamation and leapt toward him, but the vampire's arm whipped backward to knock him aside just as Macey gave Sebastian a shove and pivoted out of his grip.

"I'm not going to hurt her," Sebastian snarled, whirling onto Grady, his hand still in an angry fist, then back to Macey. "I need to know where you got this!" He brandished the fist in her face, and that was when she saw the faint glitter of beads on it. The rosary. Wrapped around his hand and fist.

"They're coming!" shouted Grady, looking down the street.

Sebastian cursed, but bolted off. Macey followed, but at a slower pace to keep Grady with her.

They zigzagged through streets and around parked cars, sloshing through puddles and slipping on the pavement. They didn't stop this time until they reached the ornate newel post identifying The Silver Chalice.

Moments later, they were inside the dry, silent pub. The door had barely closed when Sebastian had Macey slammed against the wall once more. "*Where did you get this?*" He was out of breath, his eyes were wild—but unglowing—and the rosary was still looped around his wrist. "Did Wayren give it to you? *Wayren!*" he bellowed, spinning away to shout at the room at large while still holding Macey flush against the wall. "Wayren!"

"No, it's not from Wayren," Macey said. She held up her hand to stop Grady, who looked as if he were ready to plunge his stake into Sebastian's back. "I—it came from—an old woman gave it to me."

"An old woman?" Sebastian straightened up, his expression one of astonishment and confusion. He released her. "An *old woman*? How? Where?"

"At Old St. Patrick's Church, over on—"

Sebastian's cry of shock and amazement was clearly one of comprehension. "My God," he breathed, looking down at the rosary wrapped around his hand. He staggered, bracing himself against the wall. "*My God.*"

If Grady thought it odd that a vampire was calling for the Divine, he didn't react. He merely watched, his eyes dark and steady as he lowered the stake to his side.

"Sebastian?" Macey reached to touch her colleague's arm, no longer the least bit concerned that his vampiric tendencies would overtake him. Something had happened…and it had to do with that rosary. "What does it mean?"

"It's got an extra bead on the tail part," Grady commented, looking from one of them to the other—but Sebastian was clearly no longer interested in conversation.

"I've…" He turned and strode off—no, he *ran*—out of the pub.

If Macey had to guess, she'd wager his destination was Old St. Patrick's Church.

Twenty-Nine

A Promise Fulfilled

G IULIA!"
Macey heard Sebastian shouting even before she got through the doors of St. Patrick's.

She burst into the sanctuary and stopped, panting, soaked from the rain, and wondering how many other times tonight she was going to be out of breath and trembling with exhaustion. Other than Sebastian, the place was silent—of course it was; it was well past midnight on a stormy, miserable night.

Candles in opaque red containers flickered in rows on either side of the pews. Flames in clear glass sent off a mellower, bright light from the altar. A massive crucifix loomed over the dais. The colorful stained glass windows were dull and monochromatic. The pews were silent and empty.

"*Giulia!*" Sebastian shouted, his voice echoing violently throughout the arched space. He stood in the center of the aisle, spinning around to look in all directions.

The door bumped into Macey from behind, and Grady came in, also out of breath from running. He automatically made the sign of the cross.

"You all right?" he asked in a low voice. "Do you know what's going on? How did a vampire even cross the threshold?"

Macey shook her head. "Sebastian is a special case." An odd, prickly sort of understanding was beginning to settle over her. It was as if she knew what was happening, but couldn't quite put words to it—even in her own mind.

Something moved near the side of the church, and Macey saw a stooped figure emerge from the shadows. Macey felt her heart swell and something big and warm blossom over her, followed by a strong, warm sensation.

She grabbed Grady's hand without thinking, staring as Sebastian turned as if pulled by a string, and faced the elderly woman. Even from here, she could see his torso heaving, and his hands trembling.

"Giulia?" he whispered, taking a step toward the frail, veiled woman. "Is it you?"

Macey and Grady were easing slowly up the aisle, drawing near Sebastian—who suddenly seemed unable to move any further.

The crone pushed back her ever-present veil and, instead of responding to Sebastian, she looked at Macey. From several aisles away, Macey was struck by the power and serenity in the woman's eyes as they fastened upon her. They were her own eyes—the Pesaro eyes.

"Thank you," said the woman. In the candlelight, her gaze glistened with tears.

"Just how old are you, anyway?" Macey blurted out, then regretted such a stupid question in the midst of—whatever this was.

The elderly woman's face wrinkled into a soft smile. "I'm 105 years old…today. Exactly today. On the day the long promise was made, I was reborn." She pulled her attention away and settled it on Sebastian. "*Mi adorate.*"

"Giulia," he whispered. "Does this mean…?"

She withdrew her hand from beneath the long, loose gown she wore. She was holding a stake. Its silver tip gleamed even in the low light. She was smiling with joy.

Macey's insides surged, and she would have leapt toward them, but Grady caught her by the arm. "No."

Heart thudding, pulse racing, Macey stilled. Every hair on her body stood on end; every muscle and tendon was taut and felt ready to snap.

"It's time," said Sebastian. "At last." He wasn't looking at anyone but the old woman—Giulia—as they walked toward each other.

"No," Macey whispered. "Sebastian!" she cried. "What are you doing? What if you're wrong? What if—"

But it was too late. The woman flung herself at Sebastian, stake raised, and as he threw himself into her embrace, she drove the pike home: hard, sharp, fast, strong.

So strong for such a frail, old creature.

Macey shrieked; she couldn't help it, for it felt as if she herself had been stabbed in the heart as Sebastian froze, impaled on the silver stake. He jolted, his head thrown back, his beautiful bronze and amber self—bruised and bloody and beaten—illuminated by the golden candlelight in that arrested moment.

A great rush of energy filled the church, a cyclone of wind catching up a cloud of glittery ash and dust in a swirling column that surrounded Sebastian and Giulia…

It spun and illuminated, and in the midst of it, Macey saw their two figures—Sebastian and his love—embracing, twining, becoming one…and in the middle of the storm, there was a flash, a sharp, specific moment where the old woman metamorphosed into the beauty of her youth: with long, lush, dark hair, an unlined face, and big, dark eyes. Dark eyes that looked just like Macey's.

They fastened on her, connecting with her from the distance. Macey felt the shock of warmth and comprehension—and perhaps love—explode over her as the young, beautiful woman held her gaze until she swirled back into the figure of the old crone.

And then, all at once, they were gone.

The two figures had exploded into a glittery silver dust that wafted throughout the sanctuary, settling over the pews and aisles like starlight rain. The scent that lingered was not the foul, musty one of death and evil, but something pleasant and beautiful.

Something like eternity.

The dust settled and the church became silent. And all that remained was the silver-tipped stake, the glittering rosary, and five copper rings.

Twenty-Nine
Decisions and Answers and a Compliment

NOTHING'S CHANGED," Macey said, her voice taut with emotion.

She and Grady had made their way back to The Silver Chalice. Dawn was just breaking and the storm was over. The two of them were alone in the pub. All was silent and dark.

"*Everything's* changed," Grady shot back. He yanked away the collar of his shirt, soaked by rain and blood. "I was fed on— multiple times—by your redheaded friend. Don't tell me nothing's bloody changed."

She balked a little at the sight of the raw vampire wounds. "Salted holy water," she began.

"Already done. I had some in the heels of my shoes last night. Along with lock picks. And a small smoke bomb tucked inside my stocking, with matches to set it off—which, as you recall, was the reason we were able to escape undetected. I had a stake in my pocket and *this*," he said, producing a series of three finger-sized pieces of wood. "It's a stake—you see, you screw the pieces together, but they come apart so they can fit in a smaller place. Like the inside of my shoe." His blue eyes blazed. "Don't tell me I don't know what I'm doing, or what I've gotten myself into, Macey. You can't use that as an excuse anymore."

She could only gape at him in astonishment, even as terror bubbled inside her. "You don't understand," she said, taking him by the arms. "My father—"

"The hell I don't." As when he was truly angry, there was no trace of the Irish—just hard, sharp words. "I understand more than you can possibly realize after seeing you fighting for your life—for my life, and for Sebastian's. *I saw you*—I saw what you experienced, how powerful you are, and how much responsibility you have. I understand."

"So did my mother," Macey whispered. Tears filled her eyes, causing his dear, handsome face to become blurry. "And she became the target of the undead, simply because she was married to my father. They tortured her, Grady. What they did to her… it was worse than what Iscariot did to Mrs. Gutchinson. And it destroyed my father." She was shaking her head. "I don't want you to be hurt…and I don't want to be destroyed. I have work to do." She tried to make her voice sound cold and hard, but failed miserably.

This was hard. This was *so hard*.

"Sounds like a little bit of cowardice to me," he said flatly. "But I guess I should take it as a compliment that you care so much."

You have no idea how much I care. "You saw what happened last night—you saw the horror and the violence and the evil. But what you don't understand, you *can't* understand, is that it's like that *every day* for me. *Every* day. *Every* night. I don't get to rest. I don't get to sleep. I don't get to take time off. I don't get to walk away. *Ever.* But you can, Grady." The tears were coming faster now, and her voice shook with emotion. "You don't want that kind of life—lonely, violent, and dark. You don't deserve it."

"Macey," he said, pulling her into his arms. "What *you* don't understand is that I'm in love with you. I willingly take on that life to be with you, to be by your side, to support you—and, when there is a chance—because you know there must be—I'll be there to make love to you, to hold you, to drive away the demons… if only for a short time. Your father had that with your mother, didn't he?"

She, so much stronger and more powerful than Grady, suddenly felt unaccountably weak and fragile in his arms. Her tears were soaking his shirt, and she could smell the familiar scent of his skin, taste the salt from both of them, feel the warmth of his body.

"You forget, *a rún*," he murmured into her hair, "I was in the War. I've seen violence for days and weeks and months on end. I grew up on the streets of Dublin surrounded by misery and greed and death."

"It's not the same." She pulled away. "This war—my war—it never ends. It won't end until I'm gone."

"And I'd be there with you till then, Macey, lass."

Something shuffled softly behind her and they both turned. Macey blinked, for Wayren stood there. This was the first time Macey had seen her since receiving her *vis bulla*.

The first time in almost a year.

It must be because of Sebastian.

"I'm Wayren." She spoke to Grady.

He looked at her for a prolonged moment, then said, "Somehow, I'm certain you already know my name."

She gave a brief smile and inclined her head. "May I speak with Macey for a moment?"

Grady nodded and turned away, walking to the other side of the room.

"What do you want?" asked Wayren. She looked at Macey with pale, clear blue eyes.

As always when in the presence of this enigmatic being, Macey felt a rush of comfort and peace. And strength. "I want him to be safe. I don't want to be like my father, risking the life of someone I love so I can selfishly be with him."

Wayren held her eyes. "Loving someone is never selfish."

Macey shook her head. "That may be, but I am not going to be my father. I won't be responsible for Grady being hurt."

"And if I could fix the problem…is that what you truly want?"

"How?" Macey asked cautiously.

Wayren dug in the small pouch that dangled from her chatelaine's belt and produced a delicate chain with a flat, golden disk on it. "This has been used for centuries to help remove the memories of people who unwittingly—or even purposely—have become exposed to the world of the Venators and the undead."

Macey looked at it and felt a shiver of the power emanating from it. "This is the pendant that belonged to Victoria's aunt Eustacia?"

"It was given to her for her use. Would you like me to use it, Macey?"

She didn't have to think about it. "If it will keep him safe, keep him from seeking out the vampires, then do it. Yes."

"Even if it will erase all of his memories in relation to this—including those of you?" Wayren's gaze bored gently into Macey's. "He would no longer know you."

Her heart thumped unpleasantly, and she glanced over at him. The little knot inside her tightened, but she nodded. "Yes. But"—she grabbed Wayren's arm—"it might make him forget everything, but Iscariot and Flora—they'll still remember him. He'll still be a target for them, won't he?"

Wayren cocked her head like a bright-eyed bird. "Unlikely, if there is no longer a connection between the two of you. But if it makes you feel better, I can give him something that will help. He won't know what it means, but it will help him sense when there is a danger or threat."

"Yes, please, Wayren."

"You're certain? You're certain you wish to release him, to give him up, to erase all his memories of you and everything that has occurred?"

Macey's throat was tight, and it burned, but she nodded. "Yes. Please. Do it, Wayren. Do it now."

"Very well then."

"Wayren."

The woman turned back expectantly. "You've changed your mind?"

"No, no…just…do you know…will Linwood live? I don't want—well, he shouldn't lose him too." Macey's eyes stung once more.

Wayren looked up and to the side, as if listening or waiting, pausing for a moment. Then she returned her attention to Macey. "He'll live."

"Thank you."

Macey watched as the slender blond woman seemed almost to glide over to Grady. She spoke softly to him, placing a hand on his arm. He didn't look over at Macey. Instead, he nodded, and Wayren led him away.

Goodbye, Jameson Grady.

Macey wiped her tears roughly and turned sharply…and nearly walked into Chas.

"You'll get over it, lulu," he said, and drew her into his embrace with his one good arm. "I just hope you don't have to travel a century to do so."

"Are they the real Rings of Jubai?" Macey asked.

She set the five copper rings on the bar counter in the silent, empty Silver Chalice.

It was late the next day, and in some ways, she felt like a new person: cleaned up, rested, finally rid of Al Capone, and no longer worried about Grady. Back where she belonged.

But in other ways, Macey felt completely bereft. Lost. And alone.

And filled with questions.

The one about the rings happened to be the simplest of them all.

"They came from Sebastian, didn't they?" said Temple. Her face was drawn and her eyes echoed the weariness and grief they were all feeling, now that Sebastian was truly gone. She of them all had spent the most time with him in the last months. "Why wouldn't they be?"

It was just the two of them, sitting in the pub—Macey on a stool and Temple behind the counter. In honor of the place's proprietor, Temple had poured each of them a shot of a rosy-amber-colored liquor they found under the counter.

"Never seen this one before," Temple had said when she pulled out the square, glass-cut bottle. Its topper was a black pyramid shape. She sniffed inside before pouring to make certain it wasn't one of his blood-whiskeys. "Must have been something special he kept hidden from Chas."

"Must've been. To Sebastian." Macey lifted her glass and sipped. The liquor was very smooth, very warming. She'd never tasted anything like it. When she replaced the glass on the counter, she explained to Temple about the copper ring she'd found in Sebastian's bedside table. "I wonder if he had an extra made so that if Iscariot did dust him, he wouldn't have all the rings. Maybe he *was* able to take off one of the rings, and used a fake one as a replacement. Or maybe he was just prepared to be able to do so, if a miracle ever happened."

"But then Iscariot would have been searching for the missing one," said Temple. "And you know he'd come after you first."

"True. But then he wouldn't know it wasn't the real one until he tried to use the fake one, right? At the pool at Munții Făgăraș. And from what I know about that pool, if you put your hand in without the proper protection…you might not even live to seek revenge on someone who tricked you." She shrugged.

"That is an excellent point, sister." Temple lifted her glass. "Sebastian was very clever." She blinked rapidly, then ducked to put the square bottle beneath the counter, thus averting her gaze. "I didn't get to say goodbye."

"I didn't either. It happened so quickly. But he was…joyful at the end. Because he was with her."

"He saved her, you are sure, aren't you?" Temple asked. "You have no doubt?"

"If I see Wayren again, I'll ask her to be certain, but I am sure of it."

"You'll ask me what?"

She and Temple turned. Somehow, Macey wasn't surprised that Wayren was there once more, having somehow arrived with no fanfare and without even using the door. To her surprise and pleasure, however, Chas was there as well.

"Whether Sebastian's long promise has been fulfilled?" The ethereal blond woman made her way over to the counter. "You know it has. You saw it for yourself, Macey. You need not second-guess what you already know—now and in the future."

"You shouldn't be out of bed, Chas," Temple told him with a dark look. "Even for a Venator, you need time to heal."

"I'm fine. Just a little sore." Chas settled onto a stool at the bar, moving gingerly. "Macey's questions might be answered, but I have some of my own, if you please." He looked pointedly at the empty glasses on the counter, but Temple either didn't notice, or chose to ignore him. Macey suspected it was the latter.

"Those are the rings?" Chas said, poking them with a finger. "Who's going to put them on and wear them for the next century?" They all chuckled, but when he reached as if to gather them up, Wayren stopped him with a quiet clearing of the throat.

"That won't be necessary, Chas. We'll return them—yes, they are the original Rings of Jubai—to St. Patrick's, where they will be safe until and unless we need them. The rings and the rosary both. You, however, should keep the stake." This last was spoken to Macey.

"Speaking of the rosary…I'm not sure I understand what happened. Why did that seem to repel Sebastian when the big silver cross didn't?" she asked.

"But did it? Did the rosary repel him?" Wayren replied.

Macey thought back, bringing the moment back to the front of her mind. "*No.* No, it didn't repel him so much as it seemed to…well, wake him up. It was like a light switch—as if the button was pushed and Sebastian went from mad and desperate and evil to…himself." The hair on the back of her arms lifted with a gentle prickle. "It seemed to jolt him from out of a dream."

"Indeed."

Macey went on, for things were becoming clearer. "It was as if he recognized the rosary—with its distinctive extra bead and the tiny cross." A rush of certainty flowed through her, and she smiled. "I understand now. It was Giulia's—she must have had one like it when he knew her. The extra bead made it special.

And the cross…it was like a *vis bulla*. He recognized it, and it reminded him of Giulia—she was the one who gave it to me. Or, rather, the reborn, reincarnated version of herself gave it to me. She said she was born on the day Sebastian made the long promise—so it wasn't really her, was it?"

"It was her soul," Wayren said. "Manifested into a new person, simply waiting for the day when she could rest again."

"And now they're both at rest." Macey smiled, though she still felt a horrible stab of grief when she realized Sebastian was really gone.

"Are you pouring any of that for me?" Wayren gestured to Temple. "Since you'll be taking over as proprietor, you should get used to doing thus."

"So now I'm to be pub-owner as well? Venator trainer, apprentice milliner, and now speakeasy proprietor? I'm going to be awfully busy." But Temple seemed to like the idea, for she spread her hands over the smooth, battered wooden counter as if caressing it. "I could do that. For him." She blinked rapidly, then turned to pouring for Wayren and—finally—Chas as well.

The four of them lifted their glasses at once.

Macey's eyes filled and she blinked hard. Two farewells in two days were far too much.

But that was her life. This was the choice she made. The legacy she must fulfill. And now, she would move forward: stronger, resolved, and unencumbered by guilt and attachment.

"To Sebastian Vioget," said Chas, lifting his drink high. His dark Gypsy eyes were damp as he stared unseeingly at the glass. "The strongest man I've ever known."

Epilogue
Indigestion and an Unpleasant Incident

A S WAS HIS HABIT, Al Capone had eaten far too much for dinner. Despite the sour taste left by Macey Gardella's defection, he'd been in a celebratory mood because—hell, he'd lived through the thievery at the Art Institute, and the damned counterfeiters who took him for a million large ones were in jail.

Thus, he'd washed down multiple helpings of osso bucco, pasta, and garlic bread with carafes of Chianti. And then there'd been the cannoli…and the coffee with lots of cream. And sugar. Not to mention the cigars.

But a man hadda enjoy life—especially when he was rich as Croesus and had more than a few bullets with his name on them—and plenty of good food was paramount to living life to the fullest. After all, wasn't that in the Church's teachings? Man's purpose on earth, as taught by the Catechism, was to live life to the fullest.

Al Capone couldn't be accused of shirking his Catholic duty in that, at least. And whatever else he did that might be sinful… well, it got washed away in the confessional every week.

Nevertheless, his overly full belly made it difficult to sleep. Mae was in Cicero tonight with her sisters, so at least he had the room at the Lexington Hotel penthouse to himself. He could fart and belch and moan from heartburn and indigestion without restraint.

Al was more comfortable without his trousers or shirt on, so he stripped down to his boxers and undershirt, leaving everything in a heap on the floor by his shoes and socks. His *vis bulla* was clearly outlined by the too-tight undershirt straining over his distended belly, and he looked down at the small cross-shaped bump rising over his navel with a wry smile.

Without the confidence and power given to him by the tiny amulet, he didn't know whether he'd ever have become the man he was today: feared, respected, and filthy rich. Powerful. He suspected the tiny cross also kept his infection by syphilis at bay, for he hadn't had an outbreak in years.

And, dammit, in exchange for such an abundant life, Al did his part for charity—more than anyone knew, in fact, but him and God. He even did his part to keep the peace in this lawless world of Prohibition. No matter what people said about his greed and illegal ways, his control over the black market liquor distribution in Chicago helped keep violent crime to a minimum, and restricted mostly to between him and his rivals. And, sure, he'd slain a few vampires over the years—hand to hand, the old-fashioned way. But that wasn't something he felt it necessary to do anymore.

His thick brows drew together as he thought about Macey Gardella Denton. The little bitch might have won the battle, but he sure as hell wasn't finished with the war. They were in this together, him and Macey. They had a prophecy to fulfill, and he'd find a way to make her realize she couldn't finish her duty here—or, more importantly, the prophecy—without him as her partner.

His stomach rumbled alarmingly and Capone's fingers slid away from his engorged torso as he closed his eyes. He knew from experience the best remedy for overindulgence was time and rest. And a nearby toilet.

He must have slept, for the pain and discomfort receded for a time…then suddenly he became aware. His eyes opened. He was facing the window, where a single beam of moonlight made its way from between gapping drapery that fluttered in the night's breeze.

A wave of icy fear rushed over him, for the window had *not* been open when he retired, and Capone reached stealthily for the pistol and stake he kept in the bedside drawer.

"I wouldn't do that."

The quiet command was accompanied by something sharp and metal poking his bare, meaty shoulder.

Al looked over and behind him to see the shadowy figure standing next to the bed. He was holding a long, slender metal object with a point that was clearly lethal in nature. Some type of arrow.

"You," he breathed, his insides shifting and sloshing with a combination of fear and relief. Not a vampire. Not one of his rivals. But…an unpleasant, unexpected visitor nonetheless. Someone he truly thought he'd never set eyes on again.

The metal tip of the arrow that was poking him prodded Al to roll over onto his back as the nighttime visitor loomed over him.

"I'm not very pleased with you, Alphonsus." The man's powerful shoulders were outlined by the stray beam of moonlight as he stood with the metal tip now pressed into Al's belly. One little shift, and there would be a lot of blood. He'd be split open like a fatted calf.

"How did you get in here? Through the window? Impossible."

A flash of white teeth accompanied his visitor's low chuckle. "Through the door, like anyone else. I found it necessary to open the window on arriving, however, in order to air out the room a little."

Through the door? How the *hell*…? It was all Al could do not to bolt upright in shock and alarm, but he managed to restrain himself. The arrow most likely wouldn't kill him, but it would be messy and painful.

"You might want to consider replacing your security team," continued his visitor. "They didn't pose much of a deterrent—at least to me." Another low chuckle.

"What do you want?"

That seemed to be the signal for all levity and cordiality to evaporate. The very air in the room changed to something dark and dangerous. "I want to know why you didn't deliver my letters."

He shifted the hand holding the arrow. The tip was sharp enough to split the straining cotton of Al's undershirt…and then it settled on his bare skin. Just above his navel, where the silver *vis bulla* now gleamed, unfettered, in the low light.

"I was waiting for the right time," Al replied. He was aware of the mad racing of his heart and a mortal fear he rarely ever experienced.

"I entrusted you with them. And you've betrayed me as well as our legacy."

The arrow tip danced gently over his skin and settled at the *vis bulla*. Al tensed, but when he would have moved, another flash of metal caught his attention. A second arrow, long and lethal, settled at his throat. He swallowed, and felt the dangerous tip scrape against his Adam's apple.

"You aren't fit to wear the *vis*."

Al felt a tug at his belly and, though he dared not lift his head to look, he realized the first arrow tip had skewered the small ring of his amulet. "You have no—"

"*I have every bloody damned right.*" And with a sharp jerk, the arrow moved and the *vis bulla* was torn from Al Capone's skin. When the arrow lifted, his small silver cross dangled from its tip.

"You—" The protest was strangled in his throat as the second arrow remained in place, pinning him to the bed. Dark, furious eyes held him pinioned with just as much force as the weapon, and Al dared not move.

The loss of the *vis bulla* hadn't been painful so much as draining. Al felt the deficit of power as if it seeped into the bedclothes beneath him, and though no other man on earth would know how he'd been handicapped, *he* knew.

And so did his visitor.

"Stay away from my daughter." The soft, icy command had no need for an accompanying threat.

There was a soft clink, and the arrow with the *vis bulla* moved sharply. The tiny amulet glittered briefly in the light before it was snatched from the air by his visitor and tucked away. "Goodbye, Alphonsus. In the interest of your well-being and my tight schedule, I hope this is the last time I will ever visit you."

And then he was gone—out the open window in a blur of dark clothing and the soft clink of crossbow bolts.

Al lay there for a long moment, his belly quivering with relief that he was still alive and no one had been there to witness his set-down. The small amount of blood gathering at his navel was incidental, but all at once, his bowels were dangerously, unpleasantly loose. He barely made it to the toilet in time, and as he sat there, cold sweat running down his face and body, Al had his own private Come to Jesus moment.

Things were going to be a lot different in Chicago going forward.

Al Capone was no longer a Venator.

Sebastian Vioget was gone.

And Max Denton had arrived.

So you thought Max Denton was dead, did you?
Read more about him in the short novel

Raging Dawn
Now available!

"If Buffy visited Downton Abbey."
--New York Times bestselling author Laurie London

England, 1922
When the vampires Max Denton hunts brutally murder his wife, he is nearly destroyed himself. He spends his life in solitude, violence, and revenge.

But when sensitive information about his young daughter falls into the hands of the vampires, Max is forced to team up with the woman whose father ultimately caused the death of his wife.

Savina Eleaisa has secrets of her own, and she's determined to do whatever it takes to clear her father's name: even if it involves seducing the most dangerous of vampires--with or without the help of the arrogant, brooding Max Denton.

Prologue
Horror

THE RAGE—THE PAIN—WAS SO INTENSE he couldn't hold back a howl. It rose from deep in his gut, long and keening and empty.

Max Denton's knees gave way as he stared at the carnage.

What was left of his wife Felicia was hardly recognizable. The vampires had torn into her flesh with fangs and nails. They'd raped and fed on and destroyed the woman he loved. The mother of his child.

Because of him.

What have I done?

My God…what have I let them do to you?

His powerful hands—slick with the blood of his wife, glistening dark and sticky, smelling of heavy rust—curled into themselves as he sank to the floor…buried his face in her matted, blood-crusted blond hair…and sobbed.

Max didn't know how long he was there before soft, light hands touched his shoulders, drawing him up and away from Felicia's cold, lifeless body.

Despite his gut-deep agony and the dull, numbing pain, Max recognized Wayren's presence. Her very essence settled around him like a soft, light blanket. He indulged for just a moment…a breath. He tried to find an island of calm and clarity.

Then the realization hit him.

"*Macey*," he said, dragging himself to his feet, terror shuttling through him. "Oh God, *no. No.* Is she—?"

"She is safe." Wayren was tall and slender, hardly more substantial than a will-o-the-wisp next to him and she helped Max steady himself with her own capable hands. Though he fought her ever-present compassion, Wayren's presence and the touch skimming his hands nevertheless brought warmth and comfort. Yet both were sensations he did not currently desire.

Dressed as always in the centuries-old, outmoded style of a medieval chatelaine, Wayren appeared even more ageless and ethereal than usual. Her straight silvery blond hair reached past the narrow braided belt she wore over a loose, floor-length gown of undyed fabric, and a trio of finger-thick braids were pulled back from each of her temples, somehow fastened at the crown of her head. From the loose belt around her waist hung a small leather pouch, a collection of keys that seemed much too bulky for such an elegant figure—yet they didn't seem to clink or shift audibly—and other accoutrements. He didn't immediately see her ever-present satchel that was usually filled with books, though it never seemed heavy or bulging.

Wayren possessed the most calming of demeanors and the warmest, kindest pale blue eyes. Her features were pleasing, and her words were always compassionate and wise.

And at the moment, Max did not want any of it from her: neither comfort nor warmth, not wisdom nor peace.

He wanted to be out of his body, away from this world, no longer facing this reality.

He wanted revenge. He wanted violence—brutal, ugly violence. He wanted to be alone.

He wanted to *hate.*

He wanted to kill, but really, most of all…he wanted to *die.*

Max opened his mouth to say all of those things, to send her away, but Wayren merely looked at him with steady cornflower eyes. It was as if she read everything dark in his heart and in his mind, and she didn't care.

"Max," she said quietly. Their eyes met, and he felt her sorrow and her grief…and it was a balm. Just for a moment, it was a balm for him.

"I have to keep her safe," he said finally. "I have to send Macey away. They can't find her too."

It was intolerable, it was a *nightmare* seeing his beloved Felicia destroyed by his enemies—the beings he was sworn to hunt and slay…but he simply could not conceive of a world in which the vampires ruled by Nicolas Iscariot would do the same to a beautiful eight-year-old girl. And they would. Given the chance, they would: if for no other reason than to destroy Max Denton. To bring their most powerful enemy, their greatest threat to his knees.

If something happened to Macey, he would go mad. He was dancing with insanity at this very moment, and that would be the last step before tipping him into complete madness.

Even now, all he wanted was to load up with his lethal ash stakes, his silver-tipped arrows and crossbow, his silver cross, and destroy. In his mind, he saw himself as a medieval berserker… dead-minded, wild, and brutal. Unforgiving.

"I have to send her away. I can't ever see her again…not until Iscariot is dead." Through the pain and anguish, Max found clarity and determination—at least for now. "That's the only way Macey will be safe."

"Max—"

"*No.* There's no other way to keep her safe. You know it. And if she's to follow in my footsteps…if she too is called to be a Venator and wear the *vis bulla*…" His voice trailed off. Max didn't know whether his daughter, his only child, would be blessed—no, *cursed*—with the powerful family legacy of vampire hunting… but surely Wayren knew whether Macey would be called to hunt as a Venator. Wayren knew everything.

He looked at the pale woman, and that was all he needed. He read the answer in her eyes.

A shiver rattled through him. *Macey.* His bright-eyed, curly-haired imp would someday face the same horror and the same evil he did. And she would be responsible for destroying it.

As long as she remained alive.

As long as she knew about her legacy…

He stilled.

Perhaps she could yet be protected.

Perhaps she need never know.

Perhaps he could somehow keep her safe.

"Send her away. Take her, Wayren—I don't want to know anything about her: where she is, what she's doing, who she's with…unless—" He stopped, unable to say the words. *Unless she dies.* "Take her. Go." The words were thick and choked. "And leave me alone."

The soft swish of Wayren's gown was the only signal of her acquiescence. He felt rather than heard her leave…and with her went the last vestiges of peace and comfort.

Max swallowed, his eyes settling on the carnage Iscariot's men had left for him to find. The brutal message. The only recognizable part was one delicate hand still wearing her two favorite rings: her delicate diamond wedding band, and a heavy cabochon-cut stone. If it weren't for them, he might believe there'd been a mistake.

Ah, Felicia. Tears stung his eyes, and the dark, heavy ball of rage settled deep inside…then swelled, encompassing him and enveloping him.

Today he had lost the two people he loved more than anything.

But he must go on. He had a job to do.

A life to live.

Colleen Gleason is an award-winning, *New York Times* and *USA Today* best-selling author with more than twenty novels in print. Her international bestselling series, the Gardella Vampire Chronicles, is a historical urban fantasy about a female vampire hunter who lives during the time of Jane Austen. Her first novel, *The Rest Falls Away*, was released to acclaim in 2007.

Since then, she has published more than twenty novels with New American Library, MIRA Books, Chronicle Books, and HarperCollins (writing as Joss Ware). Her books have been translated into more than seven languages and are available worldwide.

Visit Colleen at:
colleengleason.com
facebook.com/colleen.gleason.author

Or sign up for new book release information from Colleen Gleason here:
http://cgbks.com/news